RULES OF '48
A NOVEL

Other Books by Jack Cady

The Hauntings of Hood Canal
The American Writer
The Night We Buried Road Dog
The Off Season
Street
Inagehi
The Sons of Noah
The Man Who Could Make Things Vanish
McDowell's Ghost
The Jonah Watch
Singleton
The Well
Tattoo
The Burning and Other Stories
Ghosts of Yesterday

RULES OF '48
A NOVEL

JACK CADY

NIGHT SHADE BOOKS
SAN FRANCISCO

Interior layout and design by Jeremy Lassen

Cover layout and design by Claudia Noble

First Edition

ISBN 978-1-59780-085-3

Night Shade Books
http://www.nightshadebooks.com
Printed in Canada

For Pauline Cady
Mother, teacher and friend

A NOTE TO MY READER

This book began as a memoir, but from page one, characters stood up and demanded attention I couldn't make happen in a memoir. They whispered in my ear, through my dreams, and they argued with each other, or fussed. They didn't seem to ask for much: a display of seven weeks in 1948 when their worlds altered forever. It turns out they asked for a lot.

It became necessary to change characters' names while writing a novel. (Cady, for example, became Wade). The novelized memoir began as an account of doings between white men and black; and the aftermath of the greatest war in history.

Then the Samuels family got involved. I had not known them personally because no one did. I only witnessed their separate deaths. As the awful stories that lay behind those deaths surfaced, the first two drafts of the book hit the round file.

A new book appeared. If it is successful you'll get at least some feel of an American city as it was after WWII; a business-y city that after 83 years still held roots in the Confederacy. Some of what characters say comes from memory which remains acute. Some will reflect what 'had to have been', for while I could trace lives and actions, I could not fully know all thoughts. Use of racial terms, as of 1948, is precise.

Nearly all of these folks have now passed into history. I wrote with an urgency that said they deserve to be remembered.

NEW GUY IN TOWN

Wade had a mouth on him that could stun horse flies. Knock them right out of the air. It wasn't the standard cuss words that did the job, it was the elaborations; often Biblical.

There wasn't a mother's son among us: ('us' meaning Lester and Howard and Jim, and maybe even Lucky) who didn't almost admire that mouth; especially while knowing that Wade was not exactly heaven-bound. Wade could whip them off without thinking: "...sacramental cream-of-cowshit...."

His ability came from being raised in Blackford County, Indiana, where cussing among men was as necessary as church on Sunday. Except, in Wade's case, it was church on Saturday, because Wade's daddy was a religious bigot who hated Jews, Negroes, Catholics, Coca Cola (which represented frivolity and broken dietary laws), F.D.R., city people, country people, and members of his own 7th Day Adventist church. Wade's daddy believed that heaven was forty square acres surrounded by walls made of gold and only Adventists, and only the best of them, would be Chosen. He also believed that Mussolini had been misunderstood.

Wade's mom was so strict that when the preacher came to call, the preacher was nervous for fear he'd say something wrong. She threatened grandchildren with eternal fire if they so much as chewed a pork chop, or asked: "Was Joshua as good a trumpet player as Mr. Harry James?"

This pair spawned five kids, of whom Wade was the youngest. He always said it was a good thing his parents found each other, because it would have been a shame to spoil two families.

Months before WWII opened Wade got out of the dry and miserable heat of Indiana bringing a wife and two kids. Wade came to the wet and miserable heat of Louisville. He worked at a company called Tube Turns that cast engine blocks for B-17 bombers. He barely avoided the draft because he worked in vital industry, and also because he had kids. The war had drafted most working-age men. Wade claimed to be a foreman in charge of aging deadbeats, needy housewives, and lazy niggers; and maybe the foreman part wasn't a lie.

He hung on making bomber engines until war ended. When new cars came to market he ran the repair shop at Hull Dobbs Ford, back when it was still located on sleepy Broadway around 8th or 9th. He was a good shop manager, but, truth to tell, auto repair is boring. The car company was only a car company, no better, no worse.

Wade was like the car company. A working guy, a newer model, maybe. Wade would be not-a-little pleased when a snockered TV announcer (in those earliest days of TV, when one could still get by with being a little plowed at work) said "Hull Dobbs stands behind every one of his cars, and if you buy one you'll wish he stood in front of it."

In real short order, then, Wade got sick of auto repair and cast about for something new. That is when history took over.

Back in the 1920s the American Businessman had been celebrated as the new Messiah. Business had been King.

The Businessman, it was suggested by a popular writer and opportunist named Bruce Barton, stood with God at his right hand. Barton compared the Businessman to Jesus. He proclaimed the American Businessman as the Great White Hope of the world. Wade, who was only a kid at the time, bought it.

By 1948 Wade looked the part of Great White Hope. He was handsome and six feet tall in a day when a majority of men were not. He weighed in at around two hundred, and not an ounce of it fat. He sported blue eyes, brush cut hair, and a vocabulary suitable for pulpit or barnyard. On days when he was nice, he was very, very nice. Sweet smile and all. On days when he was bad, he was loud. He was also a rising force for change, in a place and time that resisted change.

Because of his mouth he had a choice of businesses. He could become an Evangelist which was mighty profitable, but preachers don't get to cuss in public. Yet, a man adroit with his mouth should use the abilities the good Lord gave. Wade was always a quick study. He became an auctioneer. "...easy as fucking ducks with a howitzer."

When he stood above an auction crowd throwing sweat and b.s. through all seasons, he was a man in control. From Louisville to Blackford County, Indiana was not all that far, but for Wade the distance was a million miles. And even a million miles was not quite far enough.

Business competition was slim. At the time there was only one auctioneer of high repute in Louisville. His name was Charlie Weaver, but Charlie was on his last legs. He could not have cared less when Wade rented auction rooms on Bardstown Road, although Charlie's rooms were only a few blocks distant. Charlie's rooms sat about halfway between Wade's place and a working-class slum on Jackson St.

Wade will shortly rise and mouth his way across these pages, and Charlie, in his quiet way will at least rise; but it is with Bardstown Road and Jackson St., plus an important man named Lucky, that our story really begins.

BARDSTOWN ROAD AND JACKSON ST.

At the intersection of Bardstown Road and Eastern Parkway, polite residences with tidy lawns gave way to dusty commerce. Tall trees clothed neighborhoods with shade, and magnolias cast warm scent into summer nights. Winds whispered before storm. In Kentucky summers the trees made Eastern Parkway coolish, while Bardstown Road fried.

The intersection hosted a sleepy drugstore, a new and yellowish Shell station, a busy White Castle from which flowed smells of fried onions and 5 cent hamburgers, while a nondescript car dealer's display windows boasted Kaisers and Fraisers, the early, lumpy models with hood ornaments of buffalos; and which looked like buffalos.

Hang a right before entering Cherokee park, and Bardstown Road ran all the way to Bardstown where stood a brickish southern mansion. In the music room of that mansion a painting portrayed Stephen Foster seated at a piano. His Muse, dressed as a diaphanous Victorian angel, floated airily above while pressing her finger to his brow. Had he been consulted, Foster might not have been totally pleased with the painting. He had, after all, been an abolitionist from back east during the War of Northern Aggression.

In the garden of the mansion a very black old man played the part of a darky and plucked a banjo. He dressed in the style of a minstrel, and his main tune was *My Old Kentucky Home* which was also the name of the house.

But, if you hung a left Bardstown Road took you in the direction of the river. It passed run-down houses and small businesses. Wade's auction house stood beside a shotgun-style house in disrepair. Further along were a few bars, an orphanage, another auction house until Charlie Weaver died, a hardware, a roller rink, dry goods, and more houses until the intersection with Broadway. At that intersection and to your right, Cave Hill Cemetery contained only the best people, but hang another left. Keep traveling, and bingo, you soon arrived at Jackson St. where the world turned black and brown and beige.

Three-story brick houses with concrete stoops lined a street where cars with flat tires outnumbered cars that ran. On windy days religious tracts and pieces of newspapers flew along the street. Top floor rooms or apartments looked out on a neighborhood of black folk leavened by an occasional white, like cream stirred into chocolate.

Mohammed Ali dwelt nearby, but was only six years old, and in those days was known as Cassius Clay; when he wasn't called 'boy', 'sugar', 'sweetness' or 'whatcha-say-little-nigger'. Jonah Jones *had* lived just down the street, but he took his magic horn and moved uptown, Chicago, New York, and around. Jackson St. also sported institutions: a Methodist church, an undertaker, a junior high school, a hock shop, and a bar painted in fading and flaking green named the Sapphire Top Spot.

Through all the jobless days, through days of canned heat strained when a man was cashless, the raggedy Sapphire Top Spot stood through Louisville weather that boiled in summer, deep-pressure-cooking sweat so abundant even

young guys almost didn't want to 'mess'. Sapphire Top Spot
served cold beer, also whiskey with ice, could you cost it.

Jackson St. and Bardstown Road: Auction houses:
Colored guys: White guys: It's in those places a man named
Lucky Collins would help two kids named Jim and Howard,
and two men named Lester and Wade, solve problems of
business and race. Lucky would also suffer hurt of the kind
that almost kills.

MEETING LUCKY

He was a Hebrew, was Lucky; a fallen Jewish angel. His nose hooked like a caricature of Shylock. In winter he dressed in pinstripe suits, pastel shirts, and ties in primary colors. In summer it was short sleeves and sweat like everybody else. When he smiled his brown eyes lighted, and when he snarled his gaze went flat. He had a purple splotch on the back of his right hand, and a bald spot where a yarmulke might have sat, but didn't.

His hockshop on Jackson St. sat next to the fading green Sapphire Top Spot. An alley ran in between. The undertaker sat next the hockshop, with the Methodist church just down the way. It was said that Jackson St. carried everything a man would need in life; a drink, a loan, a prayer and farewell.

Drivers along Jackson St. saw a freshly painted yellow building with three balls dangling; and the sidewalk cleanly swept. Across the front, in boldest black against brilliant yellow, a sign read:

Lucky Collins Loans   Best Deals   Try Me

You can tell a lot about a man by looking at his store. Hockshop customers being who they are, hockshops need be narrow with everything behind showcases. That said, the difference between Lucky's hockshop and the general run was certain splendor.

Trombones lined the walls. Vertically. They pointed to saxophones, clarinets, trumpets and bugles; gold and silver horns promising blues, echoes of cakewalks and jazz. Cases contained hair straightener, pocket knives, aspirin, hand tools, rings of all descriptions from zircon to diamonds; rings of lodges, rings for real weddings, and goldish bands for 'let's pretend'. There were colorful medals and patches and medallions from the latest war: orange and brown emblems of tank battalions, and Purple Hearts.

Cases held cameras and spy glasses, while shelves behind the counters carried kitchenware, and shoes with tassels, some new. At the back of the store hung racks of new suits, 15 bucks, sometimes 12. Two bucks down, a buck a week.

Most hockshops are predictable, thus dull, but not Lucky's; because Lucky attended auctions. He came up with merchandise of such wonder that even lots of white folk walked through his doorway, sniffing contemptuous sometimes, but interested and dickering.

He'd fetch in cases of canned peaches, nine cents a can, and cans of sardines eight cents. Feathered boas. Panama hats. He displayed new grilles for ancient Packards, used jukeboxes, a gross of votive candles, indoor ball bats, framed pictures of the 1937 Ohio River flood.

And, high above the front counter, beneath the invisible blare of trombones, perched two *Not-For-Sale* mascots of the store: a stuffed and mounted Guinea hen named Lola, smallish, plump, but matronly; and a stuffed Plymouth Rock rooster named Thomas, head pushed forward, somewhat askew, glassy-eyed, obviously daft, probably insane.

Most hockshops are the focus of the owner's life. The quick buck and hustle, the smooth slippy-slide and whisper of counted money. Most hockshops are sleaze. They are run by people named Big Jerry. There's no fun to them and 'compassion' seems a naughty word.

But in Lucky's shop a man could jive for free. A man could piss and moan with hope of sympathy. A man could cuss preachers and cops. What a man couldn't do was hock family property in behalf of a drink.

"God-bless-it, John, Milly *needs* that radio. I'll write you two bucks honor, and you get a week." Lucky would tap the suppliant on the shoulder, friendly-like. It was rare he ever lost a dime.

Because Lucky knew his neighborhood, knew the goldbricks and deadbeats, and never loaned to them without security. But to honest men he'd loan on trust, because two bucks were possible to pay back (plus interest). And two bucks would soothe a man. Two bucks, at ten cents a glass, bought enough time and beer at Sapphire Top Spot to let a man believe there was a job somewhere. Two bucks bought the sorrow-prevention it took to get through another day, another night. Colored men, last hired, first fired. No work. And, wife and kids at home in a rat-rid dump on Jackson St.

And, because he paid off the police, Lucky managed to keep a lot of those saddened men from arrest. It could be said, and with but little caution, that Lucky did more for that neighborhood than did all the churches in town.

When Lucky snarled, though, wise men took their scrawny bottoms elsewhere. Lucky would sell a pocket knife. Don't ask for a straight razor, a pistol, or a switchblade. And don't miss that buck-a-week payment on the 12 buck suit.

The shop was open 10-6 Mon-Fri and 10-7 Sat. On one special occasion, though, it was closed. That happened when Charlie Weaver died.

Lucky attended both the funeral service, and the interment at Cave Hill Cemetery where August sunlight flooded green, green grass. It also flooded somber clothing, dark suits, dark dresses of mourners. The temp stood above 90. Armpits poured sweat. Charlie was not overheated, but family and former customers were in misery.

And, yet, people seemed loathe to leave. Most of them knew each other. They watched each other. They had bid against each other for years. Charlie's auction house had been not a business, only. It had practically been a club. Even after an Episcopalian tribute by a hopeful preacher, and after the casket descended into soil, the crowd lingered. Somber colors, murmuring lips, and green, green grass.

Dirt to fill the grave lay heaped beneath canvas. A couple of working stiffs hovered, their shovels still hidden. The undertaker's assistant moved with what he hoped passed for dignified haste. The flower car was needed elsewhere. As the crowd hesitated, funeral florals were laid carefully but unceremoniously beside the canvas-covered heap. White lilies, forget-me-nots, mauve sweet peas and fragile baby's breath. The car departed. The assistant remained.

Around the grave-site the landscape spouted marble. Soldiers from the days of Presidents Davis and Lincoln lay in quiet ranks across hillsides. Victorian mausoleums in the form of Greek temples stood above grass so tended it seemed nigh artificial. The graves of children sported marble angels who bent toward the earth.

"I see nobody who's gonna take his place." A tall guy with a big belly spoke barely above a whisper. He wiped sweat with a bandanna-sized hankie; a man in the used-food business down on Market St.: beans with dented cans, insurance shipments from truck rollovers, warehouse stuff a teeney bit past pull date; profit margin seventeen percent, with plenty volume.

"Nobody will," a lanky man murmured. The man ran an Army/Navy store just past 4th on Broadway. "Stuff changes," he said, sounding helpless. He looked toward Lucky who, though Hebrew, was considered smart.

"The new guy," Lucky said, and said it brisk.

"Damn country boy, dammit."

"It's an act." Lucky also wiped sweat with a hankie, then looked into the grave where the polished coffin awaited dirt. "Nice funeral," Lucky said to the coffin. "Charlie, my boy, you had class." Lucky looked again at the lanky man. "You're right. Stuff changes. But I'm right too. Behind that country mouth, the new guy has his charms."

"I don't see 'em." The grocery-guy wiped more sweat. He now carried a 'going-away' posture, a man ready to head back to his store.

"He runs a clean sale. He's watching out for his dealers." Lucky looked once more at the coffin. "Until later, then," he said to the coffin, but in a voice that suspicioned the afterlife. He gave a small wave to Charlie's customers. As he left he slipped out of his jacket and pulled off his tie. Folks saw a white shirt wet in the armpits, white moving among pink and gray marble and above the greenest grass in town.

July 31st, 1948

Two Kinds of Ghosts

The Kentucky ghosts in this story are not bereaved spirits made of ectoplasm, and they do not moan. They are southern ghosts, which means they exist on the edge of living consciousness. They exert power, or at least, energy, at odd moments and they affect the living in sometimes useful ways. At other times they can cause a certain amount of misery.

The ghost of Charlie Weaver does not, strictly speaking, haunt; but Charlie is in attendance because of who he was. To Lucky he represented a gentlemanly Old Order that was giving way to a garish New Order. With the loss of Charlie, Lucky understood that history had stumbled and spat forth Wade. Lucky was the kind of man who thought about such things.

When he left the cemetery he headed toward Wade's place telling himself he had an errand. He knew that he mostly went because it was a rare, rare time when his store was closed. He could enjoy a break before reopening.

He drove left from Cave Hill and passed Charlie Weaver's auction rooms. The building stood dusty beneath summer sun. Windows needed washing. Charlie had been slipping these past few months. Although Charlie had departed quietly, his departure had been noticed; even if his ghostliness had not.

Sometimes newspapers get the facts fairly straight. *The Courier Journal*, rather more informal than *The Times*, did a front page memorial, second section. The *Courier* didn't say much about auctions. It just offered a courteous piece in behalf of a courteous man, plus a little bit of history of the kind that meant a lot to Lucky; and in those days, meant a lot to Louisville.

Charlie Weaver had grown when Louisville still ranked as an intimate performance on a small stage. Even back in the early century the city was somewhat raw and spraddle-legged, but Charlie, a gentleman, might not have known that.

He was a cultured Victorian. Had he been wealthy he would have funded missionary societies and museums. He would have done his bit to relieve respectable suffering, though he might have drawn the line at Aid to Fallen Women.

He was born in 1875 and lived a quiet 73 years. Charlie dressed well in suit and tie, although on sale days in winter he wore a houndstooth jacket. In spite of his auctioneering trade his face remained calm. He was a handsome man, not particularly tall, but somehow stately. He sported groomed gray hair, and gray eyes that occasionally seemed light blue. His manner shone deft, but kindly, with a flair for humorous understatement. He married at age 30, and was a man who missed wars; wisely escaping the Cuban adventure, too old for WWI and WWII. He begat and raised children. He was faithful to his faithful wife.

His auction house was geared to dignified days of yore, because his customers (the crowd) took seats in chairs arranged before the sales platform. Grips, including a colored gent named Lester, moved sale items into view; and Charlie's manner somehow imbued even mended crockery with respectability. "Think of the life of this dear old pot, mended now. Mended, perhaps by a gentle lady, or perhaps by some dear old pot...." a chuckle, and, "Do I have an offer?"

Charlie sold whilst seated, and he sold quietly. His was an aristocrat's performance, lightly comic, not a little pious, yet kindly.

His quiet dignity was notable in The Land of the Auctioneer; that is, Kentucky: where tobacco auctioneers chant over burley, where farm boys praise the haunches of swine, where auto auctions are sleek as greased reptiles, and sales of general goods clamor and yelp. Also, flamboyant in Kentucky, many auctioneers carry the title of Colonel. Some actually are Kentucky Colonels. They gain a colonel-hood by contributing to governors who then issue certificates. Charlie, reserved, never went in that direction. How different Wade was, from Charlie.

* * *

As Lucky would soon discover, some ghosts of the time were not southern, but European. Those ghosts do haunt the tale, and they haunt our lives, causing thought, sorrow, and weeping. Those few of us who remain still remember them, and though we no longer weep, or at least not much, we think about them. Those ghosts changed all of us.

Lucky, for instance, had no way of knowing that during the seven weeks from the last day of July to mid-September, his world would flip-flop and land him in darkness. People kept dying. Excessively.

Next door to Wade's auction a neighbor-lady passed and no doubt went to heaven. Her degenerate sons, according to every Bible-thumper in town, then went where souls wish for asbestos underwear. Hers was a grim tragedy, but no one had a hint. When she passed the newspaper carried no traditional obit. It just reported her death at age 67. It did not say where she came from or if there was ever a smile from her, ever a frown, ever a stare. The paper did not mention that she had been quiet and mousy and thin. Her name, folks learned from the newspaper, was Mildred Samuels. She died, folks learned from the newspaper, of complications from extended illness. People who read the report assumed diabetes.

Thus, she remained a mystery. She had been reclusive and foreign in her small house with her two grown sons. Perhaps someone, somewhere in town, knew and remembered her. If so, no one on Bardstown road ever heard from them.

Had there been a complete obit, Lucky would surely have acted, because Lucky, like everyone thoughtful, had reason to absorb newspapers at a time when radio news was trash and television nonexistent. He really could have used that obit.

There was no obit because there was no one to compose it. Mrs. Samuels' sons were not handy with language. The tall son was known as Mr. David (or behind his back 'The Yid') at the local grocery. He spoke fractured and screwed-up English. He looked pale, carried scars from burns, and walked crooked because of a serious limp.

Her other son was small and frail. No one knew his name. He sometimes puttered about the backyard where a sagging garage shielded a scorched garden from the alley. He never went anywhere.

In excess of grief at his mother's death (folks assumed) Mr. David shot himself. In further excess (folks assumed) the younger son wasted away. Their stories will never be fully known, although Lucky would eventually uncover facts surrounding their deaths. Years later, Wade's kid, Jim, full grown, would glean some facts about their histories. It turned out that they were Polish Jews from Warsaw. The full last name was Samuelwicz.

Mildred (her Polish first name was Noemi) Samuelwicz

and her husband Jakob (Jake) entered the United States legally in 1938, fleeing fears of Stalin. They worked, and with moderate success.

Mr. David escaped Poland in 1939, made his way to England, and flew a fighter plane until he was shot down and crashed on the English coast. The younger son, Isaac, miraculously survived Treblinka death camp. When they got to Louisville, only their mother was there to greet them. Jakob had died of age and overwork in 1943. The Samuels family had a problem. The two sons were illegal, having entered the U.S. through Mexico.

* * *

Some deaths caused other ghosts of the southern variety. A man named Jolly showed up butchered in an alley beside the Sapphire Top Spot. That proved extra hard for everybody on Jackson St., especially Lucky.

And a country boy from Corbin got himself righteously shot, and that proved hard for everybody on Jackson St., especially Lucky. Ghosts of Jolly and the country boy probably still flit through shadows along Jackson St.

July 31st

The Second Death
Mrs. Mildred Samuels

Lucky's '47 Fleetwood, painted money-color green, pulled up to the pumps of the new Shell station at Bardstown Road and Eastern Parkway. A kid with an amazing combination of freckles and pimples pumped gas at 24.9, while the station owner came from the lube rack.

"Lucky," he said, "you working or drinking?" The guy looked toward the Cad, saw Lucky's jacket and tie draped across the seat. "Or, where you been preaching?" He grinned. A youthful guy but experienced. Behind him sat a couple of cars for sale, blue '38 Chev at one-seventy-five and a black '41 Hudson at two-and-a-quarter.

"Laid a guy to rest," Lucky told him. "How's business?" A polite question. Anybody could see that business was singing.

"I'm for sale." The guy's brown eyes showed trouble. His dishwater blond hair carried a dab of grease from the lube rack. "Business is too good. Those horses' asses at Shell will find an excuse to break lease. Another six months, and this is a company station."

Behind the station, oaks and maples rose above houses on the parkway. An occasional white spot of magnolia peeped through dark leaves. Sun pinioned traffic to the street and a young woman came from the drugstore carrying the latest novel, rental 5 cents a day. She dressed in southern pastels, and walked stylish, knowing she was pretty.

The filling station guy watched the girl. "I'll open a drugstore. You never see a drugstore going broke."

"Sell down the inventory." Lucky looked the place over. "You can't break the lease, but dig a foxhole." He pointed toward the street, down toward the auction, then at the Chev and Hudson. "Dump everything. Leave Shell with what the little boy shot at."

The young guy also looked in the direction of the auction. "Twenty percent commission."

"He's new," Lucky told the guy. "Offer ten, pay fifteen."

Lucky looked over the lot, looked at inventory in lube and repair area: belts, parts, brake shoes....

"If you discount," Lucky advised, "Shell will catch on. If you peddle to another station the word will get around."

"Where did that noisy bastard come from?"

"Hicksville," Lucky told him. "It's somewhere in Indiana. Maybe Illinois."

A polished gray '48 Plymouth pulled onto the island. The kid on the pumps didn't know whether to stand and collect for gas, or pump the Plymouth. Lucky passed him four dollars, accepted change.

"I'm headed that way now," Lucky told the filling station guy. "Auction is setting up for a week from Wednesday." He looked at the freckled kid pumping the Plymouth. "Good help?

"For a kid, yep. Kids have got everything to learn."

"Honest?"

"... near as I can tell."

"When you lay him off, tell him to come see me."

"Where you're situated..." the station guy said, "... he won't. Those niggers will scare crap out of him. No offense."

"None taken," Lucky told him. "On the other hand, you're

both singin' in the dark." He grinned, touched the guy on the shoulder just to watch the guy flinch. "A customer," he told the guy, "is a customer."

When he parked across the street from the auction house he saw that someone was dead. A hearse stood at the curb. Two guys in dark summer suits climbed steps of the house next door to the auction. When the door opened, the two guys spoke to a tall, thin-faced man who rubbed his hand across his cheek, then his brow. He had been crying and he sniffed back snot. When he turned back to the house, he limped.

The mortuary guys entered. Lucky told himself he'd had enough funerals for one day. He murmured condolence beneath his breath, then headed for the auction house. Later, he would bitterly regret his haste.

* * *

Certain rhythms attend superior cussing. Few men, and almost no women, own them. The rhythms start out *lento*, move steadily to *con brio* and end up *forza*, as follows: "This Goddamn sonovabitchin' hunk-a-holiest-of-holies crap is blocking the fornicating and bag-balmed door to the shithouse. Get it moved." Mark Twain once had that kind of rhythm. Billy Sunday had that rhythm, but not the vocabulary; at least not in public. Wade proved proud bearer of the tradition. As Lucky entered, the cussing swelled, dwindled, came to conclusion. Two kids—a boy and a girl—yawned, while a quiet woman behind a desk made entries in a ledger. The boy pushed a five-drawer chest across the smooth-tiled floor. It was an awfully nice chest. Cherry wood, pre-Revolution, probably.

"Lucky," Wade said, "How's business?" He seemed ready to extend a handshake. Then he looked at his hand, saw soil and dust from merchandise. "Take my word for it."

Wade wore his thick hair cut short in no-nonsense country

style. His nose looked half-English and half-Hebrew. He had Scots-blue eyes and broad hands. Women thought him handsome, men thought him loud, and his boy thought him a pain-in-the-old-patooker. Lucky looked at the kids. The girl was pretty and probably thirteen. The boy was a year older, skinny, brown-haired and sullen.

"You're walking around during business hours." Wade looked to the front of his store where the hearse sat parked. He pointed toward the hearse and spoke to the boy. "Go see what's happening." He turned back to Lucky. "Who's minding the store?"

"Charlie Weaver's funeral," Lucky told him.

"I sent flowers." Wade watched his kid as the kid trudged to the front door and out. "Didn't seem quite right to attend." He sounded the least bit uncertain. "Charlie and I kept our distance."

"You made the right move." Lucky looked around the auction house, or at least as much as he could see. The difference between Charlie Weaver's house, and Wade's, was wider than the rolling Ohio River.

It had an upstairs and a downstairs connected by a long ramp. The downstairs room fronted the street and held antique china cabinets with bowed fronts; the cabinets decorated with carved Victorian flowers, or curving and chesty Edwardian lines. The china cabinets were needed because the city boasted large numbers of aristocrats and old money. Sales of estates produced fine glass of every variety from tumbler to chandelier.

Light sparkled along edges of cut glass. It reflected on cranberry pitchers, Meissen statuary, Limoges dining service, bisque, Delft, Wedgwood; blue and cream, or sometimes cream and green. Light brightened sterling silver, and softly illuminated coin silver (sad memory of a war where coins were melted and formed into spoons, so

Yankees would not steal them). The definition of 'antique' was: Item must be at least a hundred years old, and the best of its kind when it was made.

Standing against walls, and between china cabinets, stood Victorian wardrobes with carved grapes and lilacs, sleigh beds, four-posters, highboys in cherry and walnut, mirrored oak stands for cloaks and umbrellas, and sidearm bookcases. Arranged in rows down the middle of the house stood dining tables (usually walnut), lamps, end tables, Victorian love seats, roseback and ribbonback chairs, a baby grand and an upright; with small items of worth displayed on the tables.

In the back room, which was long and unpainted and shabby, sat used but useable merchandise: refrigerators, sofas, tables, ordinary chairs and chests, serviceable tools, boxes of clutter, unopened cans of paint. Louisville's small tradesmen came to the back room knowing they could add to their inventories, and profit would ensue.

Because, memory of the Great Depression still dwelt among businessmen and customers. Memory of scarcity during WWII also dwelt. The idea of "Use it up and make it do" had not departed America, and so, even in the first flush of new stuff after the war, there was a grand market for worn goods.

Happy, then, in that back room, was the auctioneer who could become a businessman among businessmen. He could say 'damn' if not 'shit', and he could announce about merchandise: "This poor thing can't help being dinged-up, but it's still got feelings, so do right by it." Or, describing a framed Victorian portrait, "Here's a chance to pick up an ancestor": always a good line because antique dealers were ever present; and antique dealers know that folks with New Money need ancestors.

All that was needed was a short stool, a whistle for quieting the crowd, a grip, and a clerk to write down prices and names of buyers. When the clerk's sheet was filled, Wade's kid carried it to his mom. She used it to make out invoices.

The stool put the auctioneer head and shoulders above the standing crowd. Instead of grips bringing items to the fore, people moved along lines of merchandise. The grip held up small items. This was barnyard selling, tobacco selling, but it worked because a standing and mobile crowd held more tensions than a crowd seated and relaxed. At its height, a sort of "oh, yeah?" atmosphere entered the bidding. Prices soared.

If Charlie Weaver's spirit attended such an auction (which seems likely) it doubtless shook its head, pursed its lips, watched the mounting prices; then, being spirit only, and out of the game, probably shrugged. The spirit might have thought the auction looked like a religious revival in its early stages.

After all, a large and handsome man would be elevated above an attentive crowd. His demeanor would be intense and serious. His eyes would flash, his mouth would pound adjectives onto nouns like a man setting rivets, and his hands would move most expressive.

"The neighbor lady died." When Wade's kid returned he tried to pretend that what he said meant *nothin'*, but he couldn't make it play. His voice trembled. The kid looked at his sister. "Don't go out there."

The girl, of course, went immediately. Then the quiet woman, Wade's wife, looked up from her ledger. She stood. "I'll see if there's anything we can do." She was as pretty as her daughter, maybe prettier, but a little dumpy.

"I got a sale to set up," Wade told Lucky, "and there's a shit-barge hearse in front of the store. How good is that for business?" He looked toward his son. "Don't move an inch. We got work."

The kid swallowed hard. Twice. "Her mouth was hangin' open," he whispered. "I got to pee." He headed for the can.

"My girl is more practical," Wade mused. "If my boy was a girl, and my girl was a boy, it would surely take a load off."

Beneath searing sunlight the mortuary men loaded the sheeted corpse. July heat caused asphalt to bubble. Some of the bubbles would burst, and later, in the cool of the evening, some would sag. The asphalt would carry tiny craters that looked like pockmarks of disease. Traffic would smooth them out next day.

"It's not my place to say it." Lucky sounded apologetic. "But the boy just saw his first dead person. Maybe somebody ought to explain something."

"He'll talk to his mom." Wade was clearly ready to go back to work. "What can I do for you?"

"I want to take a couple of weeks in late August. What's lined up I'd better not miss?"

"Warehouse. Plumbing supply house that went busted, but that's end-of-the-month."

Lucky noted the date of the warehouse sale. "See you in a week." As he left, Wade's wife and daughter returned. The woman suddenly sad and permanently tired. The girl seemed shaken.

MEETING LESTER

By the time Lucky returned to his store the work day stood well advanced; or, for lots of colored guys, already over:

From fetid rooms where electric fans flailed against night-heat of summer, and where humidity soaked old wallpaper from walls, men had emerged at dawn. They stepped silent along streets and between brick tenements as they headed for the river. On Market St., where the street joined the Clark bridge leading to Indiana, the men stood in clusters; men named Joe, Pete, Zeke, Mose, Alfonzo, Rodney, Jack.

In early a.m. the jive level flowed lower than the summer river. Men looked each other over and selected standing-spots. Big guys arranged to stand among clusters of smaller men. Big guys wore short sleeves or undershirts to show the bulk of upper arms. These were the men chosen by contractors, warehouse foremen and steel haulers. After the work day ended, these guys would speak of "Sweatin' lak a goddamn Irishman, and fartin' lak a Missouri mule."

Day labor. Pay in cash at the end of the day. Seventy-five cents an hour, on up to a buck twenty-five. If a man proved worth keeping, and if the boss had a big job, there might be as much as two weeks' work all in a row. Get ahead of the rent man; for once. Brag some to your woman who quit nagging, feed the kids, and loosen up at Sapphire Top Spot.

Stubby guys, who because of their builds could work low on loads, were taken by truck drivers to handle dry freight, furniture, drums of chemicals, sacks of produce, bags of cement (90 lbs. each, no hand truck).

Skinny men took what was left; or nothing a-tall. Their work day ended around noon when they were not chosen. They wandered off, eyes cast down, or searching for something to pick off from a parked car, something to hock with Lucky. It was either that or another day of empty pockets. Another day when a man would have to find an angle, or not dirty up a dinner plate.

And some guys, fortunate as Baptist angels, hooked onto a steady job. These were guys with something extra; a skill, a super strong back, or, in Lester's case, a personality. Lester worked, or had worked, for Charlie Weaver.

Lester—black—like they don't build 'em that black anymore. Purple lips, skin like midnight satin, reddest mouth anybody ever seen, and laughing open-mouthed.

And lithe, skinny, dancing like no dancing master could perform. A backward roll to his shoulders, arms flying, twinkle-toes like only the best of hoofers, more natural than trained. Dancing through the summers, throwing sweat, sweating out the beer at Sapphire Top Spot.

Mr. Personality. Lester packed a real smile. No accommodation attitudes. Not for Lester. Most white folks walked a little doubtful around him, because it seemed that "this boy done forgot he's a nigger."

Mr. Joyful, that was Lester.

And, when Lucky returned from the funeral to re-open his hock shop, Lester stood right there before the faded green of Sapphire Top Spot, and bright yellow paint of Lucky's; Lester busy holding down the sidewalk.

"Nice funeral?" Lester stood watching as Lucky searched his keys then opened up.

"There ain't no such thing," Lucky told him. "We got him in the ground."

"Midst all them dead folks," Lester said. "Too much company. I left instruction. When I die somebody grabs me by the big toe and tosses me in the river."

When Lucky went behind his front counter to pull a cash bag from a safe, Lester stood quiet. After Lucky got cash counted into the register Lester leaned on the counter. "Charlie was okay. Charlie knew how to treat a man." Lester's hands were broad like his mouth; hands work-worn, stubby nails. He looked up at the store mascots, the stuffed chickens. Old Lola the guinea hen seemed friendly. Thomas, the Plymouth Rock rooster, seemed crazier than usual.

"Miz Weaver always doubted me. What's gonna happen to the auction?"

"Miz Weaver is high-born," Lucky told him kindly. "The high-born doubt most things." Lucky looked toward the street where afternoon sun threatened to turn to evening. Shadows cast by tenements ran long and brickwork looked rusty. "There won't be an auction," Lucky said. "The family will close it down. They've got no auctioneer."

"I know the business," Lester told him. "I know the rap."

"And you know Miz Weaver." Lucky did not say that nobody colored was gonna make an auctioneer. Not a chance. There might even be a law against it.

"Hopeless," Lester said, "I got bucks laid back. I can go for quite a spell. But, man, I gotta have a job."

"The only job I've got," Lucky told him, "is a kid's job. Part time, sweep and polish." He paused. "Have you tried the new guy?"

"He don't look good."

"Could be you're wrong." Lucky reached to tap Lester on the hand, friendly. "He talks like an outhouse, but there's something there."

"You might could put in a word," Lester said. "Or, say it this way... would you put in a word?"

"You're straight," Lucky told him. "It's the least I can do. You two might be able to figure each other out."

* * *

Because they handle consignment, and do not own merchandise, auction houses open and close on schedules different from other business. During early set-up for sales, the house looks like a Kentucky thunderstorm swept through, piling merchandise helter-skelter. At zenith the pile is a confusion of goods from different places. Only concentrated memory tells what came from where. The house remains closed.

Once the floors are swept, and the various lots of merchandise sorted and placed, the auctioneer assigns lot numbers and tags every item. There's still work for the doing, but at least the public no longer screws things up by picking an item from one lot, and placing it in another. The auction's doors open for viewing.

Two days after Lester and Lucky talked, Wade and his kid were assigning lot numbers when Lester showed up for work, 7:57 a.m., sharp. Lester paused inside the doorway, admiring a mighty pretty sale. Wade saw a muscular nigger, somewhat skinny, who probably wasn't gonna work out, but Wade held trust in Lucky. When Lester held out a hand, Wade took it; not a little surprised. "Lucky called," he said, "and I'm fair for giving it a try. You're Weaver's boy."

Bad start, but Wade didn't know it. Wade had perfect pitch for talking among white folks, not colored. In those days 'race words' went this way: 'Colored' was polite and good. 'Colored gentleman/lady' was best. 'Negro' was respectable and technical. The newspapers, including *The Louisville Defender* used it. So did the NAACP. 'Black' was suspect, a bit insulting. 'Negra' was a polite way of saying nigger, and was used by cultured whites and preachers. 'Darky' was droll, nearly affectionate, and not a little possessive. 'Boy' was any colored male under sixty, and 'Uncle' was any colored male over sixty. With females it was 'Girl' and 'Auntie'. 'Nigger' was not used by people of Wade's quality in the presence of colored folk, though they might think it. Nigger was used in conversation with whites.

"I was Weaver's grip," Lester said, "I've done Army time and I'm twenty-seven years old." He looked toward Wade's daughter who was waxing an antique chest. "Better tell her to use paste, not that liquid slop."

Wade was, quite literally, taken aback. Black boys were supposed to grin and say 'yassuh'. "How in hell is this going to work? You're already tellin' me how to run my business."

"I'm saying liquid slop darkens wood. Ask any antique dealer."

"No shit?" Wade said. The white guy understood that this brand-new trooper, sorta skinny and midnight black, actually knew something.

"None a-tall," Lester told him. "Except for the war I been around this business since a kid."

The colored guy saw a white man who was so full of crap you could almost smell it on his breath. On the other hand, the colored guy saw that Lucky had been right; this white had something going. The colored guy looked around the auction house. He checked out the cleanest and most attractive sale he'd ever seen. This white guy knew something. "No shit?" Lester said.

"Help me finish numbering this sale," Wade told him. To his kid, Wade said, "Check with your mom. Find something to do." He turned back to Lester. "We get done here, we've got a big warehouse. Ever do a warehouse?"

"All the time," Lester told him. "Lots of times."

AUGUST 2ND

MEETING WADE'S KID

Rumor began two days after Mrs. Mildred Samuels was taken to the mortuary. On Saturday, while loitering, Wade's kid, Jim, heard it at the drugstore kitty-corner the Shell station. The kid was supposed to be getting a haircut, but took time for goofing off. He wouldn't have heard rumor at all, except the pinball sat near the soda fountain.

"We had our army in Europe," a sweaty man said. "We should've walked right on in and settled it. We'll have to sooner or later." He sat before a five cent glass of Coke. A straw farm-hat was shoved to the back of his head and sweat stained the hat above the hat band. His face look stream-lined. His nose stuck out nubby like one of the new Studebakers.

"That's quite a bit of territory," a second man said. "Russia's like us in a way. It's too big to occupy." This man sat slaunchwise on his stool. He watched the cashier at the cigar counter, a girl worth seeing; bobbed brown hair and leggy, though with skirt hitting mid-calf. The man wore a battered fishing hat tipped forward over horn-rim glasses. Neither man cussed because ladies were present. Across the counter a waitress scooped ice cream, leaning forward; the effect spoiled because of a primly buttoned high-neck blouse.

"They were allies, the Russians," the man with glasses said.

"And I believe everything I read in the newspaper." The first man lifted his cup, toyed with a saucer. "I believe in the Easter Bunny. Shucks, I believe in the Brooklyn Dodgers."

The other man chuckled. "I'm with you on the Easter Bunny. But, what's your beef?"

"Unions. Communism. Two names for one thing. Read your history. You'll find it goes back a long, long way." The man's voice sounded more impassioned than he looked. "Congress is looking into it."

"House UnAmerican Activities," the man with the glasses said. "It's a committee."

Wade's kid juggled nickels in his hand. The pinball's lighted backboard showed the picture of a cowboy; spurs that jingle-jangle-jingled.

"And I have read the history," the man with the glasses and fishing hat said. "Truth to tell, I teach it. Male High."

"Then I don't have to explain." The thin guy in the straw hat looked through the windows of the store, and into the street. "Samuels," he said, "what kind of name is Samuels?" He watched the waitress move beyond hearing distance. "That the *hell* kind of name is Samuels? Yid?"

"It could be Jewish. Don't bet on it. It could be English or Irish."

"Or Russian. There's lots of Russian Jews. There's an underground."

"We have a spy on Bardstown Road?" The man with the glasses and old fishing hat tried not to seem amused. "It would be the world's most boring job." He looked across the street at the Kaiser-Frasier dealership. "Those have to be the ugliest cars since the Chrysler Airflow."

"On Bardstown Road," the first man said, and he sounded prim, "we have some bastards named Samuels who do not come out in daytime. You hardly never see 'em. They talk like Russians. They sound exactly like Russians. There's a radio aerial up the side of their house. So what's that about?"

"There's lots of ham radios, and otherwise. I've got an aerial, myself." The straw-hat man tapped the counter with his fingers. "Don't get me wrong. I like this town. But it's a damn slow town. There's nothing here to attract spies."

"We're a central rail station north and south. We have industries. We have a waterfront. You think Stalin's just lying doggo?" The straw-hat-man's voice dropped to a near whisper. "And, for some, the war ain't over." He smiled, but not a happy smile. "It's over for one of them. The old lady croaked."

Wade's kid turned from the conversation. He muttered under his breath. "You never saw somebody dead."

The kid left the drugstore and dawdled along the street. He was of that age when kids get sick at heart; buried beneath both truth and bull, but haven't learned to tell one from the other.

In his mind and memory it went like this:

"What's a Jew?"

"Somebody from the Old Testament," his mother told him. "Some of them are nice."

"Sharp businessmen," his father told him. "I don't like the sonovbitches, but I can do business with them."

"Pushy," the Sunday School teacher said. "They want to buy houses in neighborhoods where they don't belong."

"Lucky is okay," his father said. "He's an exception. You can learn a lot from Lucky."

"Keep the yids in line," a man at the barbershop said. "They already own Taylorsville road. Won't be long before they want the whole damn Highlands."

"What's a communist?"

"Somebody who thinks the government should run

everything," his mother said.

"Roosevelt did something great for his country," his father said. "He died. Communists are unions. Goldbricks. People who won't work."

"Evil men trying to take over the world," the Sunday School teacher said.

"A bunch of Red sonsovbitches spreading integration shit among uppity niggers." (According to the barber shop).

And in the kid's mind ran hymns, not jazz; and yes, Jesus loved the little children, all the children of the world.

He dawdled along the street, reluctant to head for the barber shop and more confusion. School would start soon. Almost a relief.

When Mrs. Samuels died his dad had told him to see what was going on. He had walked through the open doorway of the next-door house, wishing he were elsewhere. Men's voices came in sobs and whispers from a back room. He moved timidly in that direction, knowing he was doing wrong, but obedient.

Faded-flower wallpaper decorated the short hall and living room. A plain lamp wearing a paper shade sat on a low table. Overstuffed chairs and sofa were worn but clean. The house smelled funny, like perfumed candles. The kid wanted to leave, could not.

When he stood at the doorway to the bedroom, a short, pale man wept. The man's short-sleeved shirt did not cover a blue tattoo on his arm. All the kid could tell was that the tattoo wasn't a picture of anything. It looked different and clumsy.

A second man, thin and with tear-streaked face grabbed Wade's kid by the arm. The man did not seem angry, only determined. He seemed awful sickly, barely able stand. He practically staggered when he walked. He gave little gasping sounds, like he hurt just terrible, and his grip was weak. He didn't even shove, just urged.

Wade's kid only had the briefest look at Mrs. Samuels, but it was a look that would last. Her mouth hung open. Worse. her eyeballs had disappeared. Her eyes were open and nothin' but white. Did everybody do that? Or was it Russian?

He had returned to the auction house. Then his sister and mother went next door to Mrs. Samuels' place. When they returned his sister was wordless. She picked up a rag and furniture polish. His sister could pretend anything. She could pretend that spiffing up used coffee tables was interesting. She remained wordless for the rest of the day.

"I met her sons," his mother had said. "There's not much we can do." She sounded troubled. "They are taking it awful hard."

"Foreigners," Wade said, "Albanians or something. Italians. Noisy as all hell."

"Rest her soul, a woman just died."

"They'll send for a preacher," Wade told her. "More interruptions? No sense crying over spilled Italians."

"I'm not crying." The kid's mother had looked directly at Wade, looked around the auction house, then looked at her kids. "I probably should."

The kid heard something wrong. Her voice held quiet rebuke, the way it did after he did something dumb. He watched his dad, and his dad didn't pick up.

"You'll not tell me when to be neighborly," his mom said. "Those people are from someplace else, and they're alone. They look sickly, and nobody talks to them." She had returned to desk work, and she too, became wordless.

* * *

As he walked along the heat-stricken sidewalk, after leaving the drugstore, the kid fretted. His mom said the Samuels people were from someplace else. And what was this *shit* about Russia. The kid looked around, guilty because he had just thought 'shit', even if he didn't say it.

Except for windows fronting the street, all the shops had blinds pulled against the sun. A motion picture house sat next the drugstore, and after that a florist, and on the corner a barber shop. The kid had already thought *shit*, and now he thought worse, but fought against thinking it. Although confused, he almost understood why.

Because, he was about to get a haircut and that meant more confusion. Kids were supposed to show respect for grown-ups. The kid did not understand that there was no shortage of men even a dog couldn't respect. The sad sacks gathered at three kinds of meeting places:

V.F.W. lodges, both the sort for whites, and the fractured imitations for colored, were largely sites of good red whiskey and war stories. Most war stories were told by walking-wounded; brave men who had fallen down a staircase while drunk in such exotic ports as Trenton, New Jersey. The real soldiers, the true combatants, didn't talk all that much.

Stag bars (no women allowed, ever) were places where men went to cuss, and brag about the size of their apparatus. It was better than the V.F.W. because no one felt obliged to tell war stories, and no one felt obliged to believe them. In stag bars, men who lacked arms, or legs, or eyes, could get quietly drunk without offending sensitive southern belles, or discussing their wars, or listening to summer-soldier-horse-hocky.

But, it was barber shops that educated Louisville's young white boys, because boys were not allowed in the V.F.W., and only rarely in stag bars. Barber shops gave instruction in thoughts about society and women. A standard barber shop joke went:

Young and gorgeous female enters barber shop (where she doesn't belong) in quest of hubby. She speaks:

"Bob Cox here?"

Barber smiles. Answers:

"No ma'm, just shave and haircut."

A real howler. Always good for a chuckle.

Twirling barber pole, red and white twisting; a symbol not as ancient as the pyramids, but no spring chicken. In olden times barbers were half-baked doctors, bleeding patients; the barber pole a sign of wrapped cloths and blood.

There were lots of one-chair shops, and a few three-chair, but the average shop sported two chairs and two barbers. Thus, was it inevitable, that after a haircut and a brush-down by one barber, the other barber would say to the customer: "Drop by in a day or two and I'll straighten that out."

Customers came in shifts. Businessmen arrived during afternoons, lounging, talking politics. Store workers stopped in during lunch hour. Kids came in after school. The interesting day, though, was Saturday. The shop filled with all kinds of men and an occasional kid. Men sat, waiting their turns whilst spreading one crock after the other. Kids, who knew they should be seen and not heard, listened.

"Dago up the street a-way. Died'a too much spaghetti."

"Russian. I heard she was Russian."

"Couldn't be. You hear all kinds of crap."

Barbers served as neighborhood newspapers. Barbers prodded conversation, knowing if you kept your shop interesting, you kept your customers.

"It was murder," one barber would say.

"F.B.I. Those boys keep a sharp lookout." This from the second barber.

"Russian. I'm sure she was Russian."

"Hebe. Yid. Kike. Russian. Roosevelt let 'em in, and this goddamn Truman's worse."

"Stirring up the black folk. Stirring up the niggers."

"Good ones and bad ones. There's good niggers. Don't

deny it."

"The problem ain't niggers. It's white communist nigger-lovers. Good niggers know their place."

"Their place ain't been dug yet."

"If it was murder," the first barber said, "cops don't seem to be working up a sweat."

"They've been told to back off. A Russian yid. You got to believe the F.B.I. took care of it. You can say what you want about the bastard, but Hitler was right about the Jews."

School would start soon. It would almost be a relief. When the haircut was done he could go back to work. Work would not be interesting, but would be a whole lot less confusing.

Wednesday Night, August 6th

Auction

In 1948 demand for new goods caused businesses to break old, old, old tradition. Furniture stores began staying open on Sunday, and, may God help all sinners, so did bowling alleys. The Louisville Ministerial Association reacted to Godless prosperity.

Preachers went into a tiz. They demanded closing of all nonessential business. Drugstores might stay open for prescriptions only. Buses might run. Police and firemen could work.

The Ministerial Association split. One preacherly faction held that God would understand the need for 'essentials'. The opposing, or hellfire faction, saw pharmacists and cops as doomed; but that faction was willing to sacrifice the souls of the few in behalf of the many.

Businessmen reacted. They spoke of hiring lawyers. Then a sharp guy proposed a deal. Business would close on Sundays if the Ministerial Association would forego Wednesday evening services; because, such services were in restraint of trade.

A nasty dust-up followed. When the dust settled, stores opened on Sunday, while preachers made holy noises come Wednesday evening; both kinds of business healthy, like always.

Thus, on that next Wednesday evening there was joy and song at the Methodist church on Jackson St., and the excitement of an auction would come to pass on Bardstown Road. Lucky attended the latter, natch.

He drove past the church and thought how colored folk really enjoyed religion, while white folk, except for Jews, took it like medicine. Jews were still thinking things through.

His Cad drifted past brick tenements where men and women sat on stoops, and where kids played. On the corner a group of men stood talking. Jukebox music danced through the open door of Sapphire Top Spot. Folks looked like moving shadows; dance, sweat, more dance with beer, more sweat.

White guy sweat smelled different from colored guy sweat. Egalitarian stinks, because none could say which smelled worse. What one could say was that the neighborhood had its own smell, partly sweat, partly decay; but smelling pretty good, actually. Of course, he was used to it.

The windows of his Cad were open. Back in '41, when the car was built, air conditioning could be had; but the air-conditioner filled the whole trunk. Someday soon, some smart guy would engineer something that fit under the hood.

When he hung a right on Bardstown Road a moment of melancholy hit. At Charlie Weaver's closed auction house, declining sunlight made the place look like a tired and ratty tomb. It had once stood in blazing white with conservative trim. Now it was as faded as a ghost. Charlie had gone downhill the past few years. Over to Lucky's left, at Cave Hill, Charlie worked at turning to dust; but probably did it with dignity, and maybe a touch of reserved humor.

Around Lucky the world was changing, and maybe not for the better. A stench of politics covered newspapers and radio. Congress postured. Political poltroons named

Thomas and Nixon grandstanded. A man could hardly help knowing that, once more, Jews were gonna get the short end of the stick.

"Which," he told the Cad, "is business as usual."

And, it wasn't only cat fights among political-parsnips in Congress. Worse even, the European continent still overflowed with dying refugees. Governments were doing next to nothing. Even American Zionists had been willing to dump the cause of refugees in behalf of establishing the State of Israel.

To the thoughtful man, the world seemed increasingly surreal. To the thoughtful Jew, it seemed even more so. During the war Jews knew of the German death camps, but, hundreds of thousands of Americans, including Jews were being killed in combat. Reality and surreality assailed the mind, and sometimes a man could not tell which was which.

And now there was this business of refugees. More people dying. More people starving. He knew it was real, but it seemed unreal. He knew he should weep, but somehow could not. And, because he could not, he felt like weeping... figure that one out, Lucky, my man.

* * *

The new guy's auction started at 7. At 7:15 when Lucky arrived the main crowd was already in place, but he did not enter the auction house right away. It would be hotter'n fresh biscuits in there.

Lucky stood watching occasional traffic on the street. Just down the block the Shell station's lube bays stood empty. A kid manned the pumps. The station would stay open until midnight, and that was new. Stations traditionally closed at nine.

The White Castle stood like a commercial gem in the gloaming, white and gleam-y, nickle-burgers by the sack.

Lucky looked toward the house where the dead lady, Mrs. Mildred Samuels, had lived.

Her house was not large. A screened-in sun porch held a couple of tired-looking but comfortable chairs, over-stuffed. The house looked like a small creature in mourning for a dead mate. No lights showed. Shades drawn. It stood as a patch of darkness among the glowing lights of business. A man felt sad just looking at it; felt a sense of dread, felt even a sense of fear. Maybe the man he had seen, the limping man who greeted the funeral home guy, had moved on.

He turned to enter the spiffy front room of the auction. This sale was a display of post-war commerce.

Charlie Weaver's notion of commerce had been so different. Lucky told himself he could handle either version, but was gonna miss commerce-according-to-Charlie.

In the brightly lighted room sharp nose-bite of cigarettes mixed with rich and fulsome scent of cigars. People smoked everywhere: in movies, groceries, banks and cemeteries. Kentucky was a tobacco state.

Chatter mixed with the smoke. Wednesday-night auctions served the same as church socials. Men, and a few women (mostly antique dealers) who kept shop during the day, met to gab. They shook hands as if they had not met in months, exclaimed, then inquired about business.

"Business is good."

Nobody, except a fool, would say that business was bad. Because, everybody except a fool knows that no one likes to deal with losers. It was possible to say: "Business is slow this week." But never bad. And business, even when slow, must be said to be 'picking up'.

Large fans on tall stands, and under bright flourescence, churned air into the smoke. The inside-air and the smoke exchanged with outside air, swirled; both inside and outside hotter'n the hinges of hell.

People wore minimum clothes. Men were in short-sleeve shirts, no undershirt. Women wore summer blouses, and were much relaxed. Corsets had disappeared during the war.

A few of the women were more interesting than most. They did not cluster and chat with their peers. They talked face-to-face with the men, because small-business caused leveling of sexual and social mountains. These girls were as tough as the boys.

The rest of the women were society-types, present because this was an estate sale, and: "Of course we were close with dear Edna. And, isn't it sad to see her things paraded before 'these people.'"

"Lucky," a man said. "Long time." This was a scrawny guy who ran a junk shop on Market St. Known for a bad mouth. Cheap as a carnival prize. Name of Fudd. In Lucky's mind, the guy was not a credit to the Jews.

"Missed you at Weaver's funeral." Lucky looked over the heads of the crowd. He spotted one colored face. Lester stood beside a discount guy, exchanging b.s.

Fudd followed Lucky's glance. "Weaver's nigger," he said. "Wade could do better. Nobody cares for schwartzer sass."

"He knows the trade. I helped him to the job."

"You should see what walks through the front door of my place," Fudd told Lucky. "You can't teach 'em nothin'. Born stupid." He scratched his rear end, rubbed his nose, reflected. "Wade's gonna regret it."

"We're about to get going." Lucky watched Lester break off, head toward Wade and his clerk. The three walked to the front of the house, Lester carrying a short stool. People turned, watched, gathered to hear opening remarks; the same as epistles in church. Lester placed the stool. Wade ascended. Blew a sharp note on his referee's whistle, and the crowd quieted.

A charmer, this Wade, a spellbinder. Smile broad as the ever-flowing river, and movements as liquid. Open-neck shirt displaying virility of chest hair, and hands not exactly reaching, but touching forward; as though ready to pet any head in the crowd.

"Estate of Edna Jane Masterson," Wade announced. "Let's get rolling."

"Gone to glory," Lester muttered, but loud enough for those nearby to hear. Lester grinned, looked at Wade, and Wade picked up.

"Beginning with our regrets and respect to the Masterson family and friends," Wade said. "Now let's get rolling."

No two auctioneers sound alike. It's not just the chant. It's tonal. The chant, or rap, depends on agility of tongue. The tones must hold emotion. In Wade's case it went something like: fifty-fifty-fify-fity-fifty w'illa biddahalf four-bits, and now sixtyseventyfi, make it a hundred, ninety there, and five. Fiveabucka bucka, nine-five now a century, one hundred, do it. Looka there the poor thing is bawlin', cause he's worth, yep, one tenand fif-a-teena....

Auctions start with small stuff. The smart auctioneer blows off bargains quick. If an item's worth ten, he dumps it for five, even when others are bidding. He'll do that three or four times, and best bargains at a sale are most often the first items. Low prices excite the crowd. Even experienced bidders can sometimes get caught in the early rush of prices, and ten minutes later find themselves paying too much.

Not much would happen for Lucky until the sale moved to the back room. This front room held too much good stuff, and smart men know their stores. Thus: never put a big diamond in with small diamonds, and never put a Brooks Brothers in with fifteen-buck suits. Keep the stock consistent. A few really good pieces make the rest of your inventory look like garbage.

If Lucky had been a sociologist (and in a manner of speaking he was) he would have studied the crowd, and its behavior, with analytic eye.

Serious buyers crowded near the auctioneer, so that within the larger crowd a small tableaux formed. The auctioneer stood above his grip and his clerk. The clerk was a rotund lady, flowery dress, plus rouge, lipstick and face powder. When Lester picked up an item for sale, he whispered the lot number to her. Then Lester turned to watch the crowd behind Wade.

Lucky smiled because Lester was really swinging. After a week of trying to get along with Wade, and putting up with Wade's bluster, it looked like Lester had something to prove. On top of that, after quiet years with Charlie Weaver, Lester found himself in the middle of an *occasion* and was blamed well rising to it. When a bid came in, Lester yelled, "yeah, we got it, eighty-five," and Wade went for ninety. Lester clapped his hands and made motions like Mr. Fred Waring encouraging his orchestra. The auctioneer's voice and the grip's voice sailed together, mixing, ride-out, loud and quick as uptown jazz.

When the item sold, the rotund lady wrote down price and name of buyer. Beside her a guy hovered, a guy who Lucky had known for years. Name of Daniels. He was lean as a drink of water and he much admired fat ladies; was himself a ladies' man. Daniels traded, swapped, and made a super living. Legend had it that he went to town riding shank's mare with a pocket knife to trade. He came home that evening driving a Lincoln, with a hundred bucks in his pocket, and the pocket knife. Since at least the days of the Phoenicians that story had been told in one form or other about traders. Lucky figured that in Daniels' case, it was actually, probably, true.

And next to Lester, so close they exchanged sweat, was

an antique dealer name of Gloria; a tough little red-haired cookie who rented old garages throughout the entire city, even unto the west end, even southwest unto Churchill Downs. She stuffed them with stained glass windows which were otherwise headed for the dump, carnival glass that nobody wanted, vaseline glass, which was junk, and Victorian clothes closets that were firewood; cheap cast-offs that cost her almost nothing. Lucky knew that time would prove her wise. When the stuff became popular, she would have cornered the market.

Beyond the tableaux the crowd broke into groups. Two couples were interesting. A middle age tall man and a teeney lady, both overdressed and immeasurably married, stood at the far end of the crowd. Lester worked that end, and Lucky moved closer to Lester, because whatever was about to happen ought to be fascinating.

The couple near Lester no doubt perspired money, peed money, bled money; and if they blew their noses coins would surely fill their hankies. The teeney lady wore a white and unspotted dress, and a ruby necklace. She resembled a well-clothed bulldog with an ornamental collar. This couple busied themselves ignoring another couple who stood right beside the open door. Neither couple paid attention to Wade, who was up and rolling as Lester kicked a chorus behind him.

The second couple was reversed; short and chubby guy, slender and gray-haired lady who, were she not Republican, resembled Eleanor Roosevelt.

Lucky, and practically every other customer in the house, had seen it before. The only question was: how was Wade gonna handle this one?

Because the two couples were obviously heirs of the dear departed, and they obviously hated each others' gizzards. They gathered on this festive night because somewhere in the rows of sparkly merchandise dwelt a family treasure. Dear Edna had forgotten to mention it in her will. It was an odds-on bet that at one time or other, dear Edna had carelessly promised the item to each couple. Lucky figured that the teeney lady and the chubby guy were cousins, or maybe brother/sister.

Wade's problem was this: The two couples would start a bidding war. Matters would become dramatic. The price would rise far beyond the value of the item.

On the surface, that seemed good. If a four hundred buck item went for eight hundred, the commission would double. But, that was only on the surface.

Trouble wore two faces. In this kind of combat, and in the clubby atmosphere of Louisville business, it was easy for the auctioneer to make an enemy. Word got around among money-people. Lawyers, for instance, who handled estates.

Second, and worse, a bidding war interrupted the flow of the auction. It substituted one kind of excitement for another, then left the auction flat. If compared to a church, it would be like somebody cutting a loud and smelly one in the middle of a sermon.

Lucky saw that Wade had the situation wired, and Lester had also picked up. The nasty guy, Fudd, was all attention, because a guy could really 'move in' on a busted auction. Skinny Daniels, and tough Gloria, cuddled close to Wade. Whatever was gonna happen, was gonna.

The fight erupted over, of all things, an early Victorian hall tree sporting cutesy drawers, an oval mirror, carved roses and a sidearm umbrella stand. The thing had been ugly as a can of spoiled bait a hundred years before. It had not improved with time. Value, at most, thirty bucks.

"Ten," the chubby guy beside the doorway said before Wade could open his mouth.

"And fifteen," the tall guy yelled. The teeney lady beside him looked toward the other couple, and if looks could kill that hearse from last week would have to make another trip.

Wade remained silent. He kicked Daniels, just a little. The stool was not high enough for the crowd to see the kick. Daniels looked up, mildly surprised.

"Sold to Daniels, twenty." Wade intoned. Like a blessing. This, while the teeney lady shrieked and the Eleanor Roosevelt lady gasped.

Lucky chuckled. Daniels grinned. The clerk looked confused. Lester, in a fit of admiration that could not be gainsaid, stood rapt. Gloria looked pissed.

"I am about to become a rich and happy man," Daniels whispered to the clerk. What are you doing afterward?" The clerk smiled and looked snuggly.

"You can't do this," the tall gent said. "It's an open auction."

"Second that," the chubby guy yelled.

"I'd give my soul...." the teeney lady moaned.

"And we're about to see what her soul is worth," Daniels whispered to the clerk. "I'll be back."

Wade smiled beneficent as a Shriner's charity. "Since it's my house," he said quietly, "I handle this my way. The buyer is a dealer. He'll meet you out front, and the five of you can hold your own auction."

He turned to Lester, and Lester was on top of it. He held up a cranberry lamp, black hands against red.

"Estate of Mrs. Edna Jane Masterson," Lester yelped.

"With regrets to Masterson family and friends. Keep rollin," Wade called. "Let's keep rollin.'"

Gloria remained pee-oohed.

"I knows de man," Lester jived to her in darky accents. "Next time he drop one on you. Momma always say takin' turns be fair."

AUGUST 7TH

THE THIRD DEATH
CHECK-OUT DAY

In days more ancient, even, than those when bloody rags preceded barber poles, an uglier symbol strode the world. After Ghengis Khan, or Alexander the Great, or some such other savage despoiled a city, he commanded that all loot be stacked in an enormous pile. When the stack of loot reached zenith, a blood-drenched flag was placed before the heap of statuary, ornaments, gold, tapestry, rugs, rings, pots and tools. The flag announced distribution of goods to the victors. Warriors gathered, waiting their shares. Being only warriors they publicly cried victory while thanking their gods; and privately bitching.

Thus began a custom with chants somewhat religious, and economic always. The red flag would flap across history. As methods of murder became more svelte the red flag turned to a remnant from ancient times. It now hangs outside of auction houses. Sometimes it means 'Auction Today', and sometimes it means 'Check-Out Day'.

* * *

On the following morning a small van from Arnold's Moving & Storage picked up the Victorian hall tree, so it was obvious Daniels had engaged in drama. Daniels showed up right away, but any tale of 'a rich bastard stand-off' would have to wait.

50

Lucky showed up a little later, just in time to help Wade's kid who was about to walk across forty acres of misery.

It was check-out day. On Wednesday night a lot of small stuff went home with buyers. Most of the furniture, and other gear, remained among litter of cigarette butts. In the front of the store, and in back, Wade's kid had pushed a broom.

This Thursday morning the auction would see two kinds of trucks arrive: pickups belonging to local dealers who could probably get their stuff in one load, but who could make two loads if necessary. The second kind were large, usually vans, but an occasional 18-foot stake. These were dealers from downstate who bought at St. Vincent de Paul, plus stores on Market St., then topped off their loads at auctions.

"If there is gonna be trouble...", as Lester would tell you, "it will likely come from one of these country boys whose momma didn't raise him with no politeness."

Several tons of merchandise move out of front and back doors, and mostly move in the first two hours of the business day. Ninety-nine percent of customers are honest, while one percent will steal a deaf man's hearing aid.

Most members of the one percent are known to the auctioneer and everybody else. The junk dealer, Fudd, is an example. The rule is "Fudd will never make a dollar because he thinks of dimes. He'll move items around, and shift something nearly worthless into a box of worthless crap for which he paid a buck."

The country boys may cause problems because some of them are strangers. Wade, a country boy himself, can tune in with such men quicker than a pigeon can poop. Wade usually checks them out.

The buyer gets an invoice listing his purchases by description and lot number. Wade, or Wade's kid, or Lester, or Wade's daughter checks each item off with a pencil as it is loaded on a truck. When the buyer is not known, it pays to look in drawers of chests, and open the doors of cabinets. Small merchandise has a way of getting 'lost' in large containers. The general response from such buyers, is, "Wa'll I'll be gawdam, how did *thet* git in there?"

As the sale is dismantled, some buyers get impatient as they wait for a checker. If a country boy, he's liable to act the way he acts back home. That is what caused the first rough note of the day.

Lester, so black he shone brilliant, sweated into his socks as he dismantled a baby grand for loading. It's a delicate job, about like trying to carve ivory with the elephant still attached.

The lid comes off, the sound board has to be secured, and with another guy's help the instrument is tipped on its side. The legs have to come off. It must be wrapped in furniture pads. If you're lucky, the buyer owns a piano board. Without luck, you're gonna have to help boost it, not slide it. Experienced men can get the thing ready in ten minutes if the customer stays 't'hell out of the way'. Otherwise it takes half an hour. Two experienced men can boost it if the buyer doesn't assist. Otherwise, the crash can sound like Geo. M. Cohen on a real bad day.

Lester, with Daniels' help, had the thing on edge and perched on a flatbed cart. He held it steady while Wade's kid draped furniture pads and arranged furniture straps. Daniels gradually stepped aside because he didn't want to be asked to 'boost that heavy bastard'.

Beside Lester and kid, chests and tables were carried through the front doorway as Wade's daughter checked for the antique dealer, Gloria. A truck stood out front, and sunlight made the dust on its red paint seem mellow. Sunlight flooded the street, but smart men and women wrinkled their noses. Some people claim they can smell a thunderstorm hours ahead of time. Lester wrinkled his nose, and figured it for three p.m.; plenty of time to get the sale checked.

A country boy approached. He carried his small invoice like an important flag. He looked in his late thirties, and his spiky hair needed a wash job. His overalls covered a substantial tummy. His teeth were not too rotted, and his hands showed that he knew about dog-work. He did not exactly qualify as white trash, but would serve until white trash could be found.

"Need some checkmarks," he told Lester. "Couple refrigerators in back, and a stove."

"I got this here piano."

"Now," the guy said. "I got a long drive and no time for bullshit."

Lester grinned, darky-like, so as to ease away from trouble. "Better see the boss. I can't exactly stop what I'm doin'." He reached down and around, holding a furniture strap so Wade's kid could tighten.

"Now."

"See the boss."

"Where I come from," the guy said, "we don't stand for nigger sass."

Wade's kid fumbled the strap, tried to back away, then stood his ground.

"The big trouble with niggers," Lester said quietly, "is that some of the black bastards are dangerous." He looked beyond the guy as he searched for Wade. "Go find your pa," he told Wade's kid. To the country boy he said, "Fool with me and you wreck this piano. You wanna buy a piano?"

The country boy paused. In his world black bastards did not threaten white men. Black bastards were intimidated, and goddamn well should be; ever since the invention of rope.

Folks started paying attention. After all, this was no stranger. This was Lester. Folks had dealt with him for years. Wade's daughter stopped checking and also went looking for her dad. A couple of guys from the red truck gathered close. Daniels showed up from somewhere. Gloria stood watching; and Gloria, though small, had a way of making a man feel surrounded.

The country boy shifted from one foot to the other as he studied on 'how far he could take this here mess'.

When Wade showed up the country boy had about decided to back down. "What?" Wade said.

"Your boy just mouffed off a load of crap," the country boy said. "Damn poor way of doing business."

Wade looked at his kid. "What'n' baby-face hell did you say?"

"Not him," the country boy said. "Where I come from we got a sign at city limits. It says, 'nigger, don't let the sun set on you in this town.'"

"And where I come from," Wade said as he slapped the guy on the shoulder, "we got a saying. 'The customer is always right until he gets to be a pain in my main joint.' Let's get you loaded." Wade sounded so jovial that the country boy couldn't figure whether he'd been insulted, or maybe not. Then he grinned and turned away.

"Dumb-dick," Gloria offered. "Hick-dumb-dick."

"'Ef I let such get to me," Lester told her, "I'd be livin' a life of sorrow." He grinned big time, sort of phony and sort of not, speaking darky language which wasn't usual. "You bein' good folks," he said. "Steady on this," he told Wade's kid, "and I'll tight down the straps."

When the piano was loaded Wade's kid drifted away. He lingered for a minute listening to Daniels tell about last night: about how the rich bulldog lady and the rich chubby guy nearly pulled each other's hair; except the chubby guy didn't have all that much to pull, etc.

Then Daniels, who understood himself for a hero, had settled it by making everybody act like civilians. He told both sides to pitch in fifty bucks each. They could then donate the thing to a museum, gift of both couples. There wasn't a museum in the world that would "want the gad-damn thing," but he hadn't mentioned that.

Wade's kid drifted into the back room which looked nearly naked. Long rows of merchandise had disappeared. Here and there a piece of furniture looked lonesome. At the end of the day all of the stuff not picked up would be shoved into a corner. It would move out in a day or two.

The kid paused near his dad who talked about Lester with a couple of guys. "... goddamn smart for a spade. I never seen the like."

"Keep a close eye," one of the men said. "There's not a-one of them that's not a thief." This was a man who ran a restaurant supply house on Market St. He was Germanish-looking and bald.

"Not Lester," the other man said. "Charlie used to swear by him." This man handled used furniture and clothes on Market. He was just a little snip of a man, but brittle and active.

"Charlie was too trusting."

"Dunno," Wade said. "Everything I've ever heard of Charlie said he knew his shit...."

Soon it would be time for the kid to get the push broom. More cigarette butts, more clutter of squashed chewing gum wadded in gum wrappers, more junk from buyers who sorted boxes of small stuff and left what they didn't want.

He got to the back door just in time to see the country boy pull away. The man's truck was blue with wood stakes that carried remains of orange paint. Green canvas tarp lay stretched and roped across the mounded load, and a couple of heavy timbers extended beyond the bed. The timbers were flagged, small red dots waving.

The truck traveled down an alley. When the kid stepped through the back doorway of the auction, and looked left down the alley, he could see a little swatch of Eastern Parkway. The alley did a ninety at the back door of the auction. Then it stretched away a whole block and intersected Deer Park Avenue.

All along the alley were garages with narrow doors. The garages mostly had dirt floors and once held carriages, or, later, Model T's. Roofs of some garages sagged and showed missing shingles. Doors were sprung. The buildings were past usefulness, except for a kid.

The neighbor's garage was a place where a kid could wander and not be found for a while, and the kid walked toward it. Dirt floor, sagging roof beam, door nearly off its hinges, and sunlight casting little spotlights through holes in the roof. The beams of sun spotted the dirt floor.

Once inside this place a kid could feel safe, although Wade's kid did not think of it that way. This place was not confusing. In this busted garage were no grown-ups with talk that must make sense, if a kid could figure how. Grownups said one thing, then said the opposite, and acted like both were true. How did that work?

He pulled the door open hoping it would not fall off. From inside the garage sounded a rustle, like someone moving quickly. The kid paused. A creak, like rust on a hinge. The kid almost backed away. There were no more sounds. He stepped inside. Timid.

Gloom in the garage was cut by those tiny spotlights of sun. One spotlight hit directly on the forehead of a man who lay on his back. Newspapers were spread under him. The man wore a black suit with white shirt and tie. His shoes were polished. He looked like he was asleep, and what sense did that make?

The little spotlights made the gloom seem darker, and Wade's kid thought he'd better leave. If he woke the man up, the man would be mad. Then the kid looked beyond the little spot of sun, looked at the man's face. This was the man who had taken him by the arm and pushed him out of Mrs. Samuels' house. The kid understood, before he understood how, that the man was dead.

He'd ought to do something. Instead, he stood. As his eyes fully adjusted to gloom, he saw a silver pistol lying near the man. There was nothing else in the garage, except a round-point shovel leaning against a wall. A small door led to the backyard of the house, but it stood closed.

There was a dark little hole, blue, in the man's temple. It didn't seem like nothin'. This man's eyes weren't rolled back. They weren't even open. The kid could not see the other side of the man's head, just the little hole. The newspapers weren't even wet, even. The ground wasn't even damp.

The kid knew that in another minute he was going to be scared and running. Some other part of him knew that he'd better look close. He didn't want to remember this in the quick and awful way that he remembered Mrs. Samuels' rolled eyes and open mouth.

The little spots of sun lay like freckles on the soil. The man's suit was clean but worn. It had funny, square collars and extra buttons. The jacket had frays. The worn sole of one shoe needed fixing. The pistol lay a-ways off from the man's outstretched hand, and the pistol wasn't very big. Antique dealers at the auction bought lots bigger ones.

One of the man's arms was folded on his chest like a man laid out for burial. The other arm looked like it had fallen to his side. His face looked slack, and almost caved-in, like from sickness. One little speck of light, a tiny spotlight, gleamed on the tip of his polished shoe.

"Youngster," Lucky said in a low voice. "We'd better get you out of here." He touched the kid's shoulder.

The kid had not heard Lucky approach. The kid had never heard a man's voice sound that gentle. "Nothing we can do," Lucky told him. "I'll get somebody to take care of it. You come along."

* * *

The kid would remember sweeping floors, because that was what he was supposed to do, and because people didn't pay attention to kids who swept floors. He swept while crazy stuff swirled around the auction house. The worst part wasn't his father's quiet cussing. The worst part was faces.

He knew his mother's face. He had seen her face joyful or sad, tired, and even exhausted, with her bobbed hair dull. He had seen her face glow with the quiet pleasure of church service and church song, hair shiny and blue eyes intent. He had seen her angry and suppressing it, or angry and quietly speaking. He had never before seen her face filled with shame.

"We could have done something. We're always so busy. We were obliged to do something." It was like she could not raise her head all the way. It was like she bowed beneath an awful weight.

"I'm afraid not much could be done." Lucky sounded more sad than shocked. Lucky also sounded awfully guilty. "Lots of pressure," he said. "Pressure mounts up."

Nobody understood what he meant. Maybe Lucky didn't understand all of it, but he understood enough. The style of the man's clothes showed that he was European, and eastern European at that. If Jewish, the main questions were how had he escaped Europe, and how had he come to the Jewish backwater of Louisville?

"I knew those people were alone." Wade's wife nearly whispered.

Lucky should have asked more questions. Later he would curse himself because he had not. At the time, he assumed that Wade's wife meant Mildred Samuels and the dead man. Lucky did not know that Mrs. Samuels had two sons. Lucky tried to make Wade's wife feel better, and he kept an eye on Wade's kid.

Wade's kid thought he knew his father's face. He had seen that face angry, excited, and also fatigued after a long day's work. He had watched his father's droll way of spreading b.s., and he had seen the way his father looked when bullying kids, or bidders. He had never seen that face bloodless and shocked and fearful. "Sanctified cat-nuts," his father said. "Shitfire and sermons."

It was his father's prayerful cussing that defined the day, and it sort-of seemed right. If his father could pray, it would have to be in cuss words.

There were other faces and voices. When two tough cops asked questions the kid felt almost babyish: "Where were you?   What were you doing there?" The cops tried to be nice, sort-of, but one cop's face was red like a man who is liquored-up. The other cop's face looked like a lemon, like a bored lemon.

The cops asked his father questions. "Did you hear anything? The damn gun had to make a noise...funny looking gun. A pinfire, foreign, Europe... little thing, bullet didn't go all the way through... and, what about that black boy? Where he don't belong...?"

The angry cop seemed mad because "...it don't add up." The dead man wore his frayed suit and looked respectable. It looked like, maybe, someone had closed the dead man's eyes and arranged the body. Or, maybe not. The cop used the auction's phone and gave a long explanation to his dispatcher or sergeant.

Lester's face went blank. His eyes narrowed. His face

looked like a statue, hair so short it wasn't hardly even kinky. His face looked grim, like pictures of soldiers during the war. He busied himself by assembling all goods not yet picked up. As he worked he hummed, but so low only the kid heard. It amounted to a tuneless hum, like a small electric motor running without taking a load. Lester, so black he stood out clear as sunshine, did his level best to disappear. When the kid's dad asked did Lester "...want to come see," Lester turned sullen: "I done Army time. You think I don't know how it looks?"

Lots of people just left. Daniels, who might or might not accidentally trade for stolen property, disappeared before the cops showed up. Daniels' face seemed toneless. He wasn't gonna hum, and he wasn't gonna promise anything.

Gloria acted the same, except her face beneath Irish-red hair was not toneless. She looked grim as a teacher sending a kid to the principal. Gloria had a reputation as one tough little cookie, but she wanted no part of what might happen.

Lucky hung around for a while, even if it meant he would be late opening his store. He talked to the police. He talked to the kid's dad. He mostly talked to the kid's mom, like he understood her sadness. He spoke in the same gentle way he had used with the kid.

The two cops were joined by a detective. A '47 Ford, a black mariah, came for the dead man. A couple of guys rolled the man onto a stretcher and shoved him in the Ford. The kid didn't see that. His sister told him. Of course, she might have been pretending. His sister could pretend anything.

Then the cops and detective went knocking next door. They stood on the sun porch and pounded and yelled and whistled. When the door was not answered they broke in. They found no one. The cops left. The detective poked around inside, then shrugged and pulled the door shut.

"It's the damndest thing," the detective told Wade. "Those newspapers are all dated Friday the 13th. Could be coincidence."

"Any help I can give...." Wade, like any man with half a brain, was wary of Louisville cops.

"I'd be beholden," the detective said, "if you have your boy board up that door. I'll get back to this in a day." He went back to the garage. Lester, with tools and boards, went next door.

Although lots of people left, other people showed up. As news passed around the neighborhood the auction house filled with onlookers who buzzed and exclaimed.

"Murder. Around here?"

"Suicide?"

"Is this stuff still for sale? Look at this pitcher, Madge."

"Kid, where do I dump this White Castle bag?"

His father ran the curiosity-seekers away, then locked the front door. His father seemed glad for a chance to be gruff. "I could have more fun in a holy-rollin' church," he said to Lucky. "That big warehouse sale will take time. I need this sale checked. I need my people someplace else."

His father was shaken, and his father couldn't pretend as good as his sister. "Albanians," his father said, "or some damn thing. Italians. What would make a man do that?"

"Albania's not a bad guess," Lucky told him. "My guess would be Poland. If he was Polish he saw more than his share."

Outside there, on Bardstown Road, the kid watched as traffic pulled up to the intersection. Three years ago, before the war ended, there had been horses pulling brightly painted delivery wagons. Now the horses were gone. There were lots more cars.

The pavement bubbled. It was easy to see waves of heat rising above the street and off the colorful hoods of cars.

These days there were more red cars, purple ones, even yellow. Before the war there had not been so many colors. The new cars were snazzy. These days they all carried hydraulic brakes and turn signals.

Before Lucky left he paused beside Wade's kid. "Seems like a bad run of luck." His voice sounded kind. "Two dead people in under two weeks." He waited for the kid to say something, and the kid couldn't.

"Take care of your mom," Lucky said. "It's what men do. Take care of your sister." When he left, the kid yearned to go with him.

The dead man, and the fuss he caused, and all the people swirling around, had taken time. When Lucky left at about noon a storm started work. Storms never happened before mid-afternoon, or hardly ever. This storm, though, was the main bull in a big pasture. Worse, it was like a great beast of the apocalypse galloping and growling from the river.

"Missed it by three hours," Lester told the kid. "I figured it midafternoon."

The storm announced itself with artillery cracks well before the wind arrived. Ear-busting thunder, sky going black as the back closet in Hades; and as wind rose and bent plate glass windows inward, threatening to shatter, everybody paused, looked at each other, pretended work. This was more than a normal storm. This one spat ozone, broke trees and shoved cars into ditches.

When the rain arrived the colorful cars disappeared. The street disappeared. Thunder did not roll, it exploded. The building trembled. Small pockets of dust shook loose from around overhead light fixtures. China rattled in china closets, as water rose above the curbs. Water ran on sidewalks. Water flowed beneath the front door. Out there in the street nothing moved, because nothing dared move. Traffic sat parked beneath a waterfall.

Faces. Still. Paused. Waiting. Nigh breathless. These faces were alive, though, not like the dead man.

Wade's kid, who had experience of storms, knew this one was extra-awful. It was like stuff that happened in sermons. Like the wrath of Jehovah. Like punishment for hidden sin.

All of the floors were swept. There was nothing to do except, maybe, try to reassure his sister; but his sister would just give him a hard time.

Then he figured it out. He'd better get a mop. Then he figured something more. This storm was sent so's to wash that garage clean. Rain would come through the holes where had shone the little spotlights. The dead man would be, maybe, washed away.

THE DEAD MAN

David Samuelwicz, as it would turn out, entered World War II as a member of the Polish Air Force; a force not caught on the ground (as is generally believed) by the Nazis. It was a substantial and well-trained force. Although its fighter planes were slower than German bombers, it brought considerable grief to the Luftwaffe.

When Poland fell the airmen moved to Romania and thence to England. Half of them were scheduled to go to France, but that plan fell apart because France folded through betrayal, and the Nazi onslaught. Most of the Polish airmen were formed in Polish squadrons. David Samuelwicz, however, ended up with the 601 English squadron which hosted a few Poles.

At first the Poles were a problem for the English, because the English thought even less of Poles than of Russians. In short order, though, the English were given second thoughts. It became legendary that Poles could be allowed only five gallons of gas for training exercise. If given a full tank of gas, they disappeared in the direction of Germany and kept shooting until they were destroyed. They were known to hoard small amounts of gasoline until they had enough to fill one plane. Then, there went another pilot and plane, shooting up Germany.

Poles constituted the third largest combat air force engaged on the allied side. In the 601 they were first equipped with P-39s, interceptors known as the Bell Airacobra; and known to English and American flyers as, "I don't know what the hell it is, but it sure ain't (bloody well not) an airplane."

The thing had the engine behind the pilot's seat with the propeller reduction gear attached through a long shaft that ran between the pilot's legs. Its main armament was a 37 mm cannon that, when it went off, almost stopped the plane in midair. It also carried two machine guns in the nose and four in the wings. On paper, at least, it could hit 400 mph, or nearly. It was fast enough, well armed enough, and except for use as ground support at low altitude, was as handy as a boxcar.

David Samuelwicz fought in the Battle of Britain, and miraculously survived (anyone who survived the Battle of Britain survived by miracle). In 1943, while on an intercept, he tangled with the best German plane of the war, a fighter-bomber called the Junkers 88. By then he was flying a Spitfire that was agile but lightly shielded. The plane disintegrated around him and he crashed on the east coast of England, terribly burned. Pieces of his torn plane ripped him apart.

He limped from a British hospital in 1944. When war ended he returned to Poland, searching for his younger brother.

These facts surfaced over a period of many years. In August of 1948, though, no one had an inkling of who David Samuelwicz was, or what he had accomplished.

SATURDAY EVE, AUGUST 9TH

LESTER

On Saturday evening the dead man remained dead, the auction house closed, and Lester headed home to Jackson St. A week of hard work lay behind him. His week's pay rested in his pocket. He knew, and could tell the world, that a certain amount of crap came with any job, but some work was not-so-bad. When he thought about it, and he did think about it for 10-12 seconds, it had been better'n a fish-fry to see the boss shook up. The boss was a bullshit man, not-never a fighter.

The bus wasn't half full as it headed downtown, and mostly it carried colored cleaning ladies with wrinkled faces. Going-home time. A couple old white women sat on the bus. Poor as mudcats. Cleaning ladies, also.

A fine-looking, goldy-skin woman, young and sassy, watched Lester watching her. She shrugged. Lester shone dark as any citizen could. To this woman, Lester was not that much to see. She lived in a world of peroxide and skin whitener. Along with her sass was fatigue. Her painted nails were chipped and stubby. She had a little web of dust in her straightened hair, maybe from cleaning attics. She yawned open-mouth, and the yawn was sincere.

The bus pulled to a stop before Charlie Weaver's auction. The empty windows needed a wash. In the depths of the auction a couple of chairs still sat, a third tipped over. The floor lay cluttered with paper and small trash. Lester looked it over, felt a little something. Mrs. Weaver, or the Weaver family, had not wasted any time closing shop. Then Lester felt a breeze wash the back of his neck, like a whisper from Charlie, plus a little indignation.

He watched another cleaning lady board the bus. Name of Hattie. Lived on Jackson St. Older than daddy Moses and brother Aaron combined. Stooped. Gimpy from where a once-broken hip healed wrong. Crippled brown-skin lady. She carried a full pillowcase. The bus pulled away from the abandoned auction and Hattie sat beside him.

Lester had spent a good piece of his life in that auction, and he looked backward toward the auction as the bus pulled away. He could almost hear Charlie's voice chatting most amiable with an auction crowd. Charlie had been okay. Before the war Lester was just a young guy doing dogwork, but paying attention while Charlie taught him the business. Even back then Lester knew himself fashioned for big things.

The war had been an interruption. Lester cleaned latrines, then went to Germany where he drove truck with quartermaster corps. He lost his truck on the day he got closest to the front. That happened during the Bulge. Without a truck, and in the midst of confusion, he got hijacked.

For two awful weeks he pulled graves detail. The sarge who ran the show told his crew they were lucky. Winter covered Germany. Corpses were stiff, with white and frosted eyes above black and frozen blood; but no stink or rot. A man dragged them out of craters or thin snow banks.

Lester dragged while white men inventoried pockets, registered dog tags, and mostly only robbed the German corpses. Lots of rings taken. Lots of fingers cut off, because, after all, "the Kraut bastard wasn't going to need 'em any more."

An awful detail. Before he escaped back to quartermaster, Lester put in two weeks that were longer than a fancy lady's dreams. When he cut out of that detail he figured the worst was over, but it wasn't. He was held in Europe long enough to see starving and dying children. He saw emaciated refugees. He praised the luck that allowed him to swing wide of death camps.

Which meant that, back last Thursday when that white boy shot himself, Lester didn't want any part of it; not corpse or cops, nothin'. Then, when Wade asked if Lester wanted to "come see the dead man" it was like Wade was a big, loud, baby who was talking tough to a heavyweight. Still, there wasn't one damn thing a man could say. Wade was the boss. Let it pass. Like all the other crap-e-ola. Let it pass.

"White folks," Hattie said, "talkin' there's a killing at the auction." Hattie didn't have enough of a body left, hardly, to even move, but nobody had eyes so bright as Hattie. Her eyes could smile or even grin, if her wrinkles could not.

"Can't say," Lester told her. "Most like shot himself."

"Can't help but wonder. How come?"

"Folks say he was in misery." The bus pulled over and Lester watched, sort of wistful, as the goldy-skin girl got off. "His momma died and his brother disappeared. Police lookin' for the brother. All kind of talk."

"Kill himself, he's gonna burn."

There wasn't much Lester could say to that. Hellfire preacher business. That white boy had a right to kill himself, but not out of misery. If Hattie could hold on, so ought the white boy.

The bus pulled up to Jackson St. "Little mother," Lester said, "lemmie help you with that burden." He picked up the pillow case. "Weighs something."

"Missus got a new iron. That's her old one. She give me a old coat. I got a coat for winter." Hattie gimped down the aisle, one leg sort of twisty; walking crooked.

On the sidewalk Hattie gimped and Lester carried. The two went slow. In three blocks they passed Lucky's place, with Lucky still behind the counter. Lucky waved. Lola the guinea hen looked happy-clucky. Thomas, the Plymouth Rock rooster looked spooked.

"I got regular cleaning," Hattie said. "I got regular work."

"To this point I got the same," Lester told her. "All next week we working a warehouse."

"You gone dance tonight? You the best dancer."

"I should not wonder."

Saturday Night, August 9th

Lester

A nd now it was Saturday night. A man could get rid of a week's worth of shinola; cash in pocket, beer, a good cigar, not them weedy Roi Tans. Get dressed proper, then ease over to Sapphire Top Spot. Lester could drift like a big fish in a little puddle because he had steady pay and savings.

All around town were other puddles. Lester, who was always tuned in to what was happening, could have told exactly what half of the city did, and where, and with what labels on the bottles.

* * *

Beer and tobacco held their own in workingman bars. Maybe beer was gentle suicide, tobacco quiet; but they were long-range suicide for men who busted their behinds all week, made the rent, fed the kids, and looked at nigh-empty pockets; men, who, the minute they thought they were getting ahead, looked down to see a kid's feet needing new shoes.

Because a man, goddamn, had to have something; a place to hover, come Saturday night.

All during the week Louisville's beer joints prepared. While traveling men sipped or belted bourbon at hotels: The Brown, The Clay, The Seelbach, beer trucks rolled along quiet back streets and stopped before neighborhood bars. The trucks carried Sterling, Falls City, or Fehrs. And, while traveling men at the hotels went on-the-cheap with colored porters, tipping at most a quarter, but usually only a dime, the truck drivers proved the souls of generosity: without regard to race, religious, political or sexual problems.

Ritual beer. Souse-hounds and bar-flies in each neighborhood knew the beer routes and schedules. They were unerring on the time when afternoon services would begin at the local joint.

The beer truck driver arrived. His truck was slab-sided, with beer cases tiered and open to the sun. The truck shone yellow and blue, or red and white, or black and red. The driver was always built like a linebacker. He would trundle in stacks of beer cases, trundle out stacks of empty bottles. Then the driver would return to the bar. He sat, drank a beer, and bought a round for the house because it was the breweries' idea of promotion. The driver bulled-around, telling modest lies as became a hero. Then, amid fond farewells he left, headed for the next joint. The drivers who lasted were guys who could hold their beer. The trucks that lasted were generally Chevrolets.

By Saturday night extra beer lay iced. Joints along every commercial street punctured the night with neon and juke box. Electric fans churned, refrigeration grunted and wheezed, and where one lived on Saturday night dictated where and how one drank, if one drank.

Out by Bowman Field, and Strathmore, well-off Jews 'wet the bottom of the glass' with wine. These were Jews of German background who settled through the American south in the early and mid 19th century. Most Jewish immigration in those days stayed in New York City, but some did not. Ambitious immigrants had toted eighty pound packs through the middlewest and south. They peddled, succeeded, opened stores, and sent for their relatives. Small communities of Jews were established in cities across the country.

Lots of folks out there by Bowman and in Strathmore were still observant, observing Saturday. Even fallen Jewish angels, specifically Lucky, were sober. Lucky, and Mrs. Lucky (Rachel), sometimes dined out at locally famous Kaelin's; at the time a twelve minute drive.

In the midst of downtown along Market St. and thereabout, dwelt Polish Jews who settled in the late 19th and early 20th century. Lots of them were playing catch-up ball, because, unlike the Samuelwiczes, they had come from the Polish peasantry. Hardly anybody liked them, and with some reason. German Jews were disgusted because the Poles didn't know how to act civilized. The Germans felt that Poles gave Jews a bad name. Thus, the Germans thought about Poles in the same way that Ashkenazic (Spanish Jews) had thought about German immigrants back in the 18th century. The junk dealer Fudd was a good example of second generation Polish peasantry. What he drank he brewed at home.

Along Bardstown Road in the upper Highlands, well-off Catholics roosted in nice houses in the neighborhood of Saint Francis of Assisi church. There were two sorts of well-to-do Catholics; Germans and lace-curtain Irish. The Micks drank in lounges, usually too much. The Krauts generally drank at home.

Along the Parkway, down toward Saint Joe's hospital, Germantown paraded small but tidy houses, swept sidewalks, gleaming windows, and beer joints filled with heavy Dutch song. These were working men, not wealthy, but with substance.

In Butchertown, in the eastern part of the city toward the stockyards, blue collar guys belched, cussed, and hovered around the few women who had enough nerve to frequent neighborhood bars. These were white guys: English, German, French, an occasional Finn, plus mongrels. Couples sat at tables. Men fought. Lots of barfights.

In the west end, out toward Fountaine Ferry Amusement Park, well-to-do colored ladies and colored gentlemen; doctors, lawyers, undertakers, postal workers, and teachers, entertained. Their houses were generally small, and neat and clean as Germantown. There was, at the time, no more conservative person in the world than the colored gentleman, the colored lady. They raised their kids with starchy morals. They drank a little, held poker parties, laughed and were pleased.

On Jackson Street, part slum and part blue collar; with hot and cold running roaches, rented rooms and some two-room apartments (even an occasional building ratless), Saturday night moods could start joyful.

By the time folks wandered toward Sapphire Top Spot, Lucky had closed shop. Iron grills were up and locked. Small merchandise had been removed from windows. The money-green Cad bore Lucky down the street to Broadway, hung a left, then disappeared, not to be seen before Monday morning.

Folks strolled or paraded past the yellow store with black signs.

"Hymie bastard."

"Too rich for you, boy. Me, I gone open a store. Sell shit to you niggers."

"Screw by a Jew."

"Lucky okay. Lucky ain't afraid to touch a man."

"No work fo' colored."

"Jew-boys stick together."

Heat from the summer sidewalk diminished in twilight. There came no cool of evening, but scorch and burn of afternoon went shimmering. The best time at Sapphire Top

Spot was early time.

When a man stepped inside, what he saw was a short bar with fourteen stools set close. The bar, front and top, was made of painted piney-wood. The backbar the same, with flaking mirror and whiskey bottles, draft beer glasses, a little gin; beer in the cooler, and champagne in case somebody hit a number, or backed the right horse.

Behind the bar a peroxide blonde, a pearl-skin girl, worked serious; kind of skinny but the stuff of dreams. "Best lookin' woman in this damn town." Name of Blue.

At the end of the counter nearest the door sat Albert, old, obese, silent, well-dressed and watching Blue's moves at the cash register. He mostly worried because he owned the joint. Early evening was danger time. Transition from mixed to colored.

The joint sat next to Lucky's. White booze-hounds sometimes hocked stuff, and, needing a drink, couldn't wait to get to a place where they were wanted. Their presence was all right during sunlight, but not after dark. Still, booze-hounds generally were no worry. They mostly just stood at the bar with a beer, until they got tired of being ignored. They always moved on.

Other white boys showed up. Among the whites who picked up men at the Clark bridge, a few drove their help home after work. It wasn't common, but it wasn't rare, for a white to drop in and buy beer for his crew. As long as he left before dark, all right. As long as he didn't get lonesome and show up Saturday night, all right.

If he did show up he could bring a storm. Because, no matter how much or how often a man paid the cops, a hurt or dead white man would close the joint; and it was jail or worse for Albert. To the best of Albert's knowledge, cops could shoot a colored man all to hell with nothin' happening.

And badness was forevermore coming to pass. Ever since the war colored men were changing, and didn't even know it. They still backed down before whites. They still said "yassuh," but now with more sullen lines on wrinkled brows. Albert couldn't put a finger on the change, but he had a bar owner's antenna. What used to be known as New-York-Shit was becoming common. More angry talk. More loud voices. More men sinking into silence and danger. More knives and razors. More damn fights. More men cut.

Around the rest of the large room sat a mixture of tables and chairs; none matched. Toward the back end of the joint sat the jukebox, and in the middle of the joint was a space where tables could be pushed back for dancing.

And when Lester entered, half of those tables were still empty. The joint held collections of men, with a couple women at the bar. Jukebox sitting silent. Women waiting, just waiting. See what happens.

"I stroll all around this town," Lester said to a hustler named Jolly. "Everybody tell me you doin' Pittsburgh."

"Seat your ass," Jolly told him. "I done Pitt and Detroit and missus Chicago. Nobody hellos you up there. Nobody smiles."

Jolly leaned back in his chair, casual as a rich man at peace. He looked to be early thirties. He sometimes handled horse or reefers, but was mostly a gamble-man. His skin shone a little less than coffee color, his build stocky and square. He looked like a man designed to handle heavy loads, but his hands were smooth, so he surely wasn't gonna.

"Still usin' your own dice?" Lester said it funny, and that's how it was taken.

Two other men chuckled. Jolly was dressed all flashy, but the other two looked like men just off work.

Alfonso sat tired and just plain whipped. He was elderly, old, anyway nigh sixty, tough, chocolate and skinny—ropy biceps, day labor for life, goddamn little hope. Too old and too tired to dress up Saturday night.

Zeke still seemed pretty fresh. He could be no more than mid-twenties, color like medium toast; a man still not convinced that nothin' good was gonna happen, ever.

* * *

Louisville, on Saturday nights in early August was a place for murders. Still is.

If one approached in an airplane, the city would lay beneath like a plump guinea hen sitting on the curving nest of the Ohio river. Along that river low hills on the Indiana side are verdant in summer, skeletal in winter. In spring the river rises, does its dance, flooding basements with mud and pike and channel cat; houses afloat, second stories rising above muddy waters.

Then summer blows in with humid breath. Even from a plane the city would seem overheated. Should east-coast people, or west-coast people find themselves flying along the great course of the Ohio they would feel 'just right' until a Louisville-landing. Then they would suck air like fish suck water. Outlanders cannot hit a lick in such weather. Louisvillians, acclimated, can work their hearts out.

The air carries water, and water inflates the heat. Louisville turns into a giant sauna. Take a shower, put on a fresh shirt, walk from an air-conditioned house, and by the end of the block you need a fresh shirt. In 1948, though, almost nobody had air conditioning; certainly not the beer joints.

Take a group of men, tired, some busted up, wearing their lives out working nowhere jobs—jobs they don't even talk about, because everybody knows those jobs are nowhere—men who've left their women, or been kicked out; or if at home, not paid enough to support their kids....

Then add a week of work no man can respect. Then add payday. Then add beer. Add almost any catalyst: a woman worth fighting over, or a chance for theft. White men, colored men, all the same.

Then add all-embracing heat, a knife, a razor, a Saturday-night special, a Louisville Slugger. August Saturdays, prime for murder.

* * *

By eight o'clock the joint jumped, though by ten it would sit slack. Men with money would go on the town, hitting the colored clubs. Men with sorrow would drink too quick and too much, then sit with bowed heads above tables.

At eight, though, the juke box choked with nickels, dancers danced, and Lester moved graceful, fluid, smooth as a running stream. Barlight shone off Lester's skin, and he looked like he was supposed to be the evening's entertainment.

The dancers were mostly men dancing alone. They were so busy they didn't feel or hear whispers running through the joint. A mistake had been made, a matter for comment. Something mighty stupid.

Jolly acted showy, impressing Blue and trying to take that sweet girl home, despite she belonged to a man who was mean. Name of Ozzie. Due out of jail any minute.

Jolly cashed a hundred dollar bill. He did it stylish, like it didn't count for nothin'. Showboating... one of the serious flaws of gamble-men.

And Albert, slow of body but with a bar owner's quickness of mind, went to the beer-storage room pretending he had to dial a safe to get that much change. Jolly stood at the bar sweet-talking Blue.

"That boy better not try that elsewhere. Get by with it here. Maybe." Alfonzo watched Jolly. Other men watched the hundred dollar bill disappear to the back room. The bill might be in a safe, but the change was in Jolly's pocket. Alfonzo, who was old and terrible tired, could feel the evil-eye looking Jolly's direction.

Zeke sat across the table. "Didn't think Jolly that stupid. Nobody mess with Ozzie."

Zeke turned to watch Lester dance. Lester showed loose arms. Nothin' tight about Lester. Lester had shoulders moving like Mr. Arthur Murray couldn't. Lester had sweat in his hair, sweat in his shirt, sweat coming off his eyebrows, sweat just raining.

"I gone take that man on the road," Zeke said about Lester. "Be his manager." He turned from watching Lester to look at Jolly. "Blue not stupid."

Alfonzo watched Lester. The Duke did piano on the jukebox. "I used to shake pretty good."

"Good as that?"

"Pretty good." Alfonzo looked at a half-full glass of beer, looked at his hands gnarled and scarred. The jukebox rattled "Harlem Air Shaft." "A man dances to clean out the shit. You know that."

Late Saturday Night, August 9th

Lester

Saturday night lonesome. Streets near empty. A few men sitting drunk and silent at the Sapphire. Blue, tired and fussy, sweeping floors against tomorrow. Albert yawning and counting the till. Jukebox quiet. High-rollers out on the town. Lester tired as a week's work and a night's dancing can make a man. He sits with a warm beer, Lester. Having sweated abundant, he sits damn near sober.

Looks at Blue, how smooth, how sweet, but bartender sassy. Tells himself "wants none of that." Tells himself, "what a liar" wants some of that, but don't want much. Wants a woman all his own. Wants to Belong to somebody.

Lonesome. Stand up. Tap the table twice for something to do. Step away into the hot night and empty street, with pants full of lonesome, and carrying a head full of memory.

In the Army he met some sad bastards, Louisiana crackers, Florida crackers, Georgia shitheads, but mostly not. Mostly in the Army he talked to men who looked him in the eye and talked straight across. Maybe they saw color, and maybe didn't like it, but they were used to it.

So things didn't have to be the way things were. And a man didn't have to fall ass-over-appetite for a bartending woman. Not if a man was fitted out for something better.

When he got back from Europe with money in his pocket,

he wandered north to Boston and found himself offended. Everybody there must hate each other, talking short, sometimes nasty. To a southern man, Mr. Boston Yankee, be he colored or white, was nothing but a sonovabitch.

So Lester took a train across, over to Chicago, and fell in crazy love. White girl. Mona. Communist. Union. Said her prayers to the honored ghost of Mr. Eugene V. Debs.

Crazy love, and it still hurt as he walked empty old Jackson St. When he lay beside her, her brownish nipples rising from breasts like Miss Snow White, all kinds of feelings came and went. When she lay with him, enclosing him, he felt like he walked across the face of every white man who ever hollered nigger.

Turned out that was the least of it. They did bedroom a lot, her moving warm and sometimes nigh frantic against him, like she tried to be inside of him, and not the other way around. But after bedroom came other stuff... just as hot if not as ruckus. Lots of talking, walking around; him protective of her in the mean-talking streets of South Side. She, protective of him when white men muttered, spit on sidewalk, stood looking.

He came to understood that this woman was the one, the right one; but how the hell could they make it in the U.S.A.? They couldn't even make it in Chicago which was fenced-off worse than any southern city. Maybe move to Sweden. In Sweden nobody gave a damn.

He got a job in a warehouse. Carried a temporary union card, while Mr. Dave Beck straddled the Teamsters Union like the two-bit hooker he was. Colored men kept carrying that temporary card, but kept paying full time permanent dues. Never get a permanent card. Never get permanent pay.

"Give it time," Mona told him. "It's Chicago, not unions. We gotta change Chicago." In the mornings, still yawning, she was cute as a baby duck. Wouldn't let him see her walking around each day 'til she brushed her hair. Funny little duck. Serious as all hell. Pretty in that skinny Snow-White-way.

When truck drivers unloaded at the warehouse they were made to hire union help. The foreman used the temps for unloading, charged full rates to the drivers, kicked a nickel or two back to management and kept the rest. If a driver refused union help and brought his own, even members of his own family; wait until night and cut his tires.

"Workers," Mona said. "Management has got to wake up."

"He's a worker," Lester told her. "He only owns one goddamn truck. They tell me to slash his tires. I ain't gonna."

"There's gotta be rules." Mona could get sniffy when she wanted.

Lester could see how a union would help, but he couldn't get past the hinder. "Seems," he said, "like you get told what to do, no matter."

During the war unions held all the power and got corrupted. Now the working man was union-screwed. Make that double for the Teamsters. Make that triple for the working man in missus Chicago. Mona couldn't see it.

And so it came to pass that Mr. Eugene V. Debs, not color, was the Who that broke them up.

He loved her more, maybe, than she loved him. She loved a cause. Sometimes he felt like his color was her revolution. Then he felt the wrong of that. But, he just couldn't understand loving a cause, when the cause kept a man holding a temporary card....

After all got said and done, a man came home. The south was the south, and Louisville was the best of the south. He moved back to Jackson St., and Jackson St. had not changed much. Lucky's hockshop had a new coat of paint.

When he ventured back to Charlie Weaver's auction house he had a shock. The war had worked its will on Charlie.

Charlie had gone gray, and walked a little stooped. His hand trembled just a bit when he patted Lester on the shoulder. "Looks like I owe saint Jude a candle," he said, and smiled at himself. "One can indulge that kind of foolishness when one is Episcopalian."

After all got said and done, a man came home.

And so now Lester walked old worn-out Jackson St. Louisville no longer had Charlie, but it had communists and unions. Sometimes, like after beer, and riding a pack of lonesome, he thought of calling Mona. Forget it. She wanted 'equity', whatever the hell that meant. He wanted a wife and house and kids he could raise respectful.

Sunday, August 10th

Jim

Back during WWII, Calvary Lutheran Church on Bardstown Road went through a holy conniption of the type that makes Jesus weep. A family belonging to the congregation carried the last name of Rommel. Rumor held the family as distant relatives of The Desert Fox, Irwin Rommel, Hitler's most adroit general. It was proposed by no small number that the Rommels must be kicked out, excommunicated; and churchless, set on the smooth and easy road to everlasting fire.

The uneasy proposition caused wiser heads to prevail. About half of the congregation had some German blood. The holy barbecue got squelched, though indignation reigned.

Calvary Lutheran still stands firm in piled stone. Its stained glass windows are quietly flashy. Martin Luther, were he alive, could do something with it. During 1948, though, a conventional man named Robertson bullied that pulpit. He explained about the love of God, and he understood the social order. He knew enough not to use the word 'darkies' in front of the colored janitor. He, and some of his congregation, suffered not so much from hypocrisy as obtuseness.

On the other hand, he once joked that if the Jews ever

celebrated Christmas, it would come after the Christian Christmas, because of January white sales.

And to this church, each Sunday, came Wade's wife with Wade and kids in tow. Wade could pout, and Wade could cuss, and Wade could complain about work that needed doing; but the mother was in charge.

She was a country girl. Her name was Viola and she was as lovely as a stringed instrument played pianissimo at the throne of God. When it came to church she had her reasons which were mighty. She had lived through The Great Depression and seen families torn asunder. To most American women of the day church was the tie that binds. Some years later, someone (probably a preacher on the take) coined the sentence, "The family that prays together stays together." Wade's wife, and most American women, had thought that since forever.

Thus, on Sundays, Wade sat at home with a newspaper and read classified ads, giving not a holy heck or a sweet Jesus-H-Christ for the news. Classified told him directions in which money flowed, and let him know if there were any upstart auctioneers in town. He hid behind the paper, like a child under a bed praying not to be noticed. He had, after all, been the youngest of five kids, which most likely meant something.

"We don't want to be late." The mother always said that. Quiet, firm, and even though her kids were 13 and 14, she still checked to see if they'd washed behind their ears. (They always had, because if not, those ears were due for a scraping).

Wade would look up, look lost, then lay down his paper. "They need the money," he'd say about the church. "You got a comb?" he'd say to his kid. "You look like a goddamn Ubangi." And then he would reluctantly get dressed.

At church kids sometimes wiggled loose from parents.

When that happened they headed for the balcony of the church, where, if they did not giggle and carry on, they were allowed to stay during service. The colored janitor, Mr. James, always sat up there in the back row: nigger heaven among the Lutherans, and only one nigger allowed. Mr. James, a colored gentleman, watched kids play quiet games of blackjack with small cards hidden within hymnals, and probably thought well of them.

Some kids paid attention. It was from the balcony that Wade's kid learned more confusion as he heard unkind words about socialism, uneasy words about unions, and words that decried the philosophy of an old-time heretic named Ralph Waldo Emerson; a guy who, according to the saintly pastor Robertson, had displayed the depraved ideas of an atheistic mind.

August 11th

Warehouse

On Monday morning Wade's kid noticed that boards were gone from the door of Mrs. Samuels' house. When he told his dad, Wade made nothing of it. If Mrs. Samuels' last remaining son had returned home it was his own business. Or, maybe the detective had come back. Let the cops figure it out. Nobody had time for spicks or pollacks. The warehouse sale was only half set up.

The kid imagined he saw movement from behind partly drawn curtains of Mrs. Samuels' house. The windows shouldn't be shut. It was one of those dog days of mid August that start with an orange dawn, and with sleepers waking without covers on sweated sheets; a day beginning with temp in the mid 80s and climbing. The inside of Mrs. Samuels' small house would be worse than a hotbox. Anyone in there would be barely able to breathe.

Wade and his kid stood at the front window of the auction and watched the street. Lester got off the bus.

"Damndest thing," Wade said to his kid. "I never before knew any blackbird worth a plug nickel. You tell me now, how is Lester different?"

The kid, knowing he was reamed no matter how he answered, supposed Lester was a serious person.

"Lester thinks like a white man. Lester sees a thing develop,

86

like how an item set wrong blocks the flow of the crowd. Lester don't have to be told what to do."

The kid, whose answer had been on the edge of correctness, remained silent but relieved.

"So if Lester wasn't black as the ace of spades, he'd make a hell of an auctioneer."

The kid, who mortally feared the day when he would be called on to act the part of auctioneer, and face an auction crowd, kept his flapper shut.

"Which means I'm obliged to Lucky. You can learn a lot from Lucky."

Lester approached, springy of step. "He's a goddamn goldmine," Wade said. "He's like strikin' oil. Most of the help you get have hangovers."

When Lester came through the doorway Wade got businesslike. "My girl stays here. You take the truck and the kid," he told Lester. "The Mrs. and I will meet you there. We'll bust ass early. It's gonna get hotter than the Pope's hemorrhoids."

* * *

The '39 Ford truck carried a twelve foot moving-van body, rusted floorboards covered with sheets of boiler plate, and a clutter of tools in the cab. Lester slid behind the wheel like the happiest man alive. "I think to get some wheels," he told the kid. "Then I think maybe not. Maybe get a pickup. Police don't mess with a man in a truck."

...turn left on Bardstown Road, past the skating rink and bars and orphanage. When the truck got to Charlie Weaver's place, Lester and the kid saw a colored man sweeping. Chairs and a couple of lamps, plus ashtrays and other odds and ends sat on the sidewalk. An old International pickup sat at the curb. On its sideboards was painted the biggest double-entendre in coal-burning Louisville, although the owner didn't realize it. The sign said, *Ashes Hauled.*

"That's old Larry," Lester told the kid. "Clean-up man. He takes the trash, gets the spare goods, plus a buck or two for work and gas." Lester looked at the empty auction house, at the dusty windows and fading sign. "Hell of thing," he said. "Charlie, he was all right."

"My dad said he was smart."

"Your daddy is smart. Charlie is more on the quiet side. Or was."

Hang a left at Cave Hill and travel half the length of Broadway to Arnold's Moving and Storage, famous among Louisville's small businessmen and a favorite of auctioneers. When an auction is held outside the auction house, the commission goes down to ten percent, but the gross goes up. The customer base widens to include contractors, builders, even grocerymen. It all depends on what's for sale.

In a warehouse sale, as Lester would explain because he is even more experienced than Wade, people expect most anything. It is different from an estate.

In an estate the person is dead. His goods got abandoned in the midst of daily use. They sit in place in his house, his furniture, his little secrets; dust on the lintels, month-old lettuce sinking to liquid in the refrigerator. The goods, having outlasted the master, are still arranged in practical patterns. Somebody else could move in, rearrange things, and the house and property would continue.

But in a warehouse sale the goods seem to apologize. After all, the person who left them meant to return. Why else leave personal stuff? But, life gets in the way. People remarry or die. Age and failed memory send some to the poorhouse or the old folks' home. Some move or are careless. Their goods sit lonesome. Warehouse fees add up. When the bill goes unpaid for too long, the auctioneer gets a call.

If goods could feel bad these would wail...

nice-stitched linen, antique pistols, old coins, diaphragms

(always means a divorce), sentimental stuff: programs of concerts, invitations to balls, ribbons faded but pressed among pressed flowers, Bibles holding faded obits from newspapers, tissue V-mail from the war, fading blue. There are dance cards, family photos, groups of grinning soldiers, doughboys, G.I.s, pictures of ships and planes, cars and houses, and photos of Old Dog Trey.

Porn books, porn pictures, porn postcards, mostly French from the war; but also comic books on newsprint: Donald and Daisy Duck doing the deed. Tarzan and Jane. Wimpy and Popeye and Olive Oyl.

Stuff that folks save: balls of aluminum stripped from cigarette packages, balls of string, stubs of crayons, pencils, prescription bottles with a few remaining pills, plus aspirin, and always and forever, dried-out Pepto Bismol, once pink and promissory; ration stamps from the war, for meat, gas, sugar, stamps that controlled goods outside the black market, plugs of tobacco, half-bitten, tucked in brass spittoons.

Victorian pictures of the dead: mother and child, woman in wedding dress, baby in ruffles though stillborn, in fancy coffin. Plenty pictures of well-dressed corpses, youths, and businessmen.

Coffee cans filled with buttons, magnets fashioned like little scottie dogs, nosing each other, ribboned medals from eighty years of wars, crayon pictures drawn by children and folded into dictionaries, pinking scissors, darning eggs, all a-tumble; worse than an estate sale. Sad. Ghostly. Troublesome.

And (...and this is where trouble and some real ghosts would walk in on everybody that hot August day) there are lots of containers: Drawers after drawers in vanities, dressers, highboys, old-fashioned kitchen cabinets sporting flour mills (some still holding flour), tool chests, hope chests, cedar chests, plus cartons and boxes and wooden cases. There are desks and file cabinets, armoires, hidden drawers, false bottoms in fine furniture, and trinkets carefully wrapped and packed in wastebaskets.

Lester and Wade's kid brought the truck along because a warehouse sale holds a lot of unsalable stuff that goes to the dump.

Lester pulled the truck into the huge warehouse. The truck sat dwarfed beside the 'lots' (inventories) of goods being sold for storage charges. Yellow forklifts trundled here and there. Warehousemen kept their distance. To the warehousemen, the auctioneer and crew were intruders.

"We gotta," Wade said to no one in particular, "hump like a horny racehorse, 'cause we're way behind. Number as we go. The wife and I work one lot, and Lester works another."

Wade's kid, relieved, went with Lester.

Some days, as Wade would attest, are not worth cow plop on a highway. Box after box held more trash than merchandise. Junk went onto the truck, which by noon sat half full. Lunch came from brown bags. Wade's wife had fixed for the whole crew and pretended to a picnic. She was self-conscious, the kid was self-conscious, and Lester remained quiet. Out of habit maybe, or because he still mistrusted Wade, he managed to sit off some distance by himself. Lester could not go into a white restaurant.

Wade, on the other hand, chomped fast, resenting the time that eating took away from work. And then, shortly, Wade and Lester (who would likely tell you they had seen it all) found out they hadn't.

The shrunken heads appeared just after lunch, but nobody sicked. Lester pulled them, wrapped in cloth, from a dresser drawer. He unwrapped them and the heads, with eyelids sewn shut, tried to stare back. "Sweet Jesus," said Lester. "Fiji Island?" said Lester. He laid the two heads on top of the dresser. "Better come look," he told Wade.

The heads were no longer black, as when alive. Black had turned dull gray. Leathery. They were no larger than a big man's fist.

"Some soldier-boy," Lester said to nobody in particular. "Bought 'em in the Solomons."

Wade's kid, scared, backed up. He was obliged to act like a man, but nobody said he had to like it.

"Natives sold to the soldier-boys," Lester said, "mostly imitations. Mostly monkey heads. These ain't monkey heads."

"They're worth something." Wade looked ready to reach for a lot-number. Then his mind turned to problems of display. Then he hesitated because his wife took charge.

"These were people. You'll not sell people." Then she turned red, redder than Wade's kid had ever seen her.

Lester turned away so as not to embarrass her any worse. "I'll take 'em," he muttered. "Say a word over them. Give 'em a burial."

Wade, who finally picked up, stood for a moment like a juvenile delinquent caught in a hot-wired Packard. Silent, he turned back to work.

"We're trading," Wade's wife said in a voice so certain that no sane man would argue. "I'll work this lot with the boy. Lester works my place." She didn't say she had bad feelings about that lot. Didn't have to.

Just as well. Southern ghosts appeared, and the day had it in mind to stay ugly. Wade's kid next discovered a photo album in a desk. He idly opened it to a black and white glossy of a man lynched. The man dangled, not well dressed. The picture had been taken in daytime. The kid flipped pages. The same man appeared, but this time the photo showed a close-up of his face; tongue sticking out (but not much) eyes wide like he watched something spectacular; the springtime leaves of Heaven or the winter roots of Hell. This photo showed night. A glow of firelight, or flashbulb, brightened the man's brow. The skin shone dark as Lester.

The kid motioned to his mother. She looked, whispered, and the kid had never heard her voice so sad. "Wrap it in something. Bury it in the trash on the truck. Do it quiet."

And, the day wouldn't quit. In a cedar chest, right on top of sheets, lay a Klan hood. When Viola pulled it out, she gasped, then tried to hide her confusion.

"Never mind hiding it," Lester said to her. "I see the damn thing. Lemmie look." He walked easily as an actor, and took it from her hand.

Klan hoods, up close, came in considerable varieties. Some were made of cheap stuff, starched and backed with cardboard. Some, like this one, were of finest muslin with a Christian cross embroidered large. Holes for eyes stared oval, awful. Lester looked it over, felt its considerable weight. "The lady knew how to sew," he muttered. "Look at the handwork on this thing." The stitched cross, in red, lay as clean and tight and comfortable as rope. "Through the years," Lester said to Wade's wife, "a couple of these came through Charlie Weaver's place. We all felt bad." He tossed the hood onto trash in the truck and went back to work.

And Wade's kid, who was of two minds about everything, watched his father go red and speechless. As work continued Wade remained quiet. He did not cuss and he did not boss. Where Wade came from, Indiana, there were more Ku Klux than in any southern state. The best that can be said of Wade is that he had never actually been Ku Klux, because he was not a joiner. He wouldn't even join the Rotary.

By three o'clock the truck sat filled. Wade turned to Lester. "Best make a dump run. Take the kid."

August 11th

Dump Run

The dump lay out behind Butchertown. Huge trucks trundled along narrow streets, turned into a graveled road and eased over rumpled hardpan which turned greasy, thus skiddy during rain. In summer heat, smells of decay and turpentine layered the air. In some spots, nails and glass poked through muck. A guy had to figure at least one flat tire for every half dozen dump runs.

Two men ran the dump. One tended the trash-fire that burned all day, smoldered all night. The man lived like a gamble-man, except life and limb, not money, were the stakes. The game was played in a combat zone. Discarded ammunition sometimes blew off. It was usually small stuff, but an occasional 30-30 or .45 (called 'zingers') came singing out of the fire.

The other man sat in a shack at the entrance and did diddly. Before his alcoholic eyes passed garbage trucks, mostly uninteresting, and other trucks holding amazing possibilities. Louisville had industries.

Drums of used oil, aluminum scraps, out-moded office machines, broken glass, cases of bottles or canning jars, ammunition boxes from the war, boxes of paper files, rusted tools, discarded canvas, packing boxes, cases of water-damaged clothing, books, chemicals, jerry cans painted army-khaki-color, and entire inventories of smoke-stained merchandise from some store's successful insurance fire.

A few people lived at the dump and also made their livings there. Crude shacks stood on the perimeters, nailed together from used boards and roofed with discarded tin. These 'regulars' lived off the effluvia of a growing city. They swapped, sold, sometimes cornered a market in gallons of paint discarded because it had been frozen; or building materials. For amusement (and they were joined in this on Saturdays by young boys from the neighborhood) they used .22 rifles to pot rats.

And for these folks, Lester and the auction truck were a special joy. It would not be fair to say they 'lived' for the appearance of Lester, but it is fair to say the truck made-the-day for one whale of a lot of happy scavengers.

* * *

Lester drove and Wade's kid rode. The shrunken heads rested in an old pillow case on the truck seat. The kid kind of nestled toward the door, away from the heads. When the truck bounced on railroad tracks the heads sort of jounced up, then settled. Lester hummed as he drove. "My daddy," he said softly to the kid, "was a sorta mean bastard. Not much of a drinking man. Just mean."

The kid avoided the heads, and found himself speechless. Some kind of opening lay in what Lester said. Maybe. He watched Lester's hands on the steering wheel. Blackest hands the kid had ever seen. The kid thought of the lynch-pictures riding back there in the load. He told himself he'd have to get that sack he'd put them in, and get them to the fire.

"My dad ain't exactly mean," he said. "But he ain't what you'd say, polite."

"He's in a tough business." Lester still talked soft. "You got a fine momma. She treats a colored man decent."

The kid scooched away from the heads, embarrassed,

and didn't know what to say. People didn't talk about colored, not in front of colored. People pretended. "I don't understand... shit...." he muttered. It was the first time ever, in his whole life, that he had used the word 'shit' out loud. Probably headed for hell because of it. And, he didn't even know what he meant.

Lester hummed, sort of happy. "Do you know it's shit, you'll be okay. Listen to your momma."

The heads jiggled. Lester reached to pat the pillow case like a grown man patting a puppy, or maybe a kid.

"In the war. Did you see 'em chop heads?"

"I saw sad sacks cut the ears off-a other sad sacks who happened to be dead at the time." Lester went silent like he concentrated on his driving. Then he said, "Cut heads happened in the south seas. I was in Europe where t'was worse." He drove and sort of tapped the steering wheel with fingertips. Finally, "Lucky was going through something when that foreign boy killed himself. I was watching it happen. And Lucky ain't never even been to Europe."

When they pulled into the dump and Lester backed up to one of the dump piles, the kid found he'd worried and fretted for nothing. Lester got busy with old-home-week at the dump.

"My darling Lester," a gap-tooth lady said, "simply splendid to see you again." The lady was old and crazy-as-hell, but sweet. The kid had seen her on trips with his dad, but from afar. She was sort of yellowish, mouldy-white, with wilted flowers on her straw hat. One eye sort of cocked sideways, but seemed cheery.

"Goddamn it, Lester, you got you-self a diff'rent truck. Where you find this shitbox?" This from a little tub of a man with rotted teeth; also white but unwholesome.

"New job," Lester told him. "Weaver passed." Lester headed for the back of the truck, but the kid had bailed and got ahead of him. Drop the tailgate. Climb up fast. Rustle the stuff. The kid had klan hood and lynch-pictures headed for the fire, even while Lester watched. He heard, almost like an echo, Lester saying to the old lady, "... kid might be gonna amount to something."

Folks clustered as Lester and kid pushed the load. A dark- skinned man with a narrow nose talked excitedly in a foreign language. "Portuguese," Lester explained as he worked. "Sometimes falls into English. Keep away from him. Crazy as a rabbit."

And, a romantic couple, a pair of Mutt and Jeff guys; one dirty black, one dirty white, quarreled over discarded clothes. The white one wore ragged feathers in his hair. "Be polite there," Lester told the white one. To the dark one he said, "I swear to goodness, you two boys are damn near ten pounds in a five pound bag."

* * *

"Queer as bears at a fair," Lester explained to the kid as they pulled from the dump. "Those two gents have found the safest place. Every place else is dangerous."

The kid, who had heard about queers, didn't know squat what the word meant.

"I gotta drop by my place," Lester told him. Lester patted the pillow case. "Don't think it real smart to be carrying these folks on a bus."

The truck rattled along brick streets, along a short patch of cobblestones, and wound past the stockyards where cattle and swine cried; screams of beasts, no gentle moos, no contented oinks. Cattle pressed through chutes. Sheep clustered in tight packs against fences.

"Besides," Lester said, like he was excusing himself, "I'm thinking a little bit about Lucky."

Past taverns and churches, then past supply houses; electric, plumbing, printing; finally to Jackson St. The truck pulled up before a brick three-story Victorian. It looked like a regular house. Down the block, away, stood a yellow-painted building. "Lucky's place," Lester told the kid. "I'll be right back."

Wade's kid took an interest. Down a block, beside the yellow building, a half dozen colored men stood in front of a green-painted tavern. Occasionally one clapped his hands, or did a little shuffle. The men didn't seem excited, or anything; but every-other-minute one would shuffle-dance. They watched an occasional car cruise Jackson St. Sometimes a man would drift from the group like a log on the river, only to find an eddy and drift back.

Brick Victorian houses lined the street as far as the kid could see. The kid had been around enough antique dealers to know about old houses, and thus knew this had once been a snazzy part of town. He sniffed and smelled something different, but could not say what. He knew about the colored sweat which mixed in with this different smell; but the smell was more than that. If tears could give off an odor, he smelled them. If laughter could cause the mildest stink, he smelled it. The sweet part of the smell might come from church-song. His nose, more than his eyes, told him he sat watching, for him, a brand new world.

When Lester climbed back in the truck he did not start the engine. Instead he watched the street where a coffee-colored man came out of Lucky's hock shop. The man walked a little unsteady. He looked like a bum dressed in fancy hand-me-downs.

Lester pointed. "You lookin' at a damn fool. You wanta see a fool, you're seeing him."

The man walked away from the group on the corner. When he passed the parked truck he did not look up. A bruise along the side of his head looked more red then deeper black. The further he got from the men on the corner, the more he allowed himself to limp.

"Got his ass beat pretty good," Lester told the kid. "Name of Jolly. Must of got whupped on Sunday night. Just woke up in an alley. You're looking at a man what's been rolled."

"Could use a hospital."

Lester snorted. "He needs another whop alongside the head. Bat sense into him." Lester did not say that, except for Red Cross Hospital, and the basement of General, there was not a hospital in town that would treat a colored man. Lester started the engine. "Let's cruise on down to Lucky's. You ain't seen a hock shop 'til you seen Lucky's."

August 11th

Lucky's Store

Men standing on the corner; then came a bar painted flaking green, an alley, and Lucky's showy black and yellow store. First thing through the doorway, the kid found himself looking down a bright and narrow tunnel, five times wider than a bowling lane and as long. It looked like it ought to be named 'the trombone store', what with all the slip-horns along the walls. Other horns gleamed, trumpets, French horns, silver and golden saxophones, and ebony clarinets. Everything shone polished. The store had more lights than most, and every item so clean, that, if it held the least chance of sparkle, it sparkled.

When the kid looked upward he saw two stuffed chickens, and the big one looked more than a little nuts. It had its beak pushed forward like the toughest fighting rooster ever born, but it still looked chuckleheaded. The other chicken was small and plump, and had that, "I just laid this amazing-fine egg," sort of look.

"...found ourselves in the neighborhood," Lester said to Lucky. "The boy's never seen your store." To Wade's kid he said, "The girl chicken is Lola, the gentleman is Thomas."

"The best known couple in this neighborhood." Lucky leaned over the front showcase which held watches and pocket knives on bright maroon velvet. There were colors all over the place: royal blue, fire engine red. In the bright tunnel of the store, breezes from fans whipped all around.

At the far end, two people bent to their tasks. A young boy's dusky face leaned over a silver service, and his dusky hand polished. He was too far away for anybody to see him good. Also toward the back of the store, Mrs. Lucky sat at a small desk and worked in a ledger. She was lots younger than Lucky and prettier by a long shot. She wasn't tall, and she wasn't thin, but she was beautiful; a Jewish princess turned matron.

"Looks like our man Jolly sort-of bumped his nose." Lester said it tentative.

"He was defending a woman," Lucky said. "That's his story."

To the kid, he said. "It's not a little odd, but I don't think I ever heard your name."

"James." The kid almost whispered. "It's from the Bible." He felt like squirming, but didn't. "Can't say I care much for it."

"His momma calls him Jim." Lester looked toward the rear of the store. "Looks like you found a kid. Looks like Miz Esther's Howie."

"Howard," Lucky said. "He's doing two afternoons a week, then two hours a day after school starts." Lucky looked at Jim. "...takes a good bit to keep this place up." He chuckled. "... want a job?" He turned back to Lester.

The kid... not just a kid ... because in this place he was 'Jim' and not just 'hey you', stood speechless and wanting. Did he want a job? Did he wanta work for Lucky? Were there fish in the river?

But it had sounded like a joke. Sure as anything he was about to make a fool of himself. On the other hand, he hadda. "Yes," he said. "I could use a job." He felt like tugging Lucky's sleeve, but managed to hold off.

Both men turned to him. They looked at each other, like they understood something they weren't gonna say; like Wade was the north end of a southbound horse, and his kid wanted better.

"I'll talk to your dad," Lucky said, and said it kind. "Maybe we can make something happen." He touched Jim on the shoulder, real friendly. He touched Lester the same. To Jim, that touch was altogether new, a little scary, also wonderful. He would learn that colored folk were not afraid to touch; did it all the time. It was a way of talking. It was just one more thing Lucky knew and everybody else didn't.

"You might give a mention to Jolly," Lucky told Lester. "He's talking mean, and Jolly isn't mean. He might be mouthing his way into something." Lucky sounded tentative, like he wanted to say more.

"Some folks have hell's own time learning. I'll say a word." Lester paused, waited.

"All these people dying," Lucky said. "It's like a curse, and nobody needs a curse to spread to Jackson St."

"Charlie's time was come. He got old." Lester paused again.

"We both understand Charlie." Lucky shrugged. "I just fret too much, and fretting can give a man a chill. Still, say a word to Jolly."

"It'll happen," Lester told him, then turned to Jim. "We gotta haul outta here."

"Auctions are wholesale operations," Lucky mused. "Jim could use retail experience. That's what I'll tell his dad."

And that is how Jim, on Wednesday before the Saturday warehouse sale, started working two afternoons a week for Lucky.

* * *

Jim stepped off the Broadway bus to walk up Jackson St. Cars parked along the street were two kinds, old and raggedy, or big and slick. Sunlight glanced off hoods of a '38 Cad, a '39 LaSalle, a '40 Packard gleaming above the dusty street. They sat mixed in with old pickups and cars, Studebakers, Willys, Plymouths, Fords and Chevs. One snazzy pickup, a '47 Hudson, looked businesslike.

Crud littered the gutters in front of some houses, and on some steps. Brick houses rose above the street, and front steps were mostly concrete slabs. Here and there a slim-and-silver can opener sat tucked between bricks, convenient for cracking beer cans toward the cool of evening. On one stoop an old woman sat, muttering to herself in the sun. On another stoop an old man. When Jim said "Howdy," they said nothing.

Next block, next block, sunlight and dust. On the corner just ahead, a group of men stood near a tavern with a sign, Sapphire Top Spot. Beyond them the front of Lucky's yellow-painted store stood washed in sunlight. Jim figured it might be the same men who had been there on the day of the dump run. He was at least ninety percent right.

He angled his way across the street and kind of swerved to avoid the group of men.

"You lost white boy? Running away from yo momma?" A mean voice from a man who looked more gray than black. His skin looked worn out, sort-of, and his forehead was wrinkled even if he didn't look old.

"Going to Lucky's," Jim whispered. "Going to work for Lucky."

"Stand there, boy. Don' move." The man turned to the other men. "Hebe sonovabitch. He's givin' away Howie's job."

"Leave it, Ozzie," one of the men said. "Just leave it." The man looked up and down the street, like a man checking for police.

"There's a day coming," Ozzie told the men, and Jim,

"when no white boy is gonna walk this street." To Jim he said, "Boy, move your ass."

It was only a few steps to Lucky's store, and Jim stepped them without running, but just barely. When he got inside Lucky was all business.

"Retail is different. Two rules. You can't sell out of an empty wagon, so you need tons of stuff. And, second, if things look good the customer comes in often. That's the reason we clean." Lucky led Jim toward the back of the store. "Your dad has the brightest sales in town. For wholesale. We take it a step further."

They passed the desk where Mrs. Lucky worked, when she worked. Today the desk sat empty. A kid Jim's age sorted through a pile of clothes. "Howard will show you what to do." Lucky turned back to the front of the store. No introduction. Wise enough in the ways of kids to know that kids would work it out.

"We are making two piles," Howard said. "We will brush down and clean what is saleable. These are mostly coats." His diction was so precise he must have practiced. His skin was Indian-color, and his nose was thin as his face. He looked like he weighed less than the stack of clothing.

"Jim," Jim said. "Tell me how you're judging. That stuff don't look so hot."

"It will," Howard told him. "In this store a man develops a magic touch. Have you ever stepped up to an ironing board?"

"I guess I'm gonna. How long have you worked here?"

"Long enough to know I'm wanted. If a man listens he can get ahead. I will get ahead." Howard looked toward the front of the store where Lucky dealt with a youngish woman. "You can learn the trade," Howard said, "and someday own your own store."

MILDRED SAMUELS

In Lucky's mind, although he didn't really understand it at the time, Mildred Samuels became more than one person, and more than one ghost. Lucky knew lots of people who had relatives in Germany, and by now, Lucky's friends understood their relatives were dead. When war opened it had seemed that German Jews might come through the war, because it was believed German soldiers would have a hard time shooting people who spoke German. That idea fell apart as the war progressed. Gradually, people realized that no one had heard from relatives since late in 1941.

At first, Lucky could not even be sure that Mrs. Samuels was a Jew, or that she had been Polish, or German, or Russian. All Lucky knew, in the days before he planned a vacation, was that a woman had died. He had not even thought about her until her son committed suicide. When that happened Lucky felt vaguely guilty, although he might have excused himself. He was just as busy and preoccupied as everyone else. He would later feel compelled to learn everything about her. He would not learn everything, but would learn a lot.

* * *

American immigration quotas shrank all through the first half of the 20th century, so it turned out that Mrs. Mildred

Samuels and her husband got to America just under the wire. They were exceptional in another respect. Their emigration from Poland was altogether different from what had been customary.

European immigration to the U. S. traditionally happened when a son or father left his native land for streets said to be lined with gold. What the men mostly found was work at low wages, and opportunities to use creative moxie, if they had any. In the case of Mildred Samuels history was reversed. She and her husband emigrated while her sons stayed home.

She was born in 1881 and married Jakob Samuelwicz, ten years her senior, in 1901. At her death in 1948 she was 67. Her son David was 46, her younger son, Isaac, was 44. Before marriage she had been a violinist of near professional ability. While many women gave public performances in those days, she did not because her father forbid her. After marriage, she would serve as teacher to her younger son. Isaac inherited her love of music. By the time he was twelve he was a musical prodigy of piano.

In 1936, with one son already an officer in the Polish Air Force, and a younger son establishing himself as a virtuoso musician and teacher of music, Mrs. Samuels and her husband Jakob (Jake) departed Warsaw for the United States. They had two reasons. Their main reason concerned rumors about Stalin, and further rumors about Russian weapons.

It is certain that the couple appealed to their sons to leave, and it's clear from later actions that the older son, David, chose to stand and fight against whatever destiny brought. The younger son Isaac doubtless refused because he was 32 years old and assured of a brilliant concert career.

Quite likely the sons argued. They probably told their parents that rumors of Russia's increase in weapons seemed a thin excuse for leaving a prosperous way of life. And, it's

equally likely that the parents replied, "Thin, unless one is Polish."

Poland lay surrounded by Russia to the east, Germany and Austria to the west, and Czechoslovakia to the south. For all of its eleven centuries Poland's borders had been provisional. During most of the 19th century it had not even existed as a nation, having been divided up by Europe's superpowers.

If one were not only a Pole, but Jew, and if one heard rumblings from Russia while also hearing rumblings from Germany, it was time to look toward America.

Jakob Samuelwicz was a moderately successful merchant, no intellectual, but no fool. He knew how to survive. He also knew that there was not a country in all of Europe that, for ten centuries, had not at one time or other, held pogroms. If one was a Jew in Europe there had been no good place, although Poland was the best of an historically bad lot. Jews originally came to Poland after being kicked out of Spain in the late 15th century. Samuelwicz could trace his family through seven generations in Poland. As a Pole, it took a lot of threat to pry Jakob from his native land.

The couple's second reason for emigration was the promise of economic security. Jakob had an uncle in Louisville who owned a large dry cleaning business. The uncle had neither chick nor child, and his wife had died tubercular. He was an old and lonely man in a city where most Polish Jews were of the peasantry, and German Jews were snooty.

It seemed to Jakob that if he came to America he would quickly learn, and someday inherit, the dry cleaning business. That actually happened. He prospered, and could soon afford the small house on Bardstown Road. The purchase was a great act of faith, because most European Jews rented. They did not buy because governments of Europe, when financially hard up, had routinely confiscated Jewish property.

When Jakob died of age and overwork in '43, Mildred was forced to sell the business. She was 62 and alone, but with savings and money from sale of the business. She became a thin and quiet woman, apparently friendless, who was only seen when walking to the grocery. When her two sons managed to get to the States, even though illegally, one can only hope that for Mildred Samuels it was like a sunrise.

Because of the tumult and terror that had run worldwide before Stalin and Hitler, Mildred Samuels would indeed come to represent many, many ghosts. And her sons would come to represent many more.

Saturday, August 16th

Warehouse Auction Daytime

Segregation in Louisville was one doomed duck, although Louisville didn't know it. Lots of white Louisvillians hardly understood that segregation existed. Real estate salesmen knew that sales in some parts of the city could not be made to Jews, but even real estate people did not think of restrictive covenants (still in force although the U. S. Supreme Court had just ruled otherwise) as segregation.

No preacher thought of Jews as segregated. Preachers only preached that Jews were clannish. And, when it came to colored folk, whites could point to a few colored living most anywhere in town. Some colored even received their mail at the very best addresses.

That happened in the old south because the big house with white folk sat out front, watching over the street. Servant quarters for colored watched over the back alley. Same address.

Louisville did know that Mr. Barry Bingham owned *The Louisville Courier-Journal* and *The Louisville Times*. In the matter of integration both papers approved, while standing on the side of the angels; where also, at least in that matter, stood Mr. Barry Bingham. In addition, Louisville was uneasily aware of a large and annoying number of white liberals (generally called 'communists') who were pledged to bring about change.

They had a history going back as far as the 1920s. Mr. Barry Bingham, and the papers, mistrusted communists; and sort-of rode the fence when it came to unions.

Louisville also knew that the official stance of official Louisville was, "Integration will come someday, but not just yet. It's a little too early. It needs to come gradual. Today is not the time." Thus, the NAACP wanted matters settled yesterday, while official Louisville wanted 'day after tomorrow'. Both sides, mostly, remained polite.

Charlie Weaver, or Charlie Weaver's ghost, understood the official position. He also understood the wants of the NAACP. Charlie was a generous man according to his lights, although most of his lights had been lit back in the 19th century.

As a gentlemen from an elder time, and good-hearted, he would caution against haste; but would do so with sympathy. He would also point out that his auction house always held to liberal standards. He even hired one colored gentleman, and that gentleman had free run of the place, i.e. Lester could go to the can like anybody else.

Because, for most colored folk segregation meant, among other things, there was no place to pee. White restaurants and lunch counters were strictly white, though during the war a few exceptions showed up. There were no colored restrooms in department stores. Colored gents and ladies could not try on clothing to see if it fit or looked nice.

Public parks were strictly off-limits, except in Chickasaw Park for colored, as were swimming pools. Fountaine Ferry Amusement Park, where any kid would want to go, admitted only whites, although it sat near an area of prosperous colored.

On the flip side, buses were not segregated and anybody could sit anywhere. Colored folk had the vote and could sometimes swing elections. Problem was, though, that while a man could eat or smoke on a bus he couldn't pee; neither there nor in a poll booth.

Which is why the day started poorly. When he was at Wade's store Lester went to the john like everybody else. At the warehouse he didn't. Maybe he might, but the auction crew was not beloved by warehousemen. Why take a chance on crossing a warehouse foreman? The day turned into an embarrassment when a cop caught Lester peeing behind a truck door.

The cop knew that men have done this since the invention of truck doors. Before that, men peed behind their wagons. Colored men, white men, Indians; it was a sacred tradition, though, traditionally a lot of Indians didn't give a sniff, or even half-a-parsnip, and peed anywhere. The cop had nothing else to do, except be a Louisville cop: thus worthy of explanation.

Mr. Colonel Carl Heustis was Chief of Police, conservative, but running a pretty good force. He had white officers and a few colored, and the colored cops could even arrest a white man if need be: which didn't happen, since they patrolled only colored areas. Still, the fact that they could was different from most cities of the south.

White or colored, the cops could pretty much do as they wished. If a colored man, or certain brands of white men, proved inconvenient, they could be shot without causing a whole of a lot of flak. Men could get arrested for dancing on the sidewalk, which somewhat later one man did; and the case went all the way to the Supreme Court. The court proved it liked the First Amendment more than it liked Louisville cops; who, in fairness, were sometimes moderate. And, even the worst of them were not quite as loathsome as their opposite numbers in Chicago or Detroit-City.

The first thing Wade knew was that an embarrassed and intimidated Lester got shoved in front of him ten minutes before the auction started. The cop was pug-nose Irish, with hair as red as the antique dealer, Gloria's; also present; and present also, Daniels. And Fudd, the scummy junk dealer. And country-boy dealers from downstate. And Lucky. And standing beside Lucky, dusky-skinned Howard, slight of build. Plus, a gathering auction crowd.

"...boy says he works here. Pissin' in the street. Indecent exposure." The cop had the build of a man who missed his calling, being the perfect shape for a beer truck driver.

"I got a sale starting," Wade told the cop. "I need that man."

"Behind the truck door." Lester could only whisper. His Africa-black skin was not brighter, but somehow dull. He looked like a little boy being called down by a school teacher.

"I got a problem," Wade told the cop, and said it jovial, like a preacher about to address a luncheon of the Royal Order of Moose. "I got this crazy woman...." He looked at Gloria, winked, and Gloria started to swell and puff up, all ready to surround the cop. Since no bog Irishman is worth a sniff in the face of a tough Irish woman, the crowd's interest shifted.

"Known this man for years," Lucky whispered to the cop. "Let's step over here a minute."

And, in that way, both Wade and Lester once more became beholden to Lucky. Lucky had paid off so many cops his skill was unquestioned. Five bucks settled matters. The cop left. Lester dropped into silence, and when the auction started it took him the better part of an hour to get up and rolling. Still, as it turned out, humiliation kept working on Lester. Humiliation was at the root of a nasty fracas, but that didn't happen until late afternoon. First, the auction.

* * *

In a warehouse a different style of selling is wanted. Charlie Weaver had never been particularly good at the style, and

Wade had to work like a Missouri mule to pull it off. That was because the ceiling rises higher than a barn, the concrete floors stretch endless, so auctioneer and crowd are dwarfed like parishioners in an economic cathedral.

When in his auction house, with lower ceilings and brighter lights, Wade can roll his thunder. In the warehouse, his voice disappears into the far reaches of space. Wade sells to an expanding and contracting circle of people instead of a sweating and tight-packed crowd. People cluster, then drift away to buy a sandwich at the portable lunch stand run by the caterer Mr. Evans, a colored gentleman.

And there's always at least one main tragedy just waiting to bust the auction. Somewhere in that crowd stands a pathetic creature; usually an overweight lady with flowered housedress and thinning hair, or a geriatric gentleman who leans on a cane. These are people who have come to see their stored households sold to strangers. They have almost no money, and are intent on buying "Aunt Minnie's picture...." (already taken to the dump), or "The bed me and Emma made our kids in...."

One's heart goes out to them. These people really are pathetic figures in the saddest sense of the word. The auctioneer, could he know who wanted what, would gladly rifle the entire dump to reclaim Aunt Minnie's picture; and he would gladly give away a bed, be it worth three dollars or a hundred. All it takes is one set of old man's tears, or one obese lady's blubbering, and natural human sympathy busts the auction.

It's easy to see, then, why Wade values Lester. An experienced man can estimate the crowd even as the auctioneer sells. Wade's wife can't do it because she's making invoices. Since Wade sells fast (occasionally as many as seventy numbers—items—in an hour) the clerk is too busy. Wade's kid, Jim, hasn't enough experience. Wade's daughter is back on Bardstown Road minding the store. All of the weight is on Lester.

Lester rises to the occasion. He watches. He connects.

The sufferer in this case does have a flowered housedress, but is thin and sad and tired; with drawn face and stringy hair like half of the women in coal-mining-Eastern-Kentucky. Her whole life is in her face: poverty, sick kids, day-labor husband, stump-preacher religion that only promises additional hell. She's in worse shape than women on Jackson St. because at least their preachers promise hope of Glory.

And, because she's experienced when it comes to enduring ("I must carry on.") she isn't going to weep; only stand silent, a symbol of tears, as did women of ancient times who stood before conquerors.

"Find what she needs," Lester whispers to Gloria. "It'll pay."

And Gloria, tough as well-worked old leather, heads for the woman and leads her aside. Gloria treats for a small bottle of milk and a sandwich at Mr. Evans' catering table. The two women stand, one in faded flowery housedress, one in new flowery housedress. They talk. The tired woman tries to laugh, looks grateful. Gloria pats her hand.

"Old rocking chair got her," Gloria tells Lester. "Goddamn rocking chair belonged to her momma."

"Where 'tis?"

"Two lots over."

"You'll tell me?

Wade, despite being in the middle of performance, picks up. Three items later, a colonial cherry chest worth anyway a hundred, comes on the block. "Sold," Wade says, "Gloria, ten semoleons. Let's keep moving. Move along."

This, whilst Daniels and Lucky shake their heads in admiration. Lucky leans over, whispering to Howard, filling

Howard in on what just happened; and Howard clearly enjoys the inside track. He is fascinated.

"Auctioneers take care of their dealers," Lucky explains. "They depend on dealers, because the general public may come to a sale, or not. The public comes for fun, but it also goes to horse races, ball games, elections, church picnics."

Two lots later Gloria buys the chair for cheap, and Jim checks it out ahead of time. The tired lady leaves with her chair, almost happy. A small victory for everyone.

* * *

Matters got plague-y during check-out. Wade took a break, gulped water, considered his work and was pleased. A man who has just knocked off four hundred numbers in a bit under six hours has a right to be proud. Goods moved out of the warehouse. Trucks filled.

Wade yawned, looked around, saw his kid, then looked for Lester just in time to see Lester round-house a country boy. Black fist, white face.

Like in the moving pictures. The country boy, all blue overalls and chambray shirt, went sprawling, butt-over-brisket. He rolled slow-motion, over once, then lay on his back blinking at the ceiling high above. Lester stood waiting, or maybe trying to decide if he should run. The country boy stood up, his blue overalls dark-spotted with blood from a busted lip. His spikey hair stood above a face that had turned more animal than human. When he reached in his pocket for a knife, Lester decked him again. This time the country boy did not get up so fast.

"Fornicating hell," Wade said. By the time Wade arrived on the scene two other country boys were about to chip in. They looked Wade over, saw his size, and decided to observe.

"What?" Wade stood beside Lester, and Wade was sincerely baffled. No colored man hit a white man and expected to live. At least, not where Wade came from, and not where the country boy came from.

"He niggered me one time too many," Lester muttered. Then, aloud, he said, "A man's got a right to defend himself."

"That's God's truth," Gloria told everybody. She arrived, panting, having trotted halfway across the warehouse. "Self defense. I saw everything." What a liar.

The country boy collected himself. It was the same country boy who had caused trouble the week before. "Gents," he said to the growing crowd, "you are looking at one dead nigger."

"I doubt it." The voice was gentle. Lucky, with Howard in tow, stepped from the edge of the crowd. "Leave the man alone and I promise he'll leave you alone."

"Who are you, Jew-bait?"

"A man with friends at city jail," Lucky said quietly. "You seriously don't want to go there."

"I'll make a guess," Daniels told the country boy. "I'm guessing you're one of them hard-asses from Corbin, down by the Tennessee line." He looked toward Gloria. "That sign 'nigger don't let the sun set on you in this town', that's Corbin."

And Wade, who was big, but basically noncombatant, reached down inside himself somewhere and found a speck of courage. "I need you," he told the country boy, "like a preacher needs a dose of clap. We'll get you loaded. Then you drive your tail to Corbin. Don't come back."

The country boy put his hand back in his pocket. "Let's look at it this way," Wade told him. "We're standing in the middle of a bunch of nice people, but you and me, we're different. You're a sonovabitch looking at another sonovabitch."

The country boy checked the crowd, saw that odds were something worse than zero. "This ain't finished."

Wade grinned, like almost friendly. "You got a gun under your truck seat. I got a shotgun under mine." It was a reasonable assumption. Most everybody had guns under their truck seats. Wade lied, but a nice bluff.

And then Wade said something that bound Lester to him, maybe more even than Lester had been bound to Charlie Weaver. "This man works with me," Wade said, "and he's worth a dozen of you." Wade seemed mildly shocked at his own words. Stunned, actually. He turned to Lester. "I'll check this one," he whispered. "You take somebody else."

"You wanta top off your load, let's take a drive to my place." The junk dealer Fudd saw an opportunity to off-load some of his trash on the country boy. Fudd didn't mean to, but his sad salesmanship shifted and sealed the contest; and the situation ran out of gas.

And later, after the country boy left while swearing vengeance, Wade said to Lester, "You reckon he's a back-shooter?"

"He don't know where I live," Lester said, "and Lucky got him told. Like as not it'll be all right."

"Try not to do that again... tell the truth, you scared me to ten inches under my gizzard."

"Boss," Lester told him, "I did the same damn thing to myself."

August 18th to September 1st

Vacation

To the conservative Jew, which Rachel (Mrs. Lucky) was, late July or sometimes August produced a day of sadness on the Jewish calendar; a day roughly equal to the observant Christian's Good Friday. The Ninth of 'Av remembers the Christian destruction of the temples and the expulsion of Jews from 15th century Spain. Good Friday recalls the Roman lynching of a Jew named Jesus.

To the reformed Jew, which Lucky almost was, the Ninth of 'Av might be no more than a nip at memory. In Lucky's case it just made the sore spot in his soul a bit more raw. The comfort of Law, tradition, ritual, and fast were of no more use to Lucky than Martin Luther's teaching were to Wade. But, like Wade, Lucky followed his wife's directions and walked through it.

Rachel and Lucky were a strangely happy, if seemingly mismatched, couple; and they shared a sorrow. Their union produced no children. Like the Hannah of scripture, who had experienced the same childless problem and worse, Rachel did her share of weeping as she appealed her sorrows to the Lord. Unlike the scriptural Hannah, nothing came of it.

Adoption seemed first an issue, then a possibility, then an impossibility. The courts would not place a gentile child with a Jewish family. No court in the south would place a colored kid with a white family. Even lawyers could not imagine that. Jewish orphans were scarce, because when a Jewish parent died an aunt or uncle stepped in.

Yet, on a world scale, there were more than enough kids to go around. Orphans in Europe were dying of starvation. Displaced persons were herded back and forth across national frontiers in hundreds of thousands, and U. S. immigration remained almost the same as closed. The State Department exercised control of immigration, and the Department was run by men who avowedly and sincerely hated Jews. Those men were proudly on record with their detestation.

In response, Rachel worked in promoting Zionism and the work of Hadassah. Lucky endorsed her efforts, although like many Jews before the coming of Hitler he had despised Zionism. The main beef with Zionism came because Lucky knew himself as an American, and America his homeland. Zionism claimed that such was not the case.

The war had changed everything. Hitler managed to make Lucky into a reluctant Zionist.

If Lucky took an interest in matters beyond business, his interest did not come solely because he lived beside social snideness. He was a relativist. If asked about intentions and beliefs, Lucky would probably say intentions changed with each day's newspaper.

Belief was another matter. When young, he had resolutely faced the problems of a rational brain confronted with the mysteries of faith. He decided that since he had to live in a world of both rationality and faith, he would honor each without buying into either.

He also tried to deal with that sore spot in his soul. Since he was a practical man as well as a theorist, he came to understand that the world-screw was actually comprehensive. The screw was historical, having waited until the 10th century to start against Jews; but it could turn against anyone or any group at any time.

The root of the problem was not money, but the power that money bequeathed as it denied intellect. It was the cheapest and most tawdry kind of power, yet men and religions and governments scrambled for it.

Thus, if a man was on the edge of society, in a city where bigotry was common, money had charms. It meant that if push came to grunt a man could afford to get out of town.

Over the years he developed into a secret socialist and New Dealer; a businessman living around Republican businessmen who believed that Roosevelt had been, at best, the forked barb on Old Nick's tail. Then, during the war Lucky's belief in Roosevelt, and justice, and socialism, took a licking; although he remained a New Dealer. He almost understood the idea of 'faith' as he joined with every Jewish son and daughter in the world. World Jewry had to deal with the killing going on in Europe.

Mostly, everyone felt helpless. Mostly, everyone clustered in congregations. They knew they were not safe. Mostly, everyone mourned. The depth of mourning for some was so deep, and so profound, that even the best Rabbi could scarcely find words.

That rabbi could find to his disgust, though, that in the midst of sorrow a lot of people were having a party. The majority of Jews in America were just emerging from poverty. In the affluence of war they threw money around in shovelfuls. As a matter of conscience they threw a lot of it at the Joint Distribution Committee which was a main Jewish organization. Its mission was rescue, education, and lobbying Congress.

During the war Lucky tried to mourn and he wasted no

time on parties. He answered with anger, largely at himself; and the reason he was angry was because he couldn't get past feelings of surrealism. He knew Hitler was real. He knew probably millions were dying. He just couldn't connect emotionally in ways he felt that he ought. Helplessness made him furious.

He also acted with scorn while making more than his share of money. He invested in a shirt-making company with Army contracts. He also bankrolled a newsreel theater off 4th St. The newsreels were loud and obnoxious, but they sometimes contradicted government propaganda.

If he made more than his share of money it was not as much as he could have made. Had he located his store toward the center of town, up by the railroad station, he could have amassed a young fortune. G.I.s came through headed for Fort Knox. Army guys caught passes into town. Ladies of the night operated in broad daylight. Chaos. Money flowing.

Instead, he stayed on Jackson St. It was penance, but it was also missionary. Since he was helpless to aid Hebrews, and even helpless to feel the weight from a million deaths, he could help somebody. Jackson St. amounted to economic flagellation, although it offered a fair living.

After the war he read the newspapers and watched the same old evil, the killing evil, begin to crawl from the seats of power. The House UnAmerican Activities Committee began its grandstanding. And, in spite of Harry Truman's reputation as a man who aided Israel, the President remained a question mark.

So what was a man to do? Rachel fasted during the Ninth of 'Av, then turned her serious but very pretty face toward Rosh Hashanah. Lucky read the newspapers and felt the coldness of history creeping toward his soul. He knew he should weep, or rage, but could do neither. He knew it was time to take a breather.

When he talked to Rachel about vacation his mind felt clouded. "Go to Miami? Catch a fish?" He really didn't care.

"You caught one last time," she said, and was amused. When she smiled, it never failed to persuade him. "Last time you caught a fish that was too big to eat, and too little to stuff. Let's go visiting. New York. We can see a show and shop."

AUGUST 18TH TO AUGUST 31ST

JIM AND HOWARD
ON EDUCATION AND BECOMING A COMMUNIST

During the height of August heat, Louisville slowed. Even traffic ran with less force. Heat radiated in waves from the colorful hoods of cars, and leaves of huge trees drooped bug-chewed and tired. Dust accumulated in wind pockets of buildings and along gutters. Sometimes a thunderstorm came through with promise of relief while washing the gutters. The promise always proved false. Humidity rose to 100 percent, and walking in the aftermath of storm was approximately the same as a steam bath. Extreme heat slowed everyone including Jim and Howard. Perhaps because they were slowed they forgot to be kids and actually started listening to each other. It was during August that Jim and Howard tied together: the Jim-and-Howard Club, like they were twin questions, almost answered.

Before Lucky left on vacation Jim had boarded the bus two afternoons a week. Walking to the bus stop along sidewalks where discarded chewing gum actually sizzled, he always looked at the house of Mrs. Mildred Samuels. Nothing moved in or around the house. He figured the police must have returned and taken the boards down. The house stood dead, lightless, lifeless.

...cross the street, wait on the corner by the Kaiser-Frasier dealer with his lumpy-looking cars. Catch the bus past skating rink, taverns, orphanage, and finally past Charlie Weaver's old place now standing empty. Windows had been washed, painted auction signs scraped from glass, and a 'For rent' sign stood in the window. Even after being spiffed up the place looked discouraged and ready to cast long shadows.

Hang a left down Broadway and get off the bus at Jackson St. The old man who sat in the sun now raised a hand to him when he said "Howdy." The old woman looked puzzled, but waved a kerchief. Men standing before Sapphire Top Spot moved aside. Twice Ozzie muttered "white-shit" when Jim trembled past, but by then Jim understood Ozzie was just mean. Nothing to be done about it.

Fourteen-year-olds, when pressed together and left alone, can often form communion. Neither Jim nor Howard knew that in southern history there existed strong bonds, even brother-bonds, between some men of different races.

And neither knew that in the south there wasn't a pure white man or a pure colored man to be had. People mixed, and had mixed for going-on three hundred years. The myth of a pure race was just more bull-droppings that fertilized southern pastures.

Color was something else. It was strangely attractive. The main attraction, though, was the world of another. Jim knew Bardstown Road. Howard knew Jackson St.

Other differences. Jim went day-to-day, just 'getting by'. Howard planned. His speech was whiter than soap ads on the radio. He would get ahead. He would.

And gossip. Good, Lord, the gossip.

"Lester buried those heads in a wild place by the river. Lester says he could not figure any other place where they would rest comfortable." Howard's fingers were slim as the rest of him. He cleaned an antique opal ring with a pin, picking soil from around the setting. Delicate.

"Lester gave that country guy a lickin'. I think my dad worries. I think Lester worries a little."

"Jolly is healing up."

"He's still mouthing off. Lester says he's mouthing off." Jim saddle-soaped leather belts and boots.

"Jolly is acting the fool," Howard said. "He claims he knows who robbed him. He claims that what you sow you reap."

"Ozzie? Did it?"

"If made to guess, I would say, most likely." Howard finished the ring, gave it a brief polish with soft cloth.

"Lucky promises that I may start tending to customers after his vacation. I think I will do well at retail."

"Did you ever see a dead man? We had a dead man by the auction."

"I heard about it. No, never dead. I saw Ozzie cut a man once. Ozzie had a single-edge razor blade taped between his fingers. They were fist fighting."

* * *

When Lucky and Mrs. Lucky closed shop for two weeks and vacationed, the bus ran in the other direction. In late mornings Howard boarded on Broadway at Jackson, and the bus fumed its way to Cave Hill, hung a right past orphanage, skating rink, and taverns. White men looked at him and tried to figure what it was Howard intended to steal. Mostly he was ignored. When he got off the bus in front of the drug store and crossed Eastern Parkway, he did so with more courage than he believed he owned. In this white world he had to walk a good half-block without Lucky for protection. He told himself that once inside the auction a man could feel comfortable.

Which was true, because Wade knew that an extra kid was a value, and not a liability. At first he mistrusted Howard because everything Wade knew said that nigger kids stole. Still, this dusky boy who really wanted to learn brought out a small, kind streak. For the first time in his life, probably, Wade turned teacherly without being sarcastic. It wouldn't last, but it was nice while it did. For Howard, and almost for Jim, work turned into an interesting school.

"Let's say a man gives you a cold check for fifty bucks. He comes in and offers to pay it off at ten a week. Don't take it. The minute you take the ten, you've changed the cold check into an open account." This from Wade as he and Lester and the kids worked lots of merchandise at the auction house. In the heat, Wade's shirt was even wetter than Lester's. "We got to get done here. We got a plumbing supply."

Education: "Word-of-mouth is the best advertising. If you send a painted woman out of here feeling like Lady Churchill, she'll talk nice about you." This from Lester.

"Don't place anything against a wall until you've swept along the wall. The customer won't know if the floor is dirty back there, but you will. Makes you think less of what you're selling." This from Wade.

"When you hire help on a truck, don't look at a man's muscles. Watch how he walks. If he walks straight and certain, take him." This from Lester.

"There's no way to avoid all hot property. Hot merchandise is the bane of this business, and I thought I'd seen every damned grift, shill, con, screw and scam in the book, but this one's new. We cover our sweet behinds. We call the cops." This from Wade.

"Lucky has rules about hot merchandise. Lucky says a man must know his neighborhood." Howard was all attention. "What are the rules?" The kids stood beside Wade and next to a piled truckload of merchandise. The stuff was new and still in cartons. Round-face televisions, snazzy Royal typewriters with the heel-of-the-hand bar, small appliances; roughly a ton and a half of new stuff.

"Here's the scam," Wade told the boys. "Con artists are

slick, but stupid. This dumbass forgot to clean his cartons. I picked an invoice off the side of one. It said Louisville Standard Etc. I checked the address. It's sitting right next door to Louisville Standard, a top company in Dun & Bradstreet. The street numbers are one digit off."

"Then he has stolen from a big company? How can you steal from such a big company?" Howard was fascinated. Jim put up with it.

"He steals from other companies. I called a shipper. This guy is ordering on net sixty days. When the shipper asks for credit reference, the guy say 'Look me up in Dun & Bradstreet.' When the shipper looks, the address is only one digit off, which is nothin'. The scam is using a legit company's legit credit to steal."

"I think I understand. How does he meet the net sixty?"

"By shoving stuff through auctions. He's doing what is called 'kiting'. If you sell enough stuff you can make payments while ordering more. When the stack gets high enough, sell out and disappear."

"Sometimes," Howard said, "I become a little fearful. I would never have caught that."

"Comes with experience," Wade told the two boys. "Right now we head for the next job. Plumbing warehouse. This one comes through a routine roughing-up. Not a scam. A blow-off between partners. You kids ride with Lester. I'll meet you there."

And, riding in the old truck, with Lester humming, Howard said, "Mr. Wade is a very smart man."

And Lester said, "He sure has got his points."

And Jim kept his big flapper shut.

* * *

Each morning before leaving for the plumbing supply, Jim looked at Mrs. Samuels' house. It stood spooky in sunlight, and it could give a kid a chill even with temperature in the high 90s. The sun porch looked vague because it was screened, and the screens showed rust. In the back of the house dead grass lay gray between house and garage. The door leading from yard to garage was always closed. Except for dead grass, the back yard looked tidy. No junk crowded against the house or garage, no garbage cans, no nothin'.

"I got a feeling somebody lives there," he told his mom.

"Someone who does not answer a knock on the door. Stay away from there." His mom seemed nearly fearful.

"Boards are off the front door."

"I went around back," his mother said, "thinking that poor man must be scared. His mother gone, his brother gone. Stay away from there."

"He's not hurting anybody."

"I don't know what to do, but I know he's strange. Stay away." His mother was sometimes mysterious. She only told a kid what she thought a kid should know.

Curtains hung limp as tired ghosts across the windows. Paint flaked from wooden siding and shone silver-gray in sunlight. Here and there, worn siding showed cracks and crevices. Even a kid could see that the house was a goner unless lots of work got done, and quick. When he mentioned it to his dad, Wade said, "As long as that Yugoslavian jerk-off don't burn it down. Right now you can just get a leg up. Howard takes an interest in plumbing, so what's wrong with you? You're letting a jig kid show you up."

"Howard's an exception," Jim said, "you can learn a lot from Howard." It was the first time he had ever stood up to his dad, and he stuttered doing it. He stood quiet, waiting for the blast.

Wade paused, somewhat astounded. Then he grinned like a hound with a pork chop. "This family," he said, "has produced preachers, horse thieves, pig farmers and rum heads. It never produced a lawyer, before. Maybe there's still hope." He turned away. "Let's go to work."

* * *

Then, as now, the auctioneer needs to know everything about everything. On top of that he must be a quick study. His work takes him to plumbing one week, to groceries the next, to lumber yards, hardwares, car dealers, mortuaries (he must know the difference between an embalming table and a sink, because they are different but similar), frozen food factories, packing houses, breweries (though these rarely go broke), drugstores, wholesalers: everything from seed companies to kitchen cabinets, wholesalers in furniture, restaurant equipment, concrete, and marble. There are few products of a vast industrial nation that an auctioneer will not see sooner or later.

"...learning lots. Learning how it's supposed to be done." Howard murmured as the kids met at the plumbing warehouse on the second day.

"There's a fight between partners," Wade told the kids. "Any business will, sooner or later, hit a stale spot. When that happens it has to grow, or it begins to shrink. Comes from doing things the same way all the time. Comes from being too damn comfortable."

"Charlie Weaver," Lester told the kids. "Charlie got that way. Lost his hustle. Lost his brightness."

Row after row of bins stretched the length of a long building. They stood something over head-high. Racks of pipe ran along the tops of the bins, and plumbing fittings filled the bins. Tools, from pipe wrenches to power-threaders sat in a showroom-type of space. Farther back, in a work area, walls were decorated with girlie pictures from calendars. One picture wore nothing but a smile. Lester took it down, tossed it in the trash. "Time enough for that later," he said, and smiled at the boys.

All through the day, neither kid had the moxie to sneak

the picture out, though naturally both thought about it.

"So, what happened," Wade said, "is the man in charge, the senior partner, ran the business into debt. Then he lent money to keep the business afloat. Then he ran it further into debt. Then he called in the note knowing his partners couldn't pay. We sell the place out. The sale cancels the debt. The man in charge gets rid of his partners. He opens up a plumbing supply next door."

"You're kiddin'. Next door?" Lester was clearly impressed.

"Already signed a lease," Wade said. "Let's get to work."

* * *

Dusty work. Kids counting 45 degree ells, 90 degree ells, couplings, nipples, tees, reducers; half-inch, three-quarters while the men handled large stuff.

Sometimes, in a liquidation, dangerous situations develop. The auctioneer and his help need some knowledge of rigging. They must understand structural requirements for handling great weights, and have keen eyes for sloppy work. A business that has operated for a long time, then gone down hill, can turn deadly.

"Look at this," Lester told Wade. "Look at this here." The two men stood twenty feet away from the boys. On a rack above the bins iron pipe was restrained by wooden shims. Wooden posts bolted to the rack held the pipe in place. Both shims and posts showed dry rot. When Lester touched one, powder fell on his hand. "The damn fools had a roof leak and just kept mopping," he told Wade. "Wet and dry, wet and dry, and wood turns to powder." He called the boys over. "Getting set to kill somebody. When you've got a load above, suspicion it." He showed them the dry rot. "There's better'n a ton of pipe up there. Don't never trust the work of a man you don't know."

"We'll unload it from the end," Wade said. "You kids stay

way the hell back." As the men began unloading, the wood exploded into dust. Pipe rolled and fell sideways. It cascaded, clanked, crashed, cracked the concrete floor. It rolled against a second rack which remained sturdy.

"Fastest way to unload." Lester wiped sweat. "Now we got stoop work. We gotta pick it up. And, damn the sonovabitch that let things fester."

"I figured this set-up for no more than five days," Wade said, and he was sore. "Now it's gonna take six."

...work through dusty days, early morning to quitting time or sometimes past. Two dusty boys, sure that they were counting all the pipe fittings in the whole wide world.

"When you found the dead man were you scared?"

"I was too scared to be scared. That don't make no sense."

"It probably does. Will you show me where it happened?"

"Soon as we get a chance. If my dad don't catch us."

"It will need to happen soon. Lucky is due back a week from Sunday."

"That's the day after this sale."

"The dead man was nicely dressed?"

"He was ready to be buried. It would've saved money. I think he was awful poor."

Dusty work. When they finished counting fittings they cleaned office furniture and office machines. A pot-bellied Bendix radio broadcast stations WAVE and WHAS: soap opera, music, news, weather.

"When Ozzie used the razor blade did he kill the man?"

"Johnson. The man's name is Johnson. He hardly ever comes around. He has a face full of scars."

"Why were they fighting?"

"No one knows. They were drunken. I have seen a number fights. Men go mad when they drink."

"Hotter'n the Devil's armpit in here." Jim wiped sweat from his forehead. Dust from his hand made a dark streak across his brow.

"Are you allowed to swear? My mother says swearing is sorry."

"My mom says swearing is redneck. My dad says it's a free country."

"Don't dead people get dressed up at the undertaker?"

"Something weird," Jim explained. "Don't say a word. Somebody was in the garage with him. Maybe he was murdered. Those folks are just weird, and my mom knows how but she ain't sayin'."

"I'm not let to say ain't."

"Me, neither, but it slips out sometimes. Maybe the guy's a communist."

"I know a number of communist people," Howard said, and no doubt bragged a little. "They are not weird. No one gives them much attention."

"Do you know what it means? Communist?"

Howard's voice, which had showed a brag, was now subdued. It actually sounded nervous, like Howard thought he might be taking a chance. "It means that you and I could go to the park together. Or school."

And Jim, embarrassed not a little, and struck with sudden malaise, did not have the foggiest notion of what to say or do. It was also at that moment that he crossed over the first high hill of Louisville-barbershop-drugstore-cowboy bullshit. He knew that from then on, and forever, he was a communist.

* * *

Toward the end of the second day, with the truck near full of trash, and with sweat pouring off of everybody, Wade and Lester stood together looking at the job.

"Make a dump run," Wade told Lester. "Take Howard with

you. There's no sense bringing the truck back to the store, then getting on a nose-pickin' bus." Wade rubbed the back of his butt where his hip hurt a little. "I'll take my kid. Meet me back here tomorrow."

And thus was another tie placed between Wade and Lester. From then on, the auction truck parked each night on Jackson St. "The boss is a hard-ass bastard," Lester would admit over a beer at Sapphire Top Spot. "But there's a little-somethin' to him."

"Lester is a bronco-bustin' gold mine," Wade told his kid. "When you find a good man, you damn well got to treat him right." Then Wade added, "Even if he is blacker'n the inside of preacher's pocket." And then Wade paused and grinned. "Lester's an exception," he told his kid. "You could learn quite a bit from Lester."

Saturday, August 30th

War and Plumbing

During World War II the bloodbaths of ancient times were duplicated on a global scale. Whereas Ghengis Khan once destroyed the entire world of a city, World War II swept cities aside as it blew apart nations, continents, and entire peoples. No one, anywhere, could feel one hundred percent safe. No one was above suspicion. In Louisville, a German-sounding name made a man into an automatic suspect. Folks named Schmidt changed their names to Smith. Jackob Samuelwicz changed his name to Samuels.

He made the change because he lived in a town where popular opinion roughly broke down as 50 percent of people believed the Great Depression had been caused by an international conspiracy of Jewish bankers; 25 percent were too smart to buy most government and agitator propaganda, thus disagreed; 25 percent didn't give a rip.

Bigotry had been kick-started during The Great Depression when agitators spreading out from Muncie, Indiana, pretty much covered the south and middle west with hate-talk centered on Jews and Catholics; with a nod to Negroes. Those agitators were often welcomed, because desperate people were hungry and out of work. Desperate people needed someone to blame. Since there was no price of admission to the hate-talk, it was also cheap entertainment.

On top of that, a civil-sounding dandy styled: Father Coughlin, Priest of Royal Oak (Michigan) spread dreck over radio. He had once supported Roosevelt's New Deal. As his thought processes declined he began to speak of 'The Jew Deal'. Very popular man, Father Coughlin.

Preparation and execution of World War II by all nations caused dulled and staring eyes from one hundred million corpses; direct and indirect casualties; meat and bones, stinking, many thrown to lime pits. Nazi death camp operation was expensive at first, but gradually became efficient.

Mr. and Mrs. Samuels survived and prospered, but Jake did not live to see war end in Europe. He never knew if his sons survived.

Both did. Isaac was not sent to Treblinka extermination camp until late in the Nazi game. By then, starvation was as large an enemy as gas chambers.

A lot of airmen from all nations got blown up. Some of them survived, but with burns or bodies torn by shrapnel. David carried a small sliver of steel the docs missed. It would eventually turn into a killing machine as it inched through his brain, and would cause agony. All David could think of, after the war, was that he must try to find Isaac.

Miracles happen. The two men made it to Louisville through Mexico, because while Mexico was not crazy about Jews, it was less restrictive and less organized. The two men entered illegally because there wasn't a chance of legal immigration. Thus, no one at the auction knew anything about the Samuels for two reasons. First, no one had time to inquire. And, second, even if someone had inquired, the Samuels could not have answered since the sons were illegal. The misfortunes of war.

* * *

Such large war had required materiel on a level that stripped the U.S. of metal, rubber, cement and cloth.

Metal toys disappeared, along with new automobiles and appliances. Construction companies played catch-as-catch-can for building materials. A large market in used lumber and pipe appeared. No possibly functional item got cast aside. The slogan went, "Use it up and make it do."

When war ended, construction guys went happily overboard because the nation embarked on a building frenzy. As new stuff came to market, construction companies over-bought for at least two reasons. One: The smart money figured there was gonna be a war with Russia, thus more shortages. Two: There was gonna be inflation, so stock up at lower prices, and charge through the snoot later on.

"The dumbest numbnut could sell to this crowd," Wade told the boys. "But numbnuts don't know how to milk the cow." He said this in a low voice as kids and Lester watched the crowd form at the plumbing supply. Not a woman in sight. The men were mostly dressed in surplus tans or khakis, shirt sleeves rolled, smoke from cigars. Here and there a householder appeared wearing a short sleeve shirt and slacks; the householder valuable because he didn't need much.

"We're gonna sell small, then bigger, then biggest. Why?" Wade looked not at Jim, but at Howard. For the first time since meeting Wade, Howard found himself on the spot. "I have to study this." Howard spoke right up. "It must have something to do with price. By small, then big, do you mean quantity or merchandise?"

"I swear to god I'm gonna adopt this kid," Wade told Lester. To Jim he said, "If quantity, which it is, why?"

Jim stood silent, not knowing the answer, and not giving a purple damn.

"Because people who buy small pay a higher price." Howard looked like a little old man pulling at his beard, even though his chin was naturally hairless. "I have it. The small sale sets the price. That price structure stays in the crowd's mind." He looked surprised, but pleased.

"People call it psychology," Wade said, "which is a college way of saying nothin'. It's using your common sense."

"Which means," Lester added, "when you sell something like lumber, you sell by the board foot, or the square foot, not by the piece."

"Construction guys are good," Wade said about the crowd, "but most of them don't bring slide rules. A bin of parts is like a sheet of plywood. You go for one-quarter cent bids because, if you sell fast, these boys have a pig's own time figuring something like three-and-three-quarters cents times thirty-two.

"I," said Howard, "will certainly become rich." Howard was completely sincere. "I thought I liked retail best, but...." He stopped, not wishing any disloyalty to Lucky.

"Retail is just fine," Wade told him, "but retailers take title to merchandise. Auctions work with the other's guy's money. Capital investment for the auctioneer is zilch."

When the sale started Howard and Jim found themselves nearly out of work. Their only task was to run a clerk's sheet to Jim's mom, or check out purchases. Jim dawdled. Howard watched. Wade sold fittings so-much-a-piece in lots of ten. "Take as many lots as you want." Then in lots of fifty. Then, "Let's shoot off the balance."

"I think," said Howard, after a small sale, "that the price just approached retail."

"I think," Jim said, "that school starts awful soon." He turned from the gloom of the building toward the sunstruck street. "Grab clerk sheets, willya?"

On the street sunlight lay across old warehouses, some ramshackle, and all of them frame. The street sloped toward the river. Cars and trucks parked up tight, with some trucks backed into loading docks. As he walked he felt the misery of confusion, and could not even understand it was confusion. This world was the only one he knew, and it must make sense; but if people hated bull, why did they do it so much?

He stepped along red brick streets, and, toward the river saw cobblestones shining silver beneath the sun. Working trucks parked all around, positive in red and green and orange. Dust lay like sheen on the front of warehouses. Dust-coated windows glowed dull in sunlight, the windows not washed since before the war. He thought about Howard and how Howard handled bull. Howard fit right in. He could listen to Wade spread bull, ignore it, or maybe use it for his own plans.

School would start soon. It would be a relief. He could still do two or three hours twice-a-week with Lucky, and Lucky was due back from vacation tomorrow, Sunday.

He saw the truck trundling along like one old horse pulling a two-horse wagon. Painted blue, it was, with remains of orange paint on the stakes; and so much over-loaded that any cop should write a ticket. Green canvas covered the load. The truck sat on flattened helpers with the front end slightly elevated. It was a tire-busting load, a forty mile-per-hour and don't-go-a-cent's-worth-faster load. The truck moved slow, then slower as it passed the auction. The country boy's face was red, like a drinking man.

The truck jiggled, like the guy was about to release his clutch. Then it stopped jiggling. Jim looked up and down the street. A colored driver stood on a warehouse dock. He stood short but stocky, dark as worked leather. He wore Wellington boots, gray work clothes.

"Goddamn nigger lovers." The country boy's yell sounded raspy. Definitely a drinker. Definitely as tight as the curl in a little pig's tail.

The colored driver stiffened, turned. "That's me," he

hollered. "Love each and every darky. Walk this way you sonovabitch." The driver was obviously a man who owned his own truck. Nobody colored, who didn't drive north, and who was not independent, would talk that way. The driver walked toward the cab of his truck. Pistol behind the seat, sure as stink.

The country boy may have been snockered, but he had enough sense to keep moving. He drove steady enough. A-course, he drove slow. The truck traveled a couple of blocks, then hung a left and disappeared.

The colored driver looked at Jim, sneered, shrugged, and turned away. Jim turned back to the auction. This was serious.

* * *

"He might not be after me," Lester said after the sale. "He might be set on badness to the auction." He stood beside Wade who was awash in sweat. Even Wade's short hair was wet. Lester glistened black and sweaty, like a Nubian statue in the rain. The two men had more going between them than either would admit. If Jim and Howard had a club, so did Wade and Lester. Almost.

"He's a backshooter," Wade said. "I was raised with those bastards. Indiana is full of 'em." He turned to Jim. "He had a full load? A real full load?"

"Spring buster," Jim spoke to Lester.

"Could be coincidence. Could be he just happened by."

"He was drinkin' heavy," Jim told Lester.

Lester looked to Wade, and Wade to Lester. Both grinned. "I'm not about to worry," Lester told Jim. "If he's already got his load, and if he's drinking it means he's headed home or to a cathouse."

"The bastard is stupid as drainwater," Wade said, "but how stupid do you have to be to come after a man when you're drinking? Cowboy crap."

"Pure and simple," Lester said, "cowboy picture show."

"Excuse me," Howard told them, and he looked at Lester. "Drunken men act stupidly."

Lester paused. "You got a point. I expect we'll watch our backs."

Saturday Night, August 30th

Lester

From the high shelf in Lucky's store the stuffed chickens, Thomas the Plymouth Rock rooster, and Lola the Guinea Hen, stared glassy-eyed into the gloaming along Jackson St. A group of men stood before Sapphire Top Spot, as other men eased along the sidewalk toward a night of drink. From the juke in Sapphire Top Spot came the bluesy beat of "I Wonder," early rock by Mr. Cecil Grant.

Two blocks farther up stood Jackson Colored Junior High, its principal Mr. Thomas Law; a man well-named and not a little strict. The school sat among brick Victorian houses, and in those houses lived a great variety of people and their dreams: and one dream of many (including Lester) was to move the hell away from Jackson St.

Which, in 1948, seemed like it might could-be gonna happen. As men drifted toward Sapphire Top Spot, a few of them knew that the Supreme Court of the United States, in April of that year, had reversed its previous opinions. In *Shelly vs. Kraemer*, the court ruled that restrictive covenants were unenforceable.

In theory, any colored man or any Jew could now live anywhere in Louisville he could afford. Lots of luck, buddy. Still, at least one chip had been knocked off the hard wall of segregation. Even experienced cynics, and they were legion, recognized a flutter of hope. Not, though, on hot Saturday nights.

"Lucky closed. Off to Miami spending our money."

"Give the hebe credit. He hired Miz Esther's Howie."

"And a white bread."

"I doubt Miami. Folks don't head to Miami in summer."

"Alaska. North Pole. Do I give a shit?"

From a second floor apartment, two rooms with its own toilet, Lester stood near-naked and looked onto the street. His hair had been washed under the tap, was lightly oiled, and a sponge bath took care of the rest. He watched the drift of men toward Sapphire Top Spot. Slow motion. Men had moved toward the joints on Saturday night before the war, probably during the war, and now, after the war. Things just kept keepin' on.

"Time you was settling down," he told himself. "Get a place. Find a decent woman."

Beneath his window the auction truck sat between a rusty LaSalle and a busted '38 Buick. The truck looked right at home. "And in the bank," Lester told himself, "you own nigh eight hundred dollars. 'Nough for a down payment."

It seemed this job was gonna last. Maybe it was time to think of buying. He watched the street and worried the worry of every working man. Would the job hold up? If the job did not hold up, was there some good direction to jump? "A man could get in over his head real fast," he said to the empty room. He pulled on a shirt and kept looking out the window.

The cluster of men still stood outside Sapphire Top Spot. And, down the sidewalk, strutting like the damn fool he was, came Jolly dressed in white suit with white fedora, all for Saturday night; Jolly looking like a goddamn pimp and not a gamble-man. Lester watched as Jolly passed the men, Jolly acting bored; like the men were not even there. Jolly strolled his flashy ass into Sapphire Top Spot.

"Looks like our man rolled with the punch," Lester told the empty room. "Gamble-men are storefronts. But maybe they got nothin' on the shelves."

He seriously asked himself if Sapphire Top Spot was the best place to be. He reminded himself about 'curiosity killing that old cat', and then he told himself he just had to watch the show. A man only needed to stay back, stay low, stay mostly out of sight.

In the rich and dusty summer-Saturday, with nightshade falling, Jackson St. ran fulsome as memories of home. Lester stepped past folks relaxing on stoops, kids playing along sidewalks, old folks sitting together tracing kinships and spinning tales. The wealthy smell of fish-fry came from ground floor rooms. People laughed, and old women hummed hymns. Jackson St. had its hold on folks, even did they want to move.

Ozzie stood among the group of men on the corner, and Ozzie was 'oh, yes' for Saturday night. Silk shirt even grayer than his color. Hellos all around, as men greeted Lester.

"Dancer," Ozzie said. "I hear you chargin' for the show."

"Slow dance tonight." Lester helloed him. "Slow and sleepy." He drifted right on in to Sapphire Top Spot.

Alfonzo and Zeke sat at the same table, like they didn't move from one Saturday night to the next. Jolly leaned against the far end of the bar away from Albert who watched Blue handle the cash register. Albert had that 'cautious-bar-owner' look, and he was looking Jolly's direction.

"We discussing," Alfonzo said, "which is worst. Wheelbarrow with a soft tire, or wheelbarrow with a iron wheel." His ropy muscles were a-sweat, and he was dusty. "Lime all day," he said, "'bout a million bags. Goddamn lime." He looked older than old, and completely done up.

"Lemmie buy you gentlemen a beer." Lester looked toward

Jolly. "Shit storm starting?"

"I put my faith in Albert." Zeke, with medium-toasty skin, was light enough he had freckles. His freckles were kind of big, just like Mr. Trummy Young's, who even then played trombone on the jukebox; but Zeke's ears didn't stick out as good as Trummy's. "Albert owns thirty-eight caliber of bad news. Keeps it back of the bar."

"Blue ain't stupid," Alfonzo said. "Except she's tied up with Ozzie, which actually is more'n a little stupid."

Jolly leaned across the bar, saying something confidential to Blue. She gave him a look sharp as fishhooks. Started to argue. Thought better of it. Then Blue looked around the joint, checking everybody's drink, and started pulling bottles.

"He bought the bar," Zeke said. "Free beer for all. More showboat."

"Blue checkin' to make sure nobody doubles up." Alfonzo chuckled. "Some of these gents will claim they been sipping Jack-y Daniels all along."

"Company coming," Lester told them. "Looks like Jolly drifts this way." The three men watched Jolly ease toward them.

From out front, out on the sidewalk, a couple of men stepped into the bar. A free beer is a free beer.

"Ozzie ain't bitin'," Alfonzo said. "Ozzie standing there just thinkin'."

Jolly seated himself about the time Blue brought the beer. "You could make more money if you was in jail," Blue told him. Blue sounded nervous.

Up close, Jolly looked more nervous than Blue.

"Why you doin' this?" Alfonzo asked.

"Do you know how to shoot that thing?" Lester watched the doorway, watching for Ozzie.

"What?"

"Don't bullshit. Do you know how to handle what you got?"

Jolly went all bristly. "A man's got a right...." He looked toward the sidewalk. He touched the side pocket of his jacket where a pistol hung heavy. "Everybody knows who did what. Let us see who's a jackass now."

"And with that," Zeke said, "I bid you the hell a-doo." He stood, grabbed the fresh bottle of beer, and left; discretion being the better part of valor.

"That'll vex Albert," Jolly said, and said it prim. "He could lose a license letting an open bottle walk outside." (So much bull, and Jolly knew it.) In spite of his nervousness Jolly seemed almost happy.

When the jukebox changed records, silence in the joint seemed remarkable. Ordinarily, the silence wasn't even noticed because men were talking. Now, as the juke changed records, men sat quiet. Yelps and cheers and foolish-ing of playing kids came from the street. Ozzie stood outside like a gray shadow in the early dark; Ozzie making up his mind what to do.

The jukebox clicked, clicked, kids yelled happy through the night, and the gray shadow disappeared.

"I will be goddamn," Alfonzo said. "He's walkin' away."

"Wolverine Blues" on the juke. Music just pouring.

"Now who's the jackass?" Jolly said.

"I wouldn't like to say," Lester told him. "You just crossed a real bad man." Lester stood.

Slow dance. Lester's week had been better than most. Hard work, but good pay. Hardly any bullshit. A man could ease himself through the hot night when there was hardly any bullshit.

Sunday, August 31st

The Fourth Death

Louisville, sunstruck and dusty between storms, lay snuggled in the nest of its great river and to its credit was not at all content. Change drifted slow as an old hound along a sunlit path, but change could not be denied. Too many new people drifted in during the war. Too many industries expanded. Too many women, and old men, and colored folk worked at high wages, only to be laid off when the soldier boys came home. Too many foreigners were even now arriving in town.

No surprise, then, that all colors and kinds of folk were restless. No surprise, then, that many ambitions were on the rise. No surprise, then, that Miz Esther's Howard stepped from rooms on Jackson St. properly wearing summer jacket, white shirt and tie; Howard not strictly in a mood for church.

A very few young people, and Howard was one, seem to know right from the cradle in which direction they are headed. There's a calmness about such children. Questions of 'if then, what?' carry little meaning for them. They know where their noses point. They are generally not excitable, except during times when the world endorses their aims.

Howard (and he knew it) was the pet of the ladies of Jackson St. Men found him pride-y, stuck-up; but they honored Miz Esther.

She was a North Carolina lady, born just outside of Asheville from a Cherokee mother by a colored father. As a girl she worked in the snooty homes of Asheville where southern ethics said 'Treat your darkies firm but nice'. Miz Esther took advantage. She learned the styles of Asheville culture. She learned dress, and the graces. She studied her world, satisfied she could play its games, and then picked up and moved away to better herself. She tried Chicago, found it scant and wanting. She drifted back south, back where people smiled and said "good day to you Miz Esther." She married an itinerant preacher, got Howard off of him, and last heard of him; gone to his reward with pneumonia while missionary-ing in Tennessee.

Good looking women (and Miz Esther was beautiful in a most stately manner) can get by with a lot. Color does not make that much difference. Good looking women with mother-wit can make their ways. Miz Esther was neighborhood cornerstone of the church. From her kitchen, Miz Esther kept books for colored proprietors, and for some whites. In this way, she knew people and she knew business. And, she taught Howard that he must not ever demean himself. He was a cut above other folks. That is why, this Sunday morning, Howard wore that white shirt and tie.

The walk to church amounted to three city blocks, but Howard left early. He strolled instead of drifting, and in a general way hoped Lucky would show up before church. Lucky was due back. Lucky would surely drop in to check his store. The two weeks of working for Mr. Wade had been just fine, but Howard (who had never met his father, so as he could remember) missed Lucky.

Fourteen-year-old boys are just emerging from that scampish stage of kidhood into the toils of puberty. They are, most likely, some of the most wide-awake people on earth, although not a little confused. They can walk right through an earthquake without paying much attention, but catch a fly ball by watching its shadow's descending arc. They see, and don't see. Theirs is a different awareness. Sometimes they see things they shouldn't, things no one should.

A few other folks were walking Jackson St. They pretty much kept to their business, with no reason to poke around or look down alleys. No one, until Howard, looked down the alley beside Lucky's store.

He first dawdled in front of the store, hands on the black steel bars protecting windows and doors. He thought it a burglar-proof store, and approved. In the dim inside of the store Thomas, the Plymouth Rock, and Lola, the guinea hen, roosted. Old Thomas looked like he was about to lose patience with Lucky. Old Thomas looked absolutely nuts this Sunday morning.

Howard peered down Jackson St. like he willed Lucky's money-green Cad to turn the corner and cruise toward him. No cars moved on Jackson St. Up the way, next block, the auction truck stood outside Lester's place.

Howard stepped toward church, then bethought himself to check the back of Lucky's store. There was an iron-covered door back there set in a steel frame. Still, it didn't hurt to check.

He saw the shoe before he was halfway alongside the store. Empty garbage cans hid everything except the shoe. The shoe pointed toe-down and slanted. It glowed patent-leather black in sunshine. Howard paused. Thinking about it.

Maybe the man was sick. Maybe he was just drunk and sleeping. Because, there had to be a man attached. A shoe didn't stand that way, not all by itself. Maybe, Howard thought, he'd better go find Lester, or somebody.

On the other hand, if the man was sleeping one off, it wouldn't do to pester people. Howard stepped forward, real slow, and a little scary. When he got closer he saw blood that wasn't even red anymore, but black. A lot of blood.

He knew the man could not be alive even as he told himself he had to look. He thought of Jim. If Jim could handle a dead man, Howard could handle a dead man. If the man was really, truly dead.

Flies buzzed in the sunlight. It would be flies that Howard would not forget, ever. Flies perched on the tips of Jolly's ears as Jolly lay face down. Flies buzzed all around his head, and around the blood. Jolly's white suit was purple-black with blood, and flies sat in a cut along his neck. His hands were stretched out like he tried to pull himself up, and his hands were cut and covered with flies.

Howard backed away. He did not scream, and he did not turn his back. He stepped real quiet backward down the alley, and he kept his hand to the wall of the store. The store seemed like the only safe place in the world, but Howard did not understand why. He brushed his jacket sleeve along the wall and thought it would get dirty and his mother would have words. When he got close to the mouth of the alley he turned and ran. He stood before Lucky's store, ready to move, trying to decide which way to go and to whom. He looked down Jackson St. and, like the answer to a prayer, saw a money-green Cadillac.

* * *

During the war death had walked the world: guns and gas chambers, ordnance, disease and starvation. And, before the war, The Great Depression made death dreadful because many, many folks went hungry to their graves; nor could the living afford doctors. And death was dirt common in days when t.b. and cholera, scarlet fever and infantile paralysis swept neighborhoods like punishing hands.

People thought differently about death, because it was expected. At the same time, sorrow wasn't different. The tearing, ripping, anguish caused by a loved person's passing dwelt in human hearts; and some folks prayed, and some cursed God.

What was different in Louisville, was closeness. People knew each other because neighborhoods were tightly woven. People owned faces as well as names. A man might be a bum, a drunk, a ne'r-do-well, but he belonged. People might not even like him, but he had his place. When he died the neighborhood knew that, somehow, it was less.

News of Jolly's murder got known on Jackson St. within ten minutes of Lucky's arrival. Preaching and singing shortly started at church, song calling Jolly to Glory, or maybe all of Jackson St. to Glory.

In front of Lucky's store the hot street seemed empty though lots of people were around. Some were down the alley looking at the corpse, and thinking.

"When you last see him?"

"He went on the town. Maybe ten, ten-thirty."

"How the hell he get here?"

"Goddamn man, who is to know? A bad man walked him this-a-way."

"I ain't sayin' who."

"Nor me. Some New York shit from one of the clubs."

"Might could be. Might could be."

There wasn't a soul on Jackson St. who didn't know that Ozzie killed Jolly. Except, maybe, Lucky who had been away. When the cops arrived there wasn't a soul seen on Jackson St., which ran empty as a dry stream.

What was needed was colored cops but these were white. One cop was red-faced and with a beefy-butt. Old school. Head breaker. Always on the take. The other was a newer kind of cop. He was no sweetheart, but he had some judgment, having done Army time in the Pacific.

When the cops entered Lucky's store they saw Lucky sitting

beside Howard, and Howard cried. His shirt front ran wet from sweat and tears. His hands trembled. He stayed close to Lucky. Howard had one shoe kicked off. The shoe showed a spatter of blood. Howard looked at it, then wept through tightly closed eyes. Lucky watched the street and waited for Miz Esther.

"Peter," Lucky said to the experienced cop, "The problem's around back." He leaned toward Howard, protective.

"Who?" The beefy-butt cop pointed at Howard.

"He found the body," Lucky said.

"Let's take a look," the experienced cop said. He turned to the door.

"One more dead nigger," the beefy-butt said. "Hot damn for Saturday night." As the cops stepped through the doorway Miz Esther rushed in. She stepped past the cops like the cops were not there.

"I was headed for church," she told Lucky. "Give me my baby." Lucky stood, gave her his chair. "I'll try to head them off." He left the store to walk down the alley.

The two cops stood looking at the corpse. "You know him?" the experienced cop asked Lucky.

"He's called Jolly," Lucky said. "I've got a card on him in my file. His real name is Williams."

"Ordinary robbery," the experienced cop said. "Not a dime on him." He looked straight at Lucky. "You got any idea?"

"I've been away," Lucky told him. "Two weeks."

"Talk to the smoke."

"He's just a boy," Lucky said. "He can't tell anything."

"You're too damn nice to these people," the beefy-butt said. "They'll turn on you one day." The cop sounded positive, and he stayed positive right up to the time when he banged heads with Miz Esther.

"He can't say anything," she told the cops. "Can't you see."

"He's got a mouth," the beefy-butt said. "Let him damn

well use it."

At which point Miz Esther stood (and she stood anyway five-ten, or maybe five-eleven). At any rate, she looked somewhat down on the cop. Her blue and white church dress set off a face a little darker than Howard's, a face with Indian brow and framed with Indian hair. Her lips were almost thin, and even the most bigoted bastard in the world would have to admit that he was looking at a lotta woman. "You will not curse in my presence," she told the cop, "and you will not plague my child."

"Let it rest," the experienced cop said. "Take your boy home." To Lucky he said, "Lemmie use your phone."

Howard could hardly talk. "I'll be back tomorrow," he whispered to Lucky.

"Yes, you will," Lucky told him. "Indeed you will."

As the cop called for the meat wagon, Lucky stood watching the street. Howard walked crooked because he only wore one shoe.

Lucky knew there would be no investigation, or not much; certainly no more than the dead man by the auction had gotten. Cause of death for Jolly would be marked down as just another Saturday night; and may God truly damn such Saturday nights.

September 1st

Loose Ends Growing Looser

Early Monday morning the auction truck pulled away from Jackson St. as Lester headed for work. Up Broadway, hang a right, and cruise easy on Bardstown Road. He almost drove past Charlie Weaver's place, but pulled over instead.

A sign painter already worked on the windows. On the sidewalk sat small tables and restaurant equipment. A slick-looking white man in new work clothes watched the painter. The slick-guy's blondish hair looked long and sort of faggy, but it was the pink Lincoln Continental at the curb that hollered. Nobody painted a car pink. Nobody.

"Pays to advertise," Lester muttered, either to the Lincoln or the restless, or possibly now resting, spirit of Charlie Weaver.

The painter was going off half-cocked. Instead of doing the name of the joint first, he worked on blue and orangey curlicues in loud pastels. It looked like some kind of tearoom for white ladies, but that faggy Lincoln said something else. Besides, Cave Hill sat almost right next door. What kind of damn fool started a tearoom next-a cemetery?

Lester gave a low whistle and wondered how Charlie Weaver handled all this... assuming Charlie was in a state to know, which seemed likely... a man couldn't help but think of Charlie. During an estate sale, Charlie had always told gentle stories about the dear-departed. Charlie's car had been a black Lincoln Zephyr from 1939, shiny as new. His signs were black on white with dark green trim.

"Hell of a note," Lester said to the truck, and pulled away. Then Lester said, "I give the fag three months. Busted in three months."

It was still early when he parked on Barringer Ave. down a little ways from the auction. Morning shadows of trees ran long across the street. Cool of morning, or at least not as hot, dwelt under ragged leaves of those trees. Fewer white glows of magnolias among dark leaves. Brick glowed dull. Shadows ran long. The hottest part of summer faltered.

He sat in the truck waiting for Wade to open, because a colored man did not hang around a closed store on Bardstown Road. As it was, a woman passing down the sidewalk gave a suspicious look... woman taking a bus to work, woman dressed to ramrod an underwear counter at a dime store. Lester pretended not to see her. Instead, he thought of Sunday.

Folks walked wide of Ozzie, but Ozzie didn't walk wide of nobody. On Sunday afternoon he held that street corner firmly in place, talking and crapping around. Three or four men came and went. Sapphire Top Spot sat closed but Ozzie had bootleg whiskey. That bad man actually seemed cheery.

Nobody on Jackson St. would say a word to cops. Nobody on Jackson St., ever again, was gonna mess with Ozzie; 'cause it turned out Ozzie was even meaner than anybody thought. And, for another thing. Ozzie would now be carrying Jolly's pistol. It wasn't right, but there it was; and not a soul, anywhere, but was relieved when that bad Sunday got over.

* * *

When Wade and Jim parked nearby, Lester climbed from the truck. He would have to say a word to Jim. Come

Wednesday, when Jim went to Lucky's, Howard had a tale to tell.

Lots of dead people this summer. Lots, but summer was on the wane. Autumn in the air.

The house beside the auction looked somehow different. Rusty screens on the porch kept the front door from easy view. When Lester paused before the house he saw what Jim had seen earlier. Boards were taken from the door. Mrs. Samuels' son, the alive one, not the suicide, must have plans.

"We're up the crick," Wade said, when Lester entered the store. Wade had his pants on fire. He was already sweating, despite the morning cool. He looked rush-y, even though standing still. "We're getting more loads of store stuff, and I just signed a furniture factory. Three floors of genuine, mudcat trash."

"Where to?"

"Clarksville," Wade told him, talking about Indiana. "Bring the truck. My missus is at home. I'm leaving my kids here. Pick up help. Get a couple guys at the bridge." Wade turned to Jim. "Keep the damn loads separate. You know what to do. *Do* you know what to do?"

"Keep the loads separate."

"Lemmie talk to Jim a minute." Lester's voice went low. "Looks like we're this week in Indiana. When you see Howard he's been through something." Lester explained quick. Then he said, "Indiana. It ain't no place for civilized."

There were counties in Indiana that were meaner than the whole state of Kentucky. "I got to get goin'," Lester told Jim. "I know the right men to pick up if they ain't already hired."

With Wade and Lester gone Jim looked forward to a good day. Freedom almost never happened. Now that he worked for Lucky he even had a little money. Lucky paid top kid wages, 35 cents an hour.

A free day could be tricky. A kid had to be close to hand when needed, but a kid could hit the drugstore and pinball between times. As Wade and Lester pulled away, Jim turned to his sister.

"How many? Loads?"

"You," his sister told him, "are already thinking about goofing up." Nothing shy about his sister, at least not when she ran the show. It was pretty clear who had all the brains. "Front windows need washing," she told him.

He was a whole year older than her, and yet he never had a chance. Not only was she smarter, she gave a damn. He didn't.

He wandered from her, pretending he might actually go find cleaning stuff. It didn't make a lick of sense to argue. Not with Miss Pushy.

He was saved from window-wash as the Shell station's pickup pulled to the back door. There was rumor going around that the Shell station might turn into company-owned. Now it looked like the rumor was true, and the guy who leased the station was dumping inventory. Lots of it.

Starting just after the war all cars needed oil filters. Filling stations stocked lots of parts because they were also repair garages. They carried fuel pumps (older Fords went through them like toot through a tin horn) and clutches (something about pre-war Chevrolets and their vacuum shift) and tie rods (Packards with that soft front end).

As Jim sorted and stacked, working quick, the Shell guy went for another load. When the Shell guy returned with batteries and tires, his first load sat arranged and tidy. The guy, who should have been impressed, wasn't.

"This door open all the time?" He looked down the alley where nothin', absolutely nothin' ever happened.

"Nobody steals stuff." Jim started working the new load.

"I got a complete list of inventory."

"Most folks do." Jim worked the new load. "You want to go over it?"

And, like most folks, the guy didn't. He wanted to get back to work. He wanted to make a buck. He wanted what?... lube a Buick?... marry Betty Grable?... go to heaven?

By the time Jim got the second load stacked, a truck with furniture sat out by the front door. A rich lady had redecorated. She replaced her furniture. Her used furniture didn't look used very much.

You could always tell if a lady came from old money or new. New money people put covers on their couches. New money never owned fine veneer. New money had paintings of landscapes, not folks. New money was always sure it was about to get screwed. Old money, on the other hand, when screwed, stood above it; unless it was a major screw. In that case everybody needed to look sharp and stand way, way back. Lots of power ran through Louisville-town.

This load smelled of new money. The truck driver was a blondy-haired German with beer on his breath; and it no later than ten in the morning.

"Little tits," the guy told Jim about the rich lady, and Jim was shocked but fascinated. "Like pretty little pears. She kept leaning over. I should maybe go back." The driver was one of those guys proud of his strength. He boosted a heavy couch all by his lonesome. "Don't know whether 'twas invitation or not."

By the time the man left and the furniture sat in a neat stack, it turned to late morning; almost late enough to con his sister... tell her he would go to White Castle, get a bag of burgers; a sociable lunch.

"The windows," she said.

He drifted away, pretending he once more went for window-wash, but easing toward the back door. Maybe step into the alley, walk away for a while. And boy, would that jazz up Miss Pushy.

He surely had thinking to do. Lester had said Jolly was dead. Lester talked fast, but sounded sad. It came to Jim that Lester didn't bull-around all that much... Lester was like Lucky in that way.

And, Jim told himself, he didn't actually know Jolly. Jim had seen him once on that day of the dump run. Since then, though, Jim and Howard talked a lot about Jolly. In a way, Jim sort-of knew Jolly.

All Lester said was Jolly got killed. If Jolly got run over by a car, Lester would have said. Jim thought of Ozzie, and how Ozzie cut people. Maybe Ozzie did something bad. Ozzie stood pretty big in the Jim and Howard gossip. It looked like there would be lots more gossip.

Thinking of Jolly... it was weird how you felt a hurt for somebody you didn't even hardly know. It felt almost the same as when the neighbor man killed himself. Sad, like. Like stuff happened that was bad and shouldn't.

Thinking of the dead man. Jim stepped into the alley where shadows now sat short as temperature climbed. The door to the garage, that once barely hung on its hinges, was now nailed tight. Boards across it... not that anyone with brains would want to go in there. The garage sagged, like one day it would fall down all by itself.

That bad storm, on the day when the man killed himself, probably tore up the roof of that garage. The little spotlights of sun might be gone. One corner of the garage had a good-size crack because of the lean.

He'd promised to show Howard where the man killed himself. They'd gotten side-tracked because Howard rode with Lester, and Lester started taking the truck home at night. Jim stepped over to the crack. Take a look. Something to do.

The little spots of sun still threw patterns across the

ground. The roof had held up better than the building. Spots of sun cut through gloom. It ought to have been pretty and restful, but wasn't.

Wilted, sorta rotten flowers were arranged like they covered a grave, but the shape was of a man lying down. Little pieces of ribbon, and longer paper ribbons twined in the flowers, red and white. Paper ribbons hung from where they were stuck on the walls. A photograph lay at the head of the flowers. As near as he could tell, it was a picture of Mrs. Samuels' dead son, the tall, weakish one.

On the wall hung a bigger picture, mostly colored in red and gold. It showed the same man, but young and healthy; dressed in a foreign looking uniform. It was bordered in black, like the Victorian mourning pictures that came through the auction.

If the dead flowers were arranged to make a man, then the photograph was the man's head. The ribbons looked almost ragged as the flowers. Little spotlights showed dry ground around the flowers, the ground almost dusty.

The picture on the wall looked down on everything. Beside the picture hung a funny-looking old jacket. It was like a soldier-coat, but longer, and had some kind of medal sticking on its top pocket. A weird looking brass kettle sat beneath the jacket. The place looked like an abandoned cemetery, or maybe a junk yard.

Little dishes sat beside the kettle but they were empty. Maybe they were always empty. Or, maybe, rats.

What Jim felt was foreignness, weird, scary. Everything he knew pointed away from what he saw. It looked like a tea party in a graveyard, two pictures having tea; both dead.

His mom had said Mrs. Samuels' son, the alive one, was strange. She said to stay away. Jim suddenly felt truly afraid, and felt he must do something; maybe run, or something. He stepped away, down the alley, toward the drugstore and the pinball that jingle-jangle-jingled. The store and pinball weren't much but they were what he knew. Even the chewing-out he would later get from his sister would be a comfort. Anything normal would help.

WEDNESDAY, SEPTEMBER 3RD

AT THE FURNITURE FACTORY

Sunrise shone faded orange as Lester and Alfonzo and Zeke drove across Clark Bridge into Indiana. Orange light touched the river and painted gray water with a sheen of gold. The floating Coast Guard station, to their left and nearly under the bridge, had no boat moored. Boat crews did morning patrols. On the Indiana side where shipyards had built LSTs during the war, there was no longer much hustle and bustle. Traffic on the two-lane bridge ran sparse but quick.

"You got a handhold on what we're doin'," Zeke said to Lester. It wasn't a question. "What the hell have we been doin'?"

"It's not like a regular job," Lester told him. "All kinds of different stuff has got to work together."

"Not just push 'n carry."

"When you stack boxes keep the piles sharp," Lester told Zeke. "Sloppy stack, and the boss gets his balls bouncin'."

Forty-mile-an-hour speed caused coolish wind to rise through rusted floorboards. The truck rattled along like the old ship of Zion.

"His truck ain't real sharp." Alfonzo had his elbow draped over the window ledge, like he tried to keep the door from falling off.

"Country boys understand baling wire."

"He seems reasonable smart for a country boy." Alfonzo watched the river. A tug with coal barges beat its way upstream. "Seems kinda nervous."

"I get along," Lester told him. "He's an asshole but he ain't exactly a mean asshole." Lester sounded almost protective. Then he seemed like he'd startled himself. What'n'the world was he doing protecting Wade? "He's not used to workin' with colored. I gotta teach him something ever' day." Lester's voice still sounded protective. That protectiveness caused all three men to discover that they were almost, sorta, embarrassed.

The factory, when they arrived, stood three wooden stories with dusty windows and one whale of a pile of sawdust sitting a good piece away from the building; because sawdust can heat up. Spontaneous combustion.

Wade and the factory owner stood in the front office. Wade looked impatient with the factory owner, but tolerant. The owner looked scrawny and confused. Lester walked right on past with Zeke and Alfonzo in tow.

Ground floor of the factory held front office, shipping, and storage. Second floor held packaging and glue room. Third floor held production tools. Big factory. It measured, anyway, eighty by a hundred-twenty.

"Sob story," Wade told them after he got rid of the owner. "Let it be a lesson. Screw with big companies, and guess who gets knocked up."

"What's the lesson?" Lester gave a business-type grin.

"He made medium good bedroom stuff. Then a Kresge guy showed up wanting junk for his dime stores. Coffee and end table sets. Guaranteed ten thousand units a month. This guy retools and starts pumping out dreck. Kresge sells and sells. When sales slowed Kresge dumped the contract."

"Go back to bedroom stuff?"

"Damn fool didn't look ahead. Those customers went somewhere else."

"And now he takes a beating. You reckon he knows how much?"

Wade looked at hundreds and hundreds and hundreds of tables, boxed and ready to ship. He actually chuckled. "The sad sack is lucky he got me, and not some jack-leg. Come sale day I'll show him somethin'."

When factories go broke there is almost always tons of unfinished product lying around. It makes no difference whether it's furniture, tire re-capping, or brick-making; the place will be full of stuff caught in a halfway stage.

If the owner had brains he would continue production until stuff in process was complete. People will buy a finished table, a finished tire, a finished brick. But, what does anyone do with a junk coffee table sporting three screw inserts for legs, when the thing needs four?

There are reasons, some sad, some nasty. Owners of small factories do not have large crews. Owners know all their guys, and they know the guys will lose their jobs. The owner hangs on, minute to minute, hoping for a miracle. The miracle doesn't happen.

Or, the owner figures himself for savvy. If he tells his guys he's shutting down, they will lag on production so the job lasts longer. Cost will go up on finished product. It's a game of money-balance, cost of production opposed to "how much do I lose on half-finished...."

And, sadly, some factory owners (and this is true of small business in general) take their entire identities from the business. They watch a drooping sales curve, and instead of shutting down, mortgage their houses to keep a dying business alive. They keep coming to work. They keep smiling. Eventually they lose everything. A few kill themselves.

"So what we're gonna do today," Wade told Lester, "is sort

parts. Parts will sell. Legs, rails, tops, all good. Save back about two percent."

"Salt," Lester said to Zeke, and Zeke looked as confused as any man could possibly get. To Wade, Lester said, "Uh, huh."

Industry is messy. No way out of it. Too much material flows in and out. There's too much scrap, left-overs, and stuff that got mismatched or flawed: glue joints cockeyed, pieces of laminate too small for use and too big to throw away, pieces of wood with splits, and little cut-offs of wood. It doesn't look like much when sprinkled across a large factory floor. Then a man arrives with a push broom.

"Make one big pile," Lester told Zeke. "Sweep one side, then salt good parts in with half-finished. Then sweep the other side. We toss in more parts. Then sweep the middle. We top it off with a few parts. People just love to dig in piles."

"He's gonna sell a pile of junk?" Alfonzo sounded like a man who couldn't decide did he want to be disgusted or impressed.

"He'll even sell that pile of sawdust outside." Lester gave a little hop, happy-dance, and looked at Zeke. "Push fast, my man, before that country sonovabitch sells your broom."

Wednesday, September 3rd

At Lucky's

On Monday Jim had checked in loads, and on Tuesday shoved furniture this-way'n-that as Miss Pushy directed. His sister already knew how to set up a sale. She shoulda been a boy.

Also on Tuesday, a load of hotel stuff arrived, heavy as a wagonload of rocks. Mattresses came with beds. Illegal to sell a used mattress, but you could sell the bed and say you gave the mattress to the guy who bought the bed. The back room looked like overflow.

Wednesday morning found a full auction house and no time to do a thing with it. Flyers for the factory sale, eleven days away, had to go in the mail. Jim folded flyers. His mother addressed envelopes. His sister stuffed envelopes and licked stamps.

When he left for Lucky's at noon he felt guilty. A kid couldn't be in two places at once, but what difference did that make when it came to feeling guilty? None. Actually.

The bus carried older ladies who dressed nice and headed for a couple hours' shopping. They pointed toward Fourth and Broadway, the absolute center of town.

As the bus rattled along he had time to miss Lester. Because of Lester, who he hadn't seen since Monday, the auction had turned brighter. He took time to think how he missed Howard. Then he worried about Lucky. He hadn't seen Lucky in over two weeks. Maybe Lucky forgot all about him.

The bus poked along. When it stopped before Charlie Weaver's place, everybody on the bus came to attention. Whispers started. A woman exclaimed, "Lordy," another woman, "Lord have mercy."

Windows lay in shattered pieces. Hunks of glass still hung around the edges, and some of the pieces wore curlicues of pink paint. A man wearing heavy gloves used a chisel to pull hunks from the window frame. Inside Charlie Weaver's place, restaurant tables and chairs sat amid fragments of glass. Lots of pictures lined the walls.

"Whatever in the world. What happened?" An elderly lady looked to the bus driver.

"Somebody didn't like somebody else." The bus driver checked his mirrors, ready to pull away. A car passed. Then another. "A fellow came poking in here from back east." The driver entered traffic. He didn't say more, like he was embarrassed.

"... no reason to break windows."

"...drives a pink car." The driver muttered. As far as he was concerned, there was the end of it.

Silence in the bus. Something had just been said that, in those days, nobody with any politeness ever talked about. It was even-steven half the ladies didn't know a thing more than Jim, and Jim didn't know peanuts.

If Charlie Weaver brooded over the scene, which would be more than understandable, he probably told himself that the world had tried to pass him by; and failed. He would most likely have taken no satisfaction.

When Jim got off the bus, Jackson St. felt like the safest and most comfortable place in town. He found himself dawdling when he should be in a hurry. He really did fear

Lucky had forgotten him.

Afternoon sun struck brilliant on red bricks. The old lady with the kerchief raised it in hello. By now he knew her name, Miz Sally; and nigh a hundred years old. A plantation lady, three or four wars back. She didn't say nothin' but made him welcome.

A little bit along, an old man sat on another stoop. He hardly ever did a thing but stare. His mouth hung medium-open. He still had two teeth. His hands trembled. Name of Mr. Rufus James Whiteman. Almost as old as Miz Sally.

From a room above a woman sang. Church song, and here it was only Wednesday. The song sailed like a mockingbird above the dusty street and worn-out cars.

On the corner near Sapphire Top Spot, Ozzie stood with some other men. Jim stopped for a minute to think about it. Ozzie seemed different, even if he didn't look different.

Was it worse to go ahead, or worse to cross the street and make a point of it? No good either way. Might go around the block and get to Lucky's from the other direction. That wouldn't work, either.

Walk straight ahead like a kid going to work.

"White meat," Ozzie said to the men as Jim walked past. To Jim he said, "Boy, stop your ass."

"Leave it be," one of the other men said. "Some shit ain't worth startin'."

"Going to work," Jim whispered. "Going to work for Lucky. Working with Howard."

"Howie's a little pisser," Ozzie told him. "How come you fool with a boy who pisses his pants."

"Leave it, Ozzie." One man backed away, looked around for cops, and seemed ready to run.

"Get along, boy, get along. Your day is comin'." Ozzie turned back to the men like he'd done nothing more than stomp a bug.

When Jim stepped into Lucky's it was old-home-week at the hockshop. Lucky and Howard stood behind the front counter. Mrs. Lucky sat at her desk. A sad-looking white couple stood toward the middle of the store. They murmured to each other.

"Leave them alone for now," Lucky explained in a low voice. "Gauge your customer. Watch his clothes and how he moves. Can you tell why I know those folks just came to town?"

Howard, excited, seemed ready to bounce. "They look at small appliances."

"Tired," Lucky said. "The man is beat. The woman is weary to the point of tears. They just rented a bad room somewhere close. There's no stove. She's gotta cook."

The moment the woman looked toward the front of the store Lucky moved.

"How's it goin'?" Jim nudged Howard.

"Shssh." Howard put a hand on Jim's shoulder, like friends, but also like, "shut up and pay attention." Howard, whether the world knew it or not, was on the road to owning his own store. "We must learn."

Lucky smooth, not oily. Conventional chit-chat, "Welcome to the neighborhood."

"...we come from down to Bowlin' Green...."

"...long trip, Bowling Green."

"...goddamn long trip...."

"Don't cuss. I can't stand it when you cuss." The woman looked to her husband.

"I have three ways to go." Lucky softened his voice but did not look at the woman. "Gas plate, two kinds of electric." He looked at the man. "Temporary place?"

"Gone from there," the man said, "soonest I get a job."

"Then I got two ways to go. Got a two burner electric for six, three burner for fourteen. Which one do you think?"

"Six?" The man looked to his wife.

"Not as heavy duty," Lucky said. "But ought to work for a good while."

"Take the six," the man said, and he talked like a man damn-determined to get a job come the morrow.

"The other would last." The woman could not hide her discouragement. Fatigue crowded all through her voice.

"Take the fourteen," the man said.

When the couple left, Lucky turned to the boys. "The kind of job he's going to find, he'll be in that room 'til the house collapses. Did him a favor. Sold him something for long wear." Lucky looked directly to Howard. "Keep any deal as straight as you can. You not only feel better, you don't get as many kickbacks." To Jim he said, "Make friends with the customer, but keep a distance. Never offer a choice of one or nothing. Always offer a choice between two. It gives less space to say 'no'.

"Who was the customer?" Howard asked a question that, never in the world, would have occurred to Jim.

"The woman." Lucky looked toward Mrs. Lucky who sat far enough away she could not hear. "When you sell to a couple, talk to the woman but act like you're talking to the man. If you talk straight to the woman, or look at her, you'll lose the man. He thinks you're running a number on his wife."

Then he said, "I have a hand of work for you gentlemen."

* * *

Sitting together polishing residue from somebody's failed store; greenish brass elephants, camels, and lions.

"Lester says Jolly got murdered. You feelin' bad?"

"Lester say anything else?" Howard, glad as anything to see Jim, spoke subdued about Jolly.

"Lester's working in Indiana this week. So, no. Except Jolly is killed."

Howard told the story as best he could. When he came to the part about the blood he didn't do so well.

"You think Ozzie?"

"Don't you ever say a word." Howard sounded more resigned than angry. "Mother says Ozzie isn't right in his head."

"The police will get him."

"It doesn't work that way," Howard said. "What happens if you tell, and the police do not get him?"

Tangy stink of brass polish—dink of a cash register as Lucky made a sale—sound of a police siren a long way off; Jim stopped polishing an elephant, whispered, "He wouldn't."

"He would," Howard said. "You dare not think he wouldn't."

"What's gonna happen?"

"I expect," Howard said, "for now, nothing will happen. Then, one day, Ozzie will get crazy with drink."

"He maybe already did." Jim told about broken windows at Charlie Weaver's auction. He told what the bus driver said. Pink car.

"That was not Ozzie." Howard's voice turned teacherly. "Colored would not do that. That was a white." Howard looked toward the front of the store, a look of longing. "I waited on three customers yesterday. I did well on one." Howard watched Lucky, like Lucky might suddenly decide to sprout wings and fly. Above Lucky on a high shelf, Lola the Guinea hen seemed ready to cluck, and Thomas, the Plymouth Rock looked totally nutsy. "I think I'll get another chance today."

"Why white?" Jim figured that one of the mysteries of Jackson St. stood ready to unfold. There was definitely a difference between Jackson St. bull and the brand on Bardstown Road.

"I can't say," Howard told him. "I can tell you that colored are more live-and-let-live about homo-sexuals. White men won't put up with it." To a disbelieving, then believing Jim, Howard explained all he knew about homosexuals; the blind more-or-less leading the blind. "There are men who do sex things with each other."

Silence. Lucky's voice low as he dealt with a dark-skin lady—sound of pages turned from Mrs. Lucky's desk. "Makes me wanta urp," Jim whispered. He could no more talk about sex-things than Lucky could fly, or Thomas could do arithmetic. "I gotta tell you," Jim said, "about that other dead man. The one in the garage."

MONDAY SEPTEMBER 8TH

LOVE AND MUSIC

School began, and life for two boys changed as new feelings erupted in minds and hearts. The minds and hearts were not exactly connected (not quite yet) with loins.

Miss Stacy Hall taught science at Highland Junior High, and Miss Sarah Jones taught the same at Jackson St. Colored Junior High. Both young women, had they been willing to wait for a kid to grow up, could have married any boy in their classes.

Miss Stacy had longish auburn hair, blue eyes, slim figure, and graceful, graceful hands. Her fingers, when doing diagrams at the blackboard, seemed like magics, dancing.

Miss Sarah had eyes sparkly as stars at midnight; but dark as midnight, also. Her skin was high-yeller Creole, her figure buxom. She answered sass with sass; the teacherly kind.

Jim would learn just enough science to squeak past, but would really learn how to make full-time, standard-type, generalized dreams: a cottage for two, flowers along a white fence; if only she would wait.

Howard took to science like a duck hunting puddles, and began making dreams with a point to them: a store of his own, and Miss Sarah in a big white house, occasionally charming customers at the store—(in the dream, Howard's mother took care of the books which was only practical). If Miss Sarah would only wait.

It wasn't gonna happen. When Jim biked from the auction to school during September, he did so with the dull ache of one who owns futile dreams. Still, it was his dream, and the very biggest. Much better than dreams of being a fireman or an airplane pilot.

Howard, walking to school, walked with the same dull ache; but the dream of a store and a big white house were parts that a man could hold onto.

And, when one stops to think about it, both boys handled 'love' about as well as everyone else. And, since commerce could not exist without valentines, Mother's Day, fluffy puppies and smiling babies, it's worth looking at how everyone else was doing.

Lucky loved Mrs. Lucky, and no fool, he. If there was a speck of emptiness in their shared lives, it came through a lack of children. Lucky solved the lack by teaching his trade to young boys. He also promoted Israel, but sanely, because he figured some Zionists were as crazy as Thomas the stuffed rooster.

Mrs. Lucky, equally practical, solved lack of kids by taking care of Lucky. She probably never realized that Lucky cared for her beyond the usual complexities of love. She didn't really know that Lucky, having read the newspapers, sometimes felt groundless. She did not know that she was his main and sometimes only reason to strive.

Wade took love for granted. If asked he would throw the question back at the questioner. "If that wasn't the point, why in the fatback hell would I be bustin' the seat of my pants?" Wade would not use the word 'love' because he couldn't. It just wasn't in the man.

Mrs. Wade, Viola, loved her kids, and supposed to herself that she loved her husband. He was, after all, tolerable on Sundays.

Lester loved the memory of a Chicago-girl-communist named Mona; a union girl so far to the left she figured Roosevelt's New Deal was a right-wing conspiracy. And, like Jim and Howard, Lester loved a dream. A house, a wife, kids of his own; but the woman couldn't be Mona, and there wasn't no other woman in sight. Saturdays nights, Lester went 'high lonesome'.

And the next door neighbor, Isaac, the one with the dead mother and the dead brother? He could only have memories, because surely dreams were silenced. Perhaps he dreamed of honor, or perhaps in those dwindling days of summer, his mind wandered back to pre-Hitler Warsaw where horse-drawn carriages still moved along quiet streets, and where markets were alive with shouts.

He had lived in a nation where the well-to-do lived very well, and the majority did not. Illiteracy stood at 50 percent, the peasantry still worked dawn to dusk, and even when there was no war (which was seldom) life expectancy was low. Entertainment in the countryside came from visiting musicians, or gypsies, or chatter among neighbors on market days.

The population was predominantly Catholic. This had been a continuing problem off-and-on for Jews. The Catholic church was smart enough not to kick an economically productive group out of the country, but popes and nobles managed to shift Jews from city to country, then country to city; always at a profit to the Church.

Hitler marched on Poland at the beginning of September 1939. By then Isaac was an established concert musician. He had performed in Vienna, which in those days was the height of artistic achievement. As Nazis swarmed across Poland two factors kept Isaac alive.

The first was music. In the late 19th and early 20th century classical music held sway in Europe. Concert musicians were treated with respect, awe, and were often as popular as superstar rockers of a later day. Jewish musicians of note were kept alive as performers for German colonels and generals.

The second was love. Her name was Hela Powlowski and she was a violinist who was capable if not notable. She was small with bright smile, dark hair, delicate face. When at her best, her hands danced on strings like clever little birds. She was 24 and shy except when playing music. He was 36 and inexperienced. The year was 1943. They agreed to marry three days before she disappeared.

Treblinka work camp changed into an extermination camp in 1943. Rumor ran rife. Isaac searched for her during every stolen and dangerous moment, but he had no power to find her, leave alone help. Still, searching kept him alive.

In late '44, a broken Isaac Samuelwicz was also sent to Treblenka. Nazis were everywhere preparing to retreat. They had no further need for amusement.

Saturday, September 13th

Furniture Factory Sale

New glass appeared in the windows of Charlie Weaver's place. Tables and chairs disappeared, and it was rumored that a longish-haired stranger left town cursing every redneck in Louisville; a group that included Mayor Farnsley, Police Chief Heustis, School Superintendent Carmichael, Ministers of The Word, doctors, lawyers, professors, river-boat gamblers (the stranger believed they still existed), and the general run of populace from (A)uctioneers to (Z)ulus.

Cops did not look for the vandal. It was quite clear that Louisville was inexperienced and not ready for a high class coffee house and art boutique. After all, the city was only just beginning to handle television, as WHAS had started its first broadcasts in March.

It would become equally clear that the ruling power of the city deluded itself. Government and institutions proudly claimed that, while segregation existed (and maybe a little prejudice) tensions did not; and even people who drove pink Lincolns could live comfortably in this city of certifiable culture. Mr. Mayor and Mr. Chief cop, and Mr. School Superintendent, though generally well-intended, sounded, more-than-a-little... well ... 'full-of-it'.

Still, the part about culture was true. Louisville had an

excellent orchestra (music not yet considered a political threat), a concert program for children, and a museum in the basement of the main library. It had a very good streetcar college, plenty of religious schools, little theater groups, and it 'put up' with nice ladies who took lots of watercolor classes.

"Knew that place would go sour from the first," Lester told Jim as they drove past Charlie Weaver's and headed for Indiana. "Figured the joy-boy would go broke. Should-of known a redneck would get him." Lester drove easy, and looked easy in his mind. As they passed Cave Hill Lester looked across the rolling acres of tombstones. "Charlie. I bet Charlie crapped himself a brick."

Jim thought he understood 'joy-boy'. "They made us buy athletic supporters for gym class," he told Lester, and wasn't sure why. "One kid told another kid it was a gas mask. The other kid draped it over his ears."

"Kids." Lester chuckled; Lester a naturally happy man. "I reckon Howie will show up with Lucky."

On the Clark Bridge two-lane traffic ran medium heavy this Saturday morning as yellow and red over-the-road trucks headed for Indianapolis. Plenty of pickups, plus Cads and Lincolns, seemed headed for the furniture factory. When Lester and Jim arrived there wasn't a parking space to be had.

"We'll settle it someplace on the street," Lester said about the truck, and started cruising. "Sweet Jesus take me home," Lester said. "Look at this here." They rolled past a parked stake truck, chipped blue paint with streaks of orange. No sign of the country boy.

"Jim," said Lester, "this is gettin' serious." He no longer sounded happy; wrinkles on his brow, his eyes deeper-brown and sad-like. "I'm takin' you back and droppin' you off. You tell your daddy."

"You gonna fight?"

"Not never, can I help." Lester still sounded sad. Then he sounded mad. "Always the same old shit. Always. I'll park a-ways off, come in the back."

"I'll come with."

"And get in the middle of somethin'? I couldn't face your momma."

A crowd of men stood in front of the factory as Lester dropped Jim. They smoked cigars, gossiped, and traded brags this Saturday morning. Furniture dealers, junk dealers, and discount guys mixed in with factory owners. The factory guys wore fine clothes, drove fine cars, and came for production tools, not inventory. Near them, but standing separate, a few women stood chatting, their dresses orange and yellow and blue; colorful as flowers growing above concrete.

He hurried to find his dad. Inside the factory, just inside the door, Mr. Evans had set up his catering stand with sandwiches and silver-shiny coffee urn. Men strolled, studied the sale, and some made notes. This crowd might be too big. The bigger the crowd, the harder it is to keep it focused.

Wade took the news in stride. "Some guys," he said to Daniels who stood with him, "are so dumb they couldn't tell sheep shit from raisins, if they found them in the same piece of pie." To Jim he said, "If that bastard comes in, you hike on over and stand in front of your mom. It's what men do." He watched the crowd and was already working up a sweat. He passed Jim his car keys. "Go get my goddamn cane."

Auctioneers use sturdy canes for pointing, not walking. It's an appliance. The auctioneer can rap with it. He can bang a machine tool to get a ring-a-dink, or a garbage can to get a rattle. He can draw a line with it, moving a crowd's attention across wide spaces. It's even more handy than a Louisville slugger, being somewhat thinner and easy to swing.

Jim came back with the cane the same moment Lester arrived. "I can't feature trouble," Lester told Wade. "Too many folks."

"The bastard wants to make noise." Wade looked over the gathering crowd as he searched for the country boy. "He don't want trouble, just wants to cause it. He wants pay-back. I know these jerk-offs."

In an all-day sale, which this was gonna be, Wade would lose five pounds sweating, and at least a pound of muscle. Lester's shirt would turn sodden, and he'd have sweat on his brow heavy as Mr. Louis Armstrong's. Fine and dandy. Fresh sweat smells nice. Stale stuff stinks.

"We sell first floor, second, third," Wade said to Jim. "Why?"

For once, Jim wasn't on the spot. He could answer that one. "Office stuff ain't worth much and you use it to warm the crowd. The check-out goes on behind you, instead of having stuff hauled through the sale."

"I got to refine the crowd. By the time we get to machinery we'll have a real small crowd. I'll work 'em different." Wade paused. Reluctant. "Your answer was okay," he admitted. "Pretty good."

"Lucky," Lester said. "Lucky and Howie just come in, and ain't that fine."

Auctions begin when the auctioneer mounts his stool, or with a big crowd, a short ladder. They always begin with announcements, and with terms of the sale while the clerk tries to get a few numbers written down ahead of time. The crowd drifts in from corners of the building, or from outside. It gradually takes a roundish shape, with men gossiping on the fringes.

The auctioneer's opening spiel resembles announcements in church; which is to say, more fun than listening to the sermon. The announcements give the auctioneer a chance to make friends with the crowd. More importantly, it's the time when he takes control, which is generally an easy job. This time turned different.

Wade began a big song-and-dance about the factory owner, who, having made a bundle, was headed for Florida and other interests. It was basic-bull and expected. Even mice hiding in the walls knew the guy had busted. Then Wade turned to terms of sale, "You buy as-is, where-is, without guarantee or warranty of any kind. You get it like you got your wife, for better or worse.

"Juice is off on the machinery. When we get there we'll turn it on so you can see equipment operate..." Wade looked toward the front doorway just as the country boy eased through and toward the crowd. Wade pointed with the cane. "And you, my friend, can turn around and walk your fanny down the road." Wade sounded amused. What an actor.

"Public place. Public auction," the country boy yelled. "Nary a damn you can do about it." The guy was red-faced, but cold sober and ready for fight.

A murmur started. The crowd's attention broke. Wade was gonna have plain misery getting it back, unless something happened quick.

"There is somethin' I can do," Wade said, and his voice sounded so amused that he might bust out laughing. "It's not a public place, but that's beside the point." He turned from looking at the country boy, and waved a slow arc with his cane. The crowd's eyes followed the arc, away from the country boy.

"This fellow is a hell of nice guy," Wade told the crowd, "but he's got a doctor problem. Brains keep drizzling out his ears." Amid laughter Wade turned back to the country boy. "...hate to see a man waste valuable time. You can make bids, my friend, and you can wiggle your nose like a bunny, but it's not about to work. I won't take your bid." Wade sounded droll, like first cousin to Mr. Bob Hope. At the same time he lowered the cane, tapped Lester to make him aware, which was not necessary a-tall.

Jim headed for the office to protect his mom. No reason to believe he wasn't gonna get killed doing it.

"Public auction," the guy yelped.

"My auction," Wade said, "Let's get rolling." He turned to a bunch of junk; warm-up stuff before starting on office equipment.

"Got a line of orphans," Lester hollered. "Cute as kittens. Twenty of 'em. Needs adopting." He picked up an end table, holding it high. A line of miscellaneous tables stood along the wall, mismatched singles.

"Ten bucks," the country boy hollered.

"Sold to Daniels, one semoleon." Wade looked to Lester. Winked. "Lemmie hear something good."

"Hallelujah," Lester yelled like a Holy Roller. "Come down through the ceiling Lord, I'll pay for the shingles."

Laughter from the crowd. Lester raised a box of miscellaneous junk real high and did a little dance.

"This ain't the end of it, you nigger-lovin' bastard." The country boy yelled, his voice high, screamy, near hysterical. "And you can kiss your pet nigger goodbye." He stomped, left, slammed the door.

A murmur. The crowd looked at Lester. The crowd looked at Mr. Evans. Mr. Evans stood quiet, his head lowered; Mr. Evans getting by, making it, a colored gentleman.

Lester pissed, and showing it. "Bring help," Lester said in the direction of door. "Bring a hell of a lot." He was past caring: half the crowd on his side, and half the crowd resentful because colored were supposed to 'yassuh'. Crowd so quiet you could hear traffic swish on the street. Sale busted.

Wade's finest moment. In his whole life. Most likely.

"I pay as good wages, or better, than any man here," he told the crowd, his voice quiet. "That means I can pick and choose. I can't get better help than who you see. And no matter how hard you looked, you couldn't either." His voice, quiet and firm, remained firm but stopped being quiet. "We are businessmen and this is business. Let's get goddamn cracking."

Murmur from the crowd. An embarrassed chuckle. Then a laugh. Wade started to sell. Lester worked quietly for a while, then gradually got off the ground. In half an hour Lester was flying high, and Wade had the crowd back in his pocket.

With Wade and Lester working, and with his mom safe, Jim went looking for Howard. It took five minutes. Howard stood by Lucky.

"Don't wander just yet," Lucky said to Howard. Something's going on." He pointed as the junk dealer Fudd pushed through the crowd and toward Wade. "Your dad is a smart man," he told Jim. "Let's see how he handles this one."

Auctioneers can get stuck in two ways:

The first is to get caught while walking a bid. Sometimes inexperienced, or just plain cheap buyers jump onto an item. They bid two bucks on something that should have an opening bid of twenty. Instead of screwing around with buck-bids, and letting the crowd fall into a cheap way of thinking, the auctioneer goes, "Got two, now ten, and twenty," and then starts calling for thirty. He doesn't really have twenty, but he's walked to where the bid should open; plus he's shut down the cheapskate. If asked about his bidder, he says the bid was left by a man who had business elsewhere.

Seldom—but it can happen—he doesn't catch another bid. In that case he marks the item down to a fictional buyer because he's bought it himself. He then runs the item through his next auction and generally takes a small loss. Walking a bid is part of the cost of doing business.

The second way to get stuck happens when an amateur buyer gets stars in his eyes, buys a whole lot of stuff, and then—because of a flat bank account, or buyer's remorse—walks away and is never heard from again. Legally, the buyer has entered a contract with his bids, and the contract is enforceable. Practically speaking, it takes time and money to sue. Meanwhile, all the stuff sits and takes up space. It's cheaper for the auctioneer to sell it a second time at another sale. Second-time stuff almost always loses money. Plus, it produces added expense in time and labor.

Thus, when Fudd got eager, and started pressing forward, he sent a signal that both Lucky and Lester caught; and one that Wade was about to catch. Fudd sent the signal because he couldn't have been more dumb had he been a doorknob.

He should have let a list of goods accumulate, twenty units here, thirty there. Instead he stepped right in as Wade knocked down nine hundred tables at a buck-seventy-seven-and-a-half. "Lots of ten," Wade said.

"Take 'em all," Fudd said.

Pause. Wade stopped like a run-down clock. Daniels whispered an amazed chorus of cuss words. Lester turned to look at Fudd, and Lester did some quick figuring. "That's more'n fourteen hundred bucks," he whispered to Fudd. "Your whole store ain't worth that much. What's happening."

"One lot of ten to Fudd," Wade said, "Pass 'em around." He started parceling out lots of ten, a stall, while Fudd started getting his back up.

"Corbin," Daniels said, talking straight to Fudd. "You figure that country bastard is actually gonna pay? He'll leave you hanging out to dry."

Fudd stood confused, his big plan busted.

"Because, the bastard really will leave you hanging out," Daniels said. "He gives nary a damn, except to drop a sour invoice on the auction. How much of that load hits you?"

"He was payin' twenty bucks," Fudd whispered, and Fudd was a mighty confused man.

"You weren't gonna get a dime," Daniels told him. "By now he's halfway over the bridge and ready to drain a beer keg."

* * *

"I give the sod buster credit," Wade said. "He surely is persistent." Wade stood with Daniels after the sale. Wade's voice sounded raspy and rough after seven hours of steady performance. "I hope to hell I'm not coming down with something."

In this late afternoon the check-out lagged. A couple of trucks loaded cartons of tables. A few small items went through the doorway. Most of the check-out would happen Monday. A day-long sale wears everybody out, crowd included.

Jim checked one truck while Howard sorta supervised. Lester checked the other. Lucky lounged his way to Wade and Daniels. "You got truck space?" he asked Daniels. "You checking out?"

"Lester's going your way," Wade said.

"I hate to ask him," Lucky said. "Long day, and everybody's beat." He turned to Daniels. "I figure half a load."

"We can squeeze it."

"Are you worried?" Lucky came straight to the point.

"Dammit," Wade said, "Yes." He looked toward Lester. "I'm driving him to where the truck is parked. I'm following him home."

"We'll be headed that way," Lucky said. "We can follow

him."

"I'm beholden," Wade told him. Wade watched Lester, then looked toward the doorway like he expected the country boy to come busting through. "I've met some meatheads in my day, but that old boy's brains are hamburger. What does it take to be that nuts?"

White Trash/Black Trash

The American south at mid-century was like God's lavender hankie, but with a glob of snot in one corner. Southerners, colored or white, rightly loved the place (though they didn't necessarily love each other). To this day, one may make sharp remarks about the middle west, and former midwesterners nod their heads and say, "Yep, oh-god-a-mighty, yep." But make cracks about the south in the presence of displaced southerns and you have a fight on your hands.

When the fool from Corbin came to the big city he did so with certain knowledge that he was "as goddamn good as any man alive," despite he wasn't worth five cents. He had certain knowledge, not opinion, but *knowledge* that he was better than any colored man who ever walked. Because he was white, he was better than men like Mr. Luther Burbank.

The country boy was raised in the squalor of stump-preacher religion that induces fear and self-hatred. The country boy knew he wasn't worth a pile of toenail clippings without the work of Jesus in his soul, but his preacher amended that by telling him he was God-anointed master of the Negro race. The country boy also learned that southern heat and southern small-town-hatred were the eleventh and twelfth commandments.

The country boy was different from professional haters who occupied cities. The city boys, white or colored, had to put up with people who held different opinions. The country boy, on the other hand, didn't know a single white man in his town who disagreed with anything having to do with hatred.

Until the day Lester slugged him at the warehouse, nothing in the country boy's whole life ever said a colored would stand up to a white. He might have taken a lesson. But, he lived around intimidated negroes who came to town days, worked, grinned, shucked and jived, and left before sundown. They, as he, were ignorant men.

How ignorant? Colored folk might talk about 'going north', but for a man to go north he has to understand that he can get on a bus, and he has to know how to get on a bus. That ignorant.

Did the country boy have a choice? You bet. Did he make a bad one? Here were his options:

In Kentucky, men were Southern Gentlemen, Colored Gentlemen, Rednecks, Hill Folk, Hillbillies, Sorry, or Trash.

Southern Gentlemen: Unlike the north, a poor man of any color could be a gentleman. A rich man of any color could be sorry.

The gentleman, rich or poor, comported himself with a sense of honor. He protected children, women, old people, and if white, protected negroes, though he might exploit them economically. Plus, he didn't screw around any more than absolutely necessary. This set of standards had been imported to the south from southern England, back in the 18th century.

Rednecks, of whom Wade was a moderate example, were generally men whose artistry lay in their work. They bulled their ways through life, were more honest than not, and though obnoxious rarely went to jail. They might have some notion of gentlemanly behavior, and might even rank somewhere on the Gentleman-scale, generally lower.

Hill People were strong, ethical, moral and decent; though, through isolation, necessarily narrow. Many could count themselves as gentlemen. Many had never seen a colored man in their lives.

Hillbillies were hill people who were sorry. They were often bootleggers and small-time chiselers.

The words Sorry and Trash were synonyms. They described a man of no honor who wheedled, shirked, blamed the whole world for his troubles; they described a coward, yellow to the bone; they called up visions of barn burnings, or cut tires, or rocks through windows at midnight. Not all white men who were sorry were Ku Kluxers, but all Ku Kluxers were sorry. If the country boy had been born colored, he would have murdered Jolly.

Not all colored men who were sorry were jailbait, but jail caught lots of them. Ignorance, and lack of any principle, were the keys. If Ozzie had been white, and raised in a mid-century, small southern town, Ozzie would have been Ku Klux.

SATURDAY NIGHT, SEPTEMBER 13TH

THE FIFTH DEATH

To a man who ends a weary work day, options are reduced. He can 'go out', or stay home and listen to radio, even if race music will not get broadcast until ten p.m. Or, a man can do both. Have a beer, crap around a little, and make an early night.

Lester stood in his rooms looking down on Jackson St. Dusk, as mellow as Howard's skin, warmed the street, and sounds were like a patchwork quilt: a woman singing, the next-door lady, Miz Julia, raking the air with yells as she gave her man hell-'n-down-the-road, phonograph playing from somewhere, and folks gossiping as they gathered on doorsteps. Kids hollered, played, and, if out of hearing distance from their mommas, cussed like little troopers.

On the corner before Sapphire Top Spot a group of men stood, but no sign yet of Ozzie. Faint call of a chorus as Mr. Lionel Hampton banged out "Hey! Ba-Ba-Re-Bop" on the juke. Lester watched Alfonzo drift past Lucky's, headed toward talk and a beer. Alfonzo looked extra tired this Saturday night, and that is what decided Lester. It makes sense to sit with somebody who needs sittin' with. Work is three times harder when a man is alone.

He paused, savoring the one great thing about the day. The boss had taken his side, and the boss had advertised him as the best help going. It seemed like no colored man could ever, completely, one hundred percent, trust a white man; but set that aside for a spell. The good feeling was there. He would not turn it down.

His pause lengthened. That country boy had sounded just crazy. The colored streets of Louisville were not many. If the country boy worked at finding Lester he could cruise until he found the auction truck. Maybe it was smart to move the truck. Then Lester thought, 't'hell with it.' It was a tired, tired evening. And, by now the country boy was likely ripped and halfway home.

When he got to Sapphire Top Spot Lester found Alfonzo and Zeke holding down the same old table. Habit maybe, or good sense. The table sat toward the rear of the room. It looked out on the street corner. If badness started out there, or in the joint, a man could head for the back room and jump out a window.

"Dancer," Zeke said. "Does you need a manager?" Zeke looked pretty fresh, and dressed-Saturday-night, spangles on his shirt like a jazzman. Then, "You get rid of all that junk?"

"Seat yourself," Alfonzo told him. "We need to know stuff." Alfonzo looked dragged-out to the point of worry. "Coal," he said, "about forty million ton of bituminous. Folks loadin' up against winter. Wheelbarrow work."

Nothing about the joint seemed different. Blue tending bar, fine-looking if a little skinny... Mona had been skinny; somethin' about skinny women... work is not only harder... it's a lot more lonesome when a man is by himself.

Toward the end of the bar Albert sat in bar-owner bliss, watching cash roll in, watching Blue at the register. Early drinkers sat around. Out there on the corner a man gave a little dance as the juke clicked, and Miss Velma Middleton poured song into the evening.

"What I gotta know," Zeke said, "is how much did my pile of sweepings sell for? I got investment in that pile."

"Thirty bucks," Lester told him. "I don't believe it either. Buyers crawled all over it."

"When you gonna need more help? That was good workin'." Alfonzo started to get a little lift from the beer; a man wanting a job with no wheelbarrows. Not desperate, just bone tired. "How much that pile of sawdust bring?"

"Four bucks," Lester told him. "I didn't believe that, neither."

"What do a man do with sawdust?"

"I couldn't say," Lester told him. "Used car lots put it in bad differentials sometimes. Muffles the roar."

"Ozzie's just come up. I think of coastin' my sweet ass outta here." Zeke looked toward Albert, as Albert checked the street. Albert beckoned to Blue, and said a few words too low for anybody but Blue to hear.

"I trust Albert to do any reconciling," Alfonzo said. "Albert is no fool."

Lester, then, began dancing; moving with the music, slow and fluid as befits a tired, tired man. Lester dancing just a little, then return to the table. Sit and talk. Music catches Lester. Moves a little more, then return to the table.

"It relaxes a man," he said to Zeke. "Works out the wrinkles." ...Lester drinking quicker than usual against an early go-to-bed. Men on the street corner sipping from half pints of Jim Beam. Cop car riding past, slowing, going on. Ozzie talking ugly against the car.

Dance some more, and then Alfonzo joins in. Alfonzo begins to move with an old-man shuffle, but you could tell how graceful, how good Alfonzo once had been. Zeke sipping, sipping, sipping, watching night come down. Red neon of Sapphire Top Spot makes shadows from men standing on the street corner.

A stirring starts among those men. They turn, watch, mutter to each other. Zeke reaches over, taps Lester on the butt, and Lester stops his dance. Alfonzo looks around, then looks to Albert. Albert don't see nothin' yet, but Albert has a bar owner's instinct. He whispers quick to Blue, and Blue lays a bar towel on the bar, with you-know-what hidden beneath the towel.

The country boy walked steady enough. Drunk, but not terrible drunk. He passed Ozzie like Ozzie wasn't even there. He stepped through the doorway of Sapphire Top Spot and stood in red light, looking around 'til he found Lester.

"You," he said. "Get your black ass to the street. We're gonna settle something." To the rest of the bar he said, "Stay damn well where you are. This here is the only boy I want." He reached a hand to one pocket. Knife? Sap? Pistol?

"White man," Albert said, and said it louder than music. "Be a shame to shoot a damn fool, but that's what's gonna happen." Albert leveled a .38 revolver silver-color. Barlight glinted red off of it. Albert sounded more tired than mad, despite this white man, this late at night, was Albert's worse nightmare.

Lester pissed. Lester ready to fight. Zeke moving away. Alfonzo looking to Lester. "Leave it be," Alfonzo said. "Leave Albert with it."

"You wanna know how many white womens I lay beside?" ...Lester so pissed he started darky-talk. He sounded ready for fight, glad for fight. "More'n you boy. Is you a little younger, I swear I is yo' daddy."

Silver pistol moving in Lester's direction. "No more mouth," Albert told him. To the white boy he said, "Walk out of where you don't belong. This is exclusive colored. Do it now."

"I can wait," the country boy said to Lester. "You got to take your black ass out of here sometime." He looked at

Albert like Albert was dogshit, then turned and walked away. When he passed the men on the corner he didn't even watch his back.

"Well, I be go to hell," Zeke said to Lester, "you knows the strangest people." Zeke was trying to get a handhold on what happened. His joke was worth nothing.

Albert crossed the room and pulled the plug on the juke. "Drink up," he said to everybody. "I'm closin'." He walked to the door, started to pull it shut.

One shot. Pistol crack. Street dark. A yell. Silence.

Men on the corner turned, looked down the street, then moved quick. In ten seconds the street corner stood deserted.

"Those gents are headed home," Alfonzo said about the street-corner men. "And Ozzie not with them."

"Get gone," Albert told the bar, though it was not necessary. Men were already moving, the bar emptying, and Zeke in the lead.

"It's gotta be," Alfonzo said, "that the white boy shot Ozzie, or Ozzie shot the white boy. Don't nothing else signify."

Crash of beer glass breaking from behind the bar. Blue leaning on the bar. Blue ready to scream.

"Either way it happened," said Alfonzo, "Blue just lost her man."

"Don't go nowhere," Albert told Blue. "Nothin' you can do." He might as well talk to the wall. Blue was around the end of the bar and gone.

"Go along," Albert said to Alfonzo. To Lester he said, "Dancer, get your sass on down the road."

Lester stepped into medium darkness. Streetlight too close. Bar signs already off. He moved quick along the front of the building like a soldier under fire. If the country boy was out there, he would pack a pistol. Lester headed for the total darkness of the alley... strip off his Saturday-night shirt and ball it in one hand. With shirt off in total darkness, a man could give thanks for being black. Nobody, except maybe God himself—and even that doubtful—could see him in that lightless alley.

If he went west it was Preston St. and too much light. Best to make a dash, hit the alley across the way, and circle back on Hancock. Major stupidity to be walking Jackson St. He took a deep breath, rabbitted like a moving shadow across the street and into the other alley.

Walk along careful, hand to a wall, then a fence, then another wall. Lester bumped into garbage cans that caused a rattle. Alley dark as the inside of a pure black cow. The mouth of the alley held a little light and he moved toward it. When he got to the end of the alley he poked his head around the corner of a building to look up and down the street. The country boy's truck sat parked. It looked like someone sat in the cab.

He stepped back into the alley and studied. Instead of stepping into the street, he eased back for another look. Beside the truck, and maybe fifty yards from a street light, all kinds of stuff lay on the sidewalk, chairs, mostly. The country boy was so damn dumb he'd parked a loaded truck. Lester was ready to bet there wasn't more than half a load left. Some pretty sorry colored now owned stuff to hock with Lucky.

But no scavengers were now around the truck. It looked abandoned, but still that half a load. The country boy shouldn't be sitting in the cab. He should be cussing and picking stuff up. But, somebody was sitting in the cab.

Lester made a quick dash across the street, over to the mouth of the next alley. He peered around the corner of a building. He had a different angle.

It looked like movement in the cab. A shadowed head bent forward. It didn't move fast. It moved like a man tired-to-death, or something worse. Lester studied. It had to be the country boy, or Ozzie.... Lester paused.

The shadow of a man moved along the sidewalk. It fell away from the street light. Then a man came from behind the truck, paused, looking up and down the street. Lester recognized Ozzie, just before Ozzie took off at a gallop.

Only a damn fool was gonna go anywhere near that truck. On the other hand, the country boy had to be a man shot. Somebody better do something. Lester moved cautiously toward the truck, and looked at what he had never seen before. During the war corpses had been frozen, with blood turned to frosty-white ice... never saw blood running, or not so much....

It dripped black from under the door and off the running board of the truck. The country boy slumped over the wheel. Little sucking noises came from that cab, and the head leaning on the wheel turned but a little. The country boy's eyes were wide and alive and maybe, sorta, puzzled. Then the sucking noises stopped, and the eyes went dead. The body shivered just a little and rolled against the door. Blood stopped flowing from where Ozzie had laid a razor across a throat.

Get the hell out. Nothing to be done. Lester raced back to his warm alley (he thought of it as his, what with all this going on), and stood figuring. It had to be that Ozzie shot the man, and the man made it back to his truck. Then Ozzie came past and finished him off.

Look down the street, down beyond the streetlight. Skinny girl standing. Blue starting to scream, the scream high and awful and as sad as the death of Jesus. Blue starting to walk forward, then understanding that she better not. Screams getting fainter as Blue walked away, walked away, walked slumping.

No place to go except turn back and go home. When he

came out the other end of the alley, Jackson St. ran empty as a dry creek. It ran soundless. No song, no murmur in the hot but cooling night. Everywhere along Jackson St. people kept to their houses, wide-awake and quiet. What with all the junk sitting on the sidewalk beside that truck, the police would discover the country boy the next time they cruised that street. All hell was gonna break loose.

And, faint and far-away, Blue screaming.

SUNDAY, SEPTEMBER 14TH

WHAT FOLKS DID

Lester waited in his rooms figuring cops would call. He reconciled himself to bumps and bruises, and a whole lot worse. Further south, men got killed when questioned. Up in Chicago men got killed while questioned. Maybe in Louisville, maybe not. It was just terrible to sit waiting, but worse to run. If he ran it would be like confessing to something. With a white man dead, there wasn't a chance a colored man would not catch a beating.

What Lester didn't count on was a colored cop named Moses who was smart as his name. When white cops claimed it time to start cracking heads, Moses told them, "Lemmie see who's missing." It took him a half an hour to get the story. "Might-a known it was Ozzie," he said, "Ozzie was gonna come to something like that."

So Lester was slated for questioning, but nobody's pants were on fire. Leave it for Monday. Invoices in the dead man's truck gave the country boy's name. His license plate said Whitley county. It was no trouble to find out who the dead man was, and where from, even if Ozzie had stole his billfold. Meanwhile, get the word out on Ozzie; send it to Hamilton and Cincinnati, Knoxville, Memphis and Atlanta as the logical places.

But Lester didn't know all that. He sat in his rooms

watching the near-silent street. As morning progressed, the street livened as folks strolled to church; everybody pretending nothin' had happened. And, if something *had* happened, nobody knew nothin' about it. Lester watched Howard walk to church beside his handsome mother, so handsome she made a sober man think wistful. Howard looked like he protected her; despite Howard was skinny and weighed little more than a mouse.

Lester had plenty of time to think, and didn't know what to think. He first thought of his job. Wade was not gonna be happy. Louisville wasn't that big of a town. Gossip would run around and around, and gossip might hurt the auction.

Lester thought of the dead man. If he hadn't seen the man it might be different. But, Lester had seen all that blood streaming black as night beneath the distant glow of streetlight. And, the look in those eyes, like the man was puzzled. Back during the war Lester saw wounded men who looked the same. Even in a damn war men could not believe it when something serious came along. Before serious hurt happened, they believed it could happen. But, after it happened, they couldn't understand.

So Lester should have been glad the man was gone, because with that man it was kill-or-be-killed. Lester found that he was not glad, but maybe, later, would be. If only he hadn't seen the man's eyes.

* * *

Howard's mother was sad. Worse, his mother was mad. She wasn't mad at him, but he kept close-mouthed. "We stand above this trash," she told him.

At the time Howard did not know what she meant, because he did not fully understand what had happened. Even after she told him, all he knew was that Ozzie killed a white man. He made no connection with the country boy.

The walk to church was so quiet. When the preacher

started, he started sad then gradually warmed: words about what you sow is what you reap; words gradually getting angry. Then there was song and the anger died away.

Sometime during the afternoon, horsing around with other young men his age, Howard learned enough to know it was the country boy that Ozzie killed. He wondered, vaguely, what Jim would say to that.

* * *

Sunday school and Lutheran church. The preacher talked about Daniel in the lion's den, and how Mr. J. Edgar Hoover compared: how Mr. Hoover walked through hordes of communists mean as lions, or something like that. Behind Jim, in the very last row of the balcony, Mr. James, the church's colored-gentleman-janitor sat listening. He seemed to frown a good bit.

It turned into the biggest Sunday Jim had ever known, because Jim, who had never heard of Marx, Engels, Lenin or Trotsky, knew himself for a communist. To Jim, being a communist meant that he and Howard could go to the park together.

What was big was the realization that the Reverend Mr. Robertson, even though trying to speak civilized, sounded just like the loud mouths at the barber shop; and the Reverend Mr. Robertson was so full of crap it drizzled out his socks; and the Reverend Mr. Robertson's feet of clay were covered with it.

* * *

Blue could holler and cry just so long, and when the hollering quit, the crying turned to dry sob. It left her so tired she slept and slept. When she woke up in afternoon the room still held Ozzie's stuff. She pretended he would return... he was such a particular man about his things. She folded his clothes, straightened the room, and sat at the window watching and waiting. She pretended he would come home any minute, and knew he would not.

* * *

Ozzie had Jolly's pistol and the white man's pistol. He had near sixty dollars, which would take a man a long way. He told himself he was smart enough not to get caught. All night he walked, following the railroad. When a freight slowed, headed south, he found an empty coal car. It was the last damn thing a man would want, rubbing up against coal dust, but not even a railroad cop would think of looking for him there.

MONDAY, SEPTEMBER 15TH

SCUFFLING

With summer slacked off and Indian summer threatening, Louisville perked up after dog days of August. In the cooling days of September business sang on high notes as the new model cars went on display. Sales of major appliances continued to boom. Tugboats chugged up and down the river, barging coal and cars; lots of Hudson autos shipping all the way to Mexico.

White newspapers reported white-folk news, *The Defender* reported colored-folk news, and all papers were sort-of aware that, in Washington D.C., the House UnAmerican Activities Committee strutted its political ambitions.

"Communists," the newspapers reported in connection with House UnAmerican and its vaunted leader, Mr. J. Parnell Thomas.

"Opportunists," Lucky said about Parnell Thomas, John Rankin, and Richard Nixon. "Grandstanders." He said this under his breath, reading the newspaper at breakfast, while Rachel was in another room.

"Murder," the newspapers reported in connection with the country boy; and, in the case of *The Courier-Journal*, conveyed, through undertones, that a very bad colored lad gave good Negroes a nasty name. The victim was a "a businessman from downstate." The word 'respectable' was not used, since reporters were close to the action. They, and the cops, figured the fool had no business doing Saturday night where he 'done-did-Saturday night'. Looking for a dark skin girl, no doubt.

* * *

So, when Lester walked through the doors of the auction Wade had already read the newspaper. He would have told you that he could care damn-less about politicians.

But, about Lester, he had decided what to do. As Wade saw it he had two choices: fire Lester, or defend Lester. It's to Wade's credit that he chose the latter. Of course, Wade was such a bulldog, and so certain of himself, the choice came natural. He may have scoffed about 'theory' and 'psychology', but he knew human nature. People could forgive a ton of stuff, if, by forgiving, they could make a buck, and Lester was valuable.

Besides, Wade had an auction scheduled for Wednesday night, and the sale was only halfway set up.

"You have anything to do with it?" Wade actually sounded interested.

"He come looking," Lester said. "A bad man did him in. I gotta figure cops. But boss, all I did was sit."

"Then let's get crackin'," Wade said. "We gotta finish this set up."

* * *

The cop showed up around ten a.m., and he already had most of the story. He dressed like a civilian and didn't act cop-like.

"Bad blood between you," he said to Lester, and it wasn't a question. The cop was thin-faced as a man in a Hopper painting, and nearly as gray. He looked to be thirtyish; was balding, and cold in his speech. He looked like a man dying of T.B.

"I threw him out," Wade told the cop about the country boy. "If the sad bastard came back I was gonna get a restraining order."

"Stay out of this until I ask," the cop told Wade. "I'm

talking to your man, here." The cop betrayed himself with his speech. Sure as shootin', and in spite of his looks, this cop was a liberal. There were lots of them around, though precious few were cops.

"The man was shot right-side from the back. Where did this man Ozzie get the gun?"

Lester told the story about Jolly, there being no sense hiding that, not now. Wade kept his big mouth shut, but listened close. He never before figured colored folk could live lives more dramatic than his. He probably figured, during off hours, they sat around playing banjos.

"He'll have two guns," Lester told the cop about Ozzie. "He'll have the dead man's gun, most surely." Lester talked quiet and nervous, as befitted.

"You're sure the man had a gun."

"Corbin," Wade said.

"That doesn't prove it," the cop said, "but I take your meaning." He turned back to Lester. "There'll be an inquest. You may be called."

And then the cop left. What seemed like a big deal had turned into nothing a-tall. Lester didn't get his expected beating. Wade didn't even know he'd expected one. Lester couldn't say he was disappointed, but he told himself he was truly amazed; most genuine.

"I'm sucking horehound," Wade mentioned. "Saturday was a bull-bitch. Voice was ready to crack."

* * *

Mixed auctions need a unifying tone. This auction had modern furniture, automobile parts, hotel furniture, plus small lots of this-and-that. An unskilled auctioneer would set it up by lots, and the overall impression would be like a rag shop filled with junk.

Skilled auctioneers know how to make things look their best. The job is not unlike drawing a picture. If you have snazzy modern stuff, and dull hotel stuff, you pick by color. Reds with browns, blues with grays, and background with uncolorful but functional stuff. Thus, pin-stripe box springs and mattresses stand along the walls, instead of lying in stacks. Before them, stand dressers with lamps. Run some extension cords. Light some of the lamps.

The best stuff goes to the front of the store. Second best to the back, and junk all the back near the alley. Keep mixing and placing, then replacing, until the sale looks right. Hit the best of the stuff with furniture polish, and get it to glow. Like Lucky, Wade and Lester know that brightness sells. Clean stuff up, make it shine. Even junk looks sort of spiffy.

As for auto parts, make them look ready-for-use. Sort the oil filters so they run by part numbers, instead of stacking them hodge podge. Lean tires against the wall, don't stack. The largest tires go to the back, then grade out to smallest. If you have room, place tires side by side, like they are rolling toward the customer. An auction needs to transmit movement, as well as color.

By the time Jim got out of school, and to the auction house, the sale was in place and ready to number.

"Take care of it," Wade told Lester. "I've got some scuffling to do."

Small businesses fail for a number of reasons, but the main reasons come from lack of imagination or drive. Too many people rent a storefront, put in an inventory, hang out a sign and wait. When nothing happens they go broke. That old garbage about "location, location, location" describes the needs of the unimaginative.

A good small business can make money even if it is run from the bottom of a mine. It depends on the drive of the proprietor. If one sells antiques, for heaven's sake, have the gumption to team up with interior decorators. If one sells carpet remnants, go looking for builders of subdivisions. If one sells groceries, set up delivery service and discounts to orphanages and old folks' homes. If you 'wait to see what happens', nothing will happen, or something bad.

When auctioneers scuffle they make appointments with estate attorneys. They befriend judges of bankruptcy courts. They read the 'business opportunities' in newspaper classified, because eighty percent of those 'opportunities' are businesses going busted. Any small business can make it, even selling nothing but rutabagas; but nobody can sit on their wide, wide bottoms.

When Wade departed Jim wandered left, wandered right, and couldn't get in the mood for work. He concentrated on his science teacher, Miss Stacy Hall. Then he hummed some "Sleepy Time Gal." Then he watched his sister coming in from school, acting all official, and getting ready to polish furniture. That finally got him in gear. He'd better help Lester, or Miss Pushy would find him work more ornery. Like wash the windows.

"Uh, huh," said Lester, and hummed a little hum. "Uh-uh, huh, who is she?" Lester passed Jim a marking pencil and tags to tie to merchandise. Lester listed numbers, matching them to sources of the lots.

"Who?"

"I see that look you got about you. Don't be telling some sinful lie." Lester, naturally happy, and now off the hook, felt prancy.

"That Howard," Jim said, "he's sentimental."

"Think of that."

"He's mooshy."

"Kids," Lester said, and Lester was a happy man. "When your age I fell for older women. Reckon Howie's making that mistake?"

Jim, hurt because of a flash of reality, stayed quiet. Miss Stacey Hall was not gonna wait. Miss Stacey Hall would marry some dumb sumbitch and never know how happy she could of been. Then, "When I see Howard come Wednesday, I'll ask."

"When you see Howard, come Wednesday, Howard will have a tale to tell." Lester's voice sounded real quiet, and a little puzzled. He sounded like a man who didn't know whether to speak or shut up. "That country boy," he said lamely, "the one who messed with the auction. Hit a run of real bad luck."

Monday & Tuesday, September 15th & 16th

Lucky Fends Off

Some folks on Jackson St., and all of them men, stepped up to shake Lester's hand. Other folks, and most of them women, muttered about Satan in their midst. After all, nothin' bad would have happened if Lester hadn't brought trouble to the street. Opinion split out fifty-fifty.

And, if Lester thought badness would go away, right away, Lester was dreaming. Cops knew Ozzie for the bad man, but felt frustrated because no heads got busted.

It seemed like a patrol car constantly cruised Jackson St. If any colored men were dumb enough to hold down street corners, cops were on them like sorghum. Men got kicked around some, and men got grilled like catfish, but nobody got killed or even beat up too bad. Still, a white man was dead. Somebody had to pay.

By Tuesday evening the cops had pretty well worked it through their systems, although street-corner society did not start up for a week. Jackson St. men, who had bulled the cops in elegant ways, were proud that the cops bought some of it. Jackson St. men had gone through a real hard time but everybody 'come out in one piece'. Jackson St. men bragged, but only in private.

Lucky, on the other hand, walked a mighty thin high wire. On Tuesday morning, stolen stuff from the country boy's truck showed up with every soul who walked through the doorway. Lucky had two regrets. The first regret was that he ran a hockshop. The second? Howard was in school. Howard could have learned something.

There were ways of handling the mess.

"C'mon, John," he would say, "you're a smart man, and not that hard up. You need to save that radio, in case you need to gift a woman."

That worked, one time out of twenty.

"Sol, my man, I wish I could help, but I'm overstocked." Lucky would run a finger up alongside his nose, like he thought deep, and then smiled like a man making a big discovery. "Take that over to Market St." (And he would name a couple of junk dealers, neither one of them Fudd.) "Guys who buy will pay more than guys who hock."

That worked about 50 percent.

"Doggonit, Lucy, the man who gave you that got it from a man who took it." Lucky peered through the front windows, like he feared a cop. "I recommend you take it to the hockshop on Fifth St."

That worked with most of the ladies.

And finally, "Samuel, my friend, don't con an old con artist. Take the stuff out of the neighborhood. You don't want a name for bringing trouble to Jackson St."

That always worked. Men walked away muttering, and bringing down curses on Hebe pawn brokers all the way back to Father Abraham. On the other hand, Lucky had moved the stuff away from the neighborhood, protecting himself and the neighborhood.

Meantime, Albert had his own crisis. He had cops sitting on Sapphire Top Spot as close as ham to the bone. He had a woman who could start wailing any minute, and Blue's good looks didn't make up for Blue's hollering. Plus, it was now no secret that Albert owned a .38, and how good was that for cops or business?

Albert told himself he was too old for this kinda shit, so he closed shop. Let Blue get through the worst of it. Let the cops get fed up with looking at closed doors of Sapphire Top Spot. He would reopen when the air cleared.

WEDNESDAY, SEPTEMBER 17TH

PAUSE BETWEEN ACTS

Heading for work and a real long day, what with a sale that night, Lester pulled over before Charlie Weaver's place. The new windows shone clean and sparkly. A bulky Diamond T van stood at the curb, equipped with hydraulic tailgate. Two men steadied a ten hole ice cream freezer, lowering the gate little by little as they eased one end of the freezer toward the street. The men let the equipment slide to them, slow and gentle. A second ten holer already sat on the sidewalk.

Leaning against the side of the building, parts of a backbar were painted like a circus poster; twirly red, mostly, with gold and orange. It looked like one bear of a high class way to sell ice cream.

And this, in a town, where even the teeniest drugstore had a soda fountain. What in the ever-loving-candy-stripe world made anybody think you could make it selling ice cream? It wasn't like White Castle. White Castle did good because people couldn't pick up a quick burger anywhere else. But ice cream? Hard to walk a block without finding somebody selling ice cream.

"And sitting smack beside a cemetery," he told the truck (but he was really talking to Charlie). "And opening up at end of summer, not beginning. He'll bust by New Year's."

At least there was no pink Lincoln parked. A shiny black Roadmaster sat at the curb. The car carried New Hampshire plates. Why all these northerners all of a sudden?

"White folks?" he said to the truck (but he was still talking to Charlie), and couldn't really say (even to himself, or to Charlie) exactly what he meant. He drove thinking about Wade and the country boy, and how Wade was a country boy himself. What was the difference? Indiana, where Wade came from? Kentucky?

But it couldn't be Indiana. Indiana was Ku Klux and white-bread all the way. Muncie, Indiana had a reputation among colored like even Chicago didn't. When Mr. Joe Louis won a prize fight, and when colored folks gathered around the radio cheering, folks knew they were defying. And if Mr. Joe Louis beat a white fighter, the cops of Muncie busted colored heads. Happened every damn fight.

So it wasn't Indiana or Kentucky. And, it wasn't religion, because Wade wasn't worth shucks at that. Maybe it was because Wade learned stuff. When Lester and Zeke and Alfonzo worked the furniture factory, Wade acted embarrassed but polite. The sonovabitch was trying.

Or maybe it was business. Business was like being in a band, and not like dancing. A man could dance all by himself, but with jazz you gotta play together, or forget it. There had been some cooperation-feeling in the army, but not as much.

So, when men knew what they were doing, and did it good, they naturally had to make room for each other. "Which is why," he admitted to the truck, "I gotta say that Mr. Country-Wade ain't as awful as most." The truck, having no opinion, chugged.

When he arrived at the auction and parked, a '38 Chev and a '41 Hudson consigned by the Shell station, sat at the curb. The Chev was one of those things that would heave itself slowly out of the gutter, proceed at a washerwoman's pace, then stop easy enough, since it wasn't goin' anywhere, anyway. The Hudson, on the other hand, would hang 60 in second gear; and only the good Lord knew where its top end lay.

"Nothin' but trouble," Lester told the parked truck, and he talked about the Hudson. Still, a bitty-bit of desire couldn't stay out of his voice.

When he got to the sidewalk he looked at Mrs. Samuels' house. If anything, it was even deader than the Chevrolet. Along the peak of the house you could see a sag in the roof line. Shingles showed themselves missing in spots. The house looked deserted.

The sun porch still held those ratty stuffed chairs. Rusty screens still kept out flies. If you squinted you could see through the screens, though sunlight glinted off the rust.

* * *

"The wife will be along later," Wade told Lester. "You hold down the fort. I got an appraisal."

"Which kind?"

"Heirs," Wade said, and was so blamed pleased with himself he couldn't hardly stand it. He told himself that a stupid bastard would have fired Lester. Instead, Wade had himself a man who knew the business. In an heirs' appraisal, the auctioneer appraises low because the family wants to buy stuff from the court. That, and sometimes a judge or lawyer wants to buy stuff; all more-or-less-barely legal. When no interested party wants to buy, the auctioneer appraises at actual value.

"If you have to move those shit-boxes," Wade said about the cars, "the keys are on the desk." He looked around. "Might give the windows a lick or two. When my kid comes in, tell him he can go to Lucky's, and come to the sale with Lucky."

When Wade disappeared Lester stood to-tally pleased. He was, by God, the man in charge. If the phone rang, he would answer. If a customer came in, that customer would deal with Lester. It was like having your own auction. It was a taste of what he had always known he was gonna be; because he had always known himself cut out for higher things. And, it is fair to say that nowhere in the entire sovereign state of Kentucky, was a store better run than was the auction on that morning.

* * *

Lucky, on the other hand, was having a miserable morning.

Trouble infested the air, and if a man was thoughtful he could see how ugliness lay just over Louisville's horizon. If that same man was a Jew, he could feel malaise of spirit sail across the entire country; sailing, as usual, under the banner of the Lord of Hosts. The morning paper still told of the House UnAmerican Activities Committee. It read like the approach of storm.

Lucky sat in his store before opening, and regretted his early morning silence. At breakfast, and reading the newspaper, he felt the malaise. When Rachel asked what was wrong, he couldn't say, so didn't say; but should have come up with something. No reason to trouble the woman.

Beyond the windows of his store Jackson St. lay light gray under mist from the river, silver when sun poured through the mist. Later, when open for business, the store would fill with more jazz, more jive, more sass. Jackson St. was a fine place in plenty of ways, but Jackson St. thought that 'long range' meant tomorrow, supper time. The folks of Jackson St. never heard of malaise, and thought of storm only when it began to thunder. In that way, they were like most whites.

He asked himself what he felt, and answered that he was

feeling 'pogrom'. In the mid-'30s in Germany, Hitler rose through denunciation of communism and Jews. Hitler welded a government, a police force, and an army out of the lowest clay. In Nazi Germany that dead Corbin goon would have been a standard-issue hero.

Because of Hitler, death had ruled the world. Extermination. Before Hitler, the word 'extermination' meant something you did to bugs.

Evil seemed to cover the street, and Lucky could not figure whether it was new, or leftovers of the war, or both. He watched colored neighbors early-to-work, walking Jackson St. They walked innocent, not knowing an umbrella of hate was opening. Most of them encountered minor kinds of hate every day, but they had no idea, none a-tall about what could happen.

The only thing needed for a pogrom was a man on a white horse, a hater with spellbinding personality. Colored would sink with Jews.

He tried to feel something and almost succeeded. It had been one year, almost to the day, since trouble began. House UnAmerican sent ten Hollywood folks, some Jews, to prison for pleading the First Amendment. Those people claimed they had a right to their own opinions and beliefs. The committee hollered Communist loud and long. The committee didn't know a thing, because it didn't want to know.

Out there on the street some of those colored called themselves communists. To them communism meant a steady job and everybody equal. One or two might have understood more. To most of them, communism was like being accepted into a labor union.

In the '30s, back during the depression, communism was an idea and not a fact. Lots of people, hundreds of thousands, belonged to the party. Lots of others belonged to liberal groups that were not communist. Not communist, that is, until House UnAmerican started redefining. With House UnAmerican it was nearly dangerous to be a Democrat, certainly dangerous to be a liberal.

Which, of course, Lucky was, had been, would be.

He was also a guy who felt guilty, and couldn't quite say why. On some days, like today, he felt guilty because he was alive and successful when so many millions were dead. On days like today, he felt that his success rose from among piles of the dead. He knew enough to know that he wasn't being logical.

He watched Miz Hattie gimp past, an old, old lady with a busted hip that had healed wrong... Hattie almost always cheerful, headed for the bus, traveling to housecleaning up in the Highlands. Hattie going day-to-day, thanking Jesus, living life. He thought how terrible it would be, Hattie stripped naked amongst hundreds the same; being herded to a gas chamber. Praying to sweet Jesus.

He thought of Howard, skinny and serious and ambitious. When he thought of Howard, who was like one of his own, he thought that he'd better stop thinking, because he was finally feeling something awful. Break the train of thought. He told himself Jews loved to make themselves miserable, or was that true? Maybe 'thinking' did it.

Jews surely loved to make themselves feel guilty. Otherwise, they wouldn't do it so much. Of course, hope was even more powerful. Otherwise, they wouldn't send so many millions of dollars to aid refugees. They wouldn't send so many more millions to build Israel.

Thinking about guilt, he wondered could he have done something to prevent that suicide last month?

Then, as he headed to unlock the front door, and thinking further, he realized it had not been suicide.

September 17th

Sleepy Time Down South

Jackson St. ran quiet as the river at low stage. Jim got off the bus, walked toward Lucky's and felt scary. He heard hardly any sound. The old, old lady, Miz Sally, still sat on her porch and raised a kerchief. Mr. Rufus James Whiteman still sat trembling and gaptoothed. Except for them, hardly a soul stirred.

The door to Sapphire Top Spot, which always stood open, was now closed. No lights shone. The street corner, where men always stood, sat empty. Jim feared the ghost of the country boy might come drifting through afternoon sunlight.

Because, by then, Jim knew as much of the story as Lester would tell. Jim knew the country boy got killed and Ozzie did it. Jim did not know about all the blood, or about Blue screaming, or about cops banging heads. Lester only said the country boy got shot.

When he stepped inside Lucky's store things looked more lively. Lola the guinea hen, contented, seemed ready to cluck. Thomas, the Plymouth Rock rooster, looked, today, to-tally critical; though nuts. Thomas disapproved of everything he saw (through glassy eyes) that was happening on Jackson St.

A light-skin lady leaned elbows on the front counter, while

behind the counter Howard stood and practiced patience. There was gonna be a time, just the right moment, when Howard would need to speak. He looked at Jim, turned his mouth down signaling for quiet and watched his customer. The lady looked at stickpins, some of them diamonds, and some glass. "These come with a little box? Don't look right without no box."

"I have two kinds," Howard told her. "A plain one like this...." he placed a small cardboard box with cotton liner on the counter, "...and for fine items I have this kind that snaps open...." He placed a velvet lined box, snazzy (wholesale cost 12 1/2 cents) beside the cardboard.

The lady eyed the snap-open box with pure desire. "Don't know 'bout fine items."

"I have a bit of leeway," Howard told her. "Which pin would you like?" He brushed the cardboard box aside like it was nothing. From beneath the counter he pulled a small square of plywood covered with padded, ivory-colored velvet. He placed a ten dollar zircon on the velvet. He left the snap-open box, open. Then he chose a six dollar pin, a flashy ruby. "I can fit this one to the nicer box." He laid it beside the ten dollar. On the ivory velvet, the ruby outshone the zircon.

"That man," said the lady, "is my man, and he is gonna love that." She reached in her purse.

Toward the back, but within earshot, Lucky piddled around, arranging merchandise. He kept an eye on a flashy looking gent who kept an eye on him. Mr. Flashy hovered around the suits, some of them double-breasted and with vests.

"This time I'll get him," Lucky whispered to Jim. "Cincy's on his way to grabbing something."

"Hard to shop lift a hockshop."

"You'd be surprised," Lucky told him. "Some guys could

lift grease out of a skillet."

To Jim, Lucky looked tired. He looked the way Wade looked after a long sale. He looked like men look when pressure has been on since just-forever. Lucky, who didn't drink, looked like he needed a drink.

"Lester told me," Jim said, as if that explained something.

"What happened to that man's truck?"

"Police took it somewhere." Then Lucky whispered. "I'm going to turn my head. You turn away, but just enough. Keep an eye on Cincy."

Quick as a-mouse-down-a-mouse-hole, a satin vest went smoothly beneath Cincy's jacket. There wasn't even a lump. Magicians couldn't pull up rabbits as fast as Cincy worked.

"Vest under his jacket," Jim whispered.

"Five bucks," Lucky said in the direction of Cincy. "Top of the line vest. Impress the womens."

"I change my mind," Cincy said. He was a small, dark man, and he wore a blue suit and knit red tie. "It seem a little large." He laid the vest on a counter and walked.

"Shop elsewhere," Lucky said. "Next time gets worse." He watched Howard, who was watching Cincy. "No sense making enemies," Lucky said to Jim. "Where possible, keep it friendly." When Howard joined them, Lucky said, "You kids take a lesson about keeping records. I've had cops in here like the plagues of Egypt. It wears on a man."

"The fire department washed the street," Howard said to Jim, and maybe Howard bragged a little. Then he remembered that the fire department had washed the alley after Jolly got killed. Howard shivered. "You can still see dark spots between the bricks." He looked toward the front of the store. His customer had long gone. Then Howard looked to Lucky, waiting and anticipating.

"Good job," Lucky said. "You listened to your customer

and gave what she wanted. She's happy, and not feeling forced into something."

Howard couldn't help showing off just a tad. He clapped his hands, then clasped them prayerful and put them to his mouth.

"Basic stuff," Lucky said. "Next time, if you want to move the higher-priced item, pull out three; one of them real high-priced. Treat that one like it isn't much, but work the middle one."

"Washed the street?"

"With fire hoses."

"The man bled to death," Lucky said. "And Mussolini didn't run Italy any meaner than the police are running Jackson St."

"Police have the man's invoices," Howard explained. "They figure Ozzie is still around hocking merchandise."

"That," said Lucky, "is an excuse. They know Ozzie went south."

"South?"

"Folks most often trust each other in the south," Lucky said. "That doesn't happen as much in Chicago. White men generally run south or west. Colored men almost always run south."

"What happens when they catch him?"

"They won't catch him," Lucky said, and he was a tired, tired man. "He'll catch himself. With the kind of temper Ozzie owns, it's a wonder he's lived this long."

Bled to death. Bled to death. Lester hadn't said anything about that. Lots of people dying this summer. Lots of barbershop men talking filthy. Plus, the preacher, Reverend Mr. Robertson turned out to be as full of crap as an elephant with the trots. Communists, him and Howard.

"It's gonna be a pretty good sale tonight," Jim told Lucky.

"Today, you guys wash windows," Lucky told him. "Use ammonia. I wanta hear those washrags squeak." He looked to the front of the store where an old, old white lady just entered. "Miz Janey," Lucky said in a low voice. "Come to hock a wedding ring." He moved away.

"She has three," Howard whispered, his voice sounding real important. "Buried three husbands. Hocks a ring at the end of each month, until the old folk's check arrives. Always redeems it."

* * *

Washing windows. No help for it. If he didn't wash 'em in one place, he washed 'em in the other. Jim rubbed and scrubbed. Howard squeegeed and tsked.

"Lester never said about bleeding."

"It was surely awful," Howard said. "Ozzie must have cut him all over."

"Lester said 'shot.'"

"That too." Howard drew his squeegee, wiped its edge, looked at a streak. Tsked. "Hopeless."

"Dry rag. Follow up with a dry rag."

"My mother defends Lester," Howard said. "A great many ladies say Lester carries blame."

"Not fair. Not fair."

"Men folk hold nothing against him."

"We're selling two cars tonight. One ain't worth a split dime."

"My mother says Lester is a credit to the race, even though not churched." Howard rubbed a dry rag at a streak. Looked at the result, real sorrowful.

"You wash," Jim told him. "I'll polish."

Working together. They kept quiet when a cop came in, looked around, stepped back out. They kept quiet when a cop stopped a brown man outside Lucky's. The man carried a small adding machine, hand-operated. The cop checked the adding machine against a handful of invoices. He spoke quietly to the brown man, the man fearful. The cop gave the man a shove, and the man headed on down Jackson St.

"Roughing people up," Lucky said, as he approached the boys. "That was Prester, and that was Prester's adding machine. He's hocked it before."

"Explain to the cop?"

"And get Prester beat bad? When cops get caught up wrong, they take it out on somebody." Lucky looked upward, toward Thomas, the crazy rooster. "That chicken has more brains than all of Jackson St. combined, cops included; them especially."

Wednesday Night, September 17th

Auction
During Which A Mountain is Climbed

Supper was a sack of burgers. Jim and Howard sat out back, in the alley behind the auction where declining autumn sun lay orange and silver on old garages. The brick alley ran straight ahead, down to Tyler Park where white kids played peggie in diminishing light.

"Lucky has something on his mind," Howard said. "I don't know what."

"Maybe he's gotta learn fractions."

"Be serious."

"That dead guy. You sorry he's dead? Maybe I ain't."

"And perhaps you are," Howard said. "My mother mourns. She says Ozzie will be destroyed. Then the man who kills Ozzie will run. It keeps adding up." Howard looked down the red brick alley like a man staring into space. "Lucky is fretful."

"That other guy, the one that killed himself... I got something spooky to show you."

When they looked through the crack in the garage, the bed of flowers, shaped like a man, lay dead and dry except for a couple of wilting mums. Slanting sun did not cause little spotlights of sun. The mums glowed white in the gloom.

The picture of a man in gold and red, framed in black, hung in shadow; the jacket with the medal, the same. "He was a soldier," Howard whispered about the dead man. "A foreign soldier. Is that his picture?"

"Maybe," Jim said. "The killed man was real skinny, sick-like."

"Someone still attends him," Howard whispered. "Those flowers were picked within the week." Howard turned away. "Someone must be very sad. But, we have work." He turned back to the auction.

* * *

Laryngitis in the mouth of a politician is lovely, but in an auctioneer it borders on tragic. Wade stood with Daniels as the crowd assembled. "I'm gonna make it," Wade told Daniels, "but it's gonna be close. Last Saturday was a double-dip-butt-wipe." Wade did not sound good, and he did sound worried.

In the crowd, the antique dealer, Gloria, red-haired and Irish, drifted slow, like ball lightning. The junk dealer, Fudd, stood at the edge of the crowd and groused at Lucky. Lucky pretended to listen, then, excusing himself, stepped outside into declining light where Lester stood. The windows of Mrs. Samuels' house were dark.

"A lot of trouble," Lucky murmured to Lester. "Things all right with you?" He touched Lester's shoulder, one friend to another.

"Still worried," Lester said. "Won't nothin' come of it, prob-ly, but a man worries." He looked toward Mrs. Samuels' house. "There's ugly tokens this year. Charlie dead, people killing themselves. Jolly dead. Ozzie doing bad. A man gets queasy." He paused, and really looked at the house. "It started there. I don't study suicide."

"I don't think it was," Lucky said, and said it careful. "Anybody who went through what those folks went through is not likely to kill himself."

"What'd they go through?"

"They're eastern," Lucky said. "Russian, Finn, Poland, who knows?" He sounded mad, but also sad. "You were in Europe. You saw what went on."

"I didn't know." Lester looked up and down Bardstown Road. The Shell station sat all yellow and glowy, the drugstore had its neon on; and White Castle shining like a full and fancy moon. In the Kaiser-Frazier dealership, a fat, round-faced car stared bulbous at the street. "I saw little of it," Lester told Lucky, "but I saw more'n a man would want." He looked at the house. "How the hell they get here?"

"Some come in legally," Lucky said. "Congregations help. The government finally allowed a few. Some come in the back door." He glanced toward the auction where Wade looked ready to start. "I expect these folks were illegal. They acted mighty shy."

"Gotta go," Lester said. "We're cranking it up."

Opening spiel. Wade's voice sounded rough but capable, like a bulldog a-woof. "Terms cash or good check, and move stuff by Saturday... goods sold free and clear of all encumbrance... dealers get open titles to cars, otherwise you wait 'til seller registers sale... now, gimmie something."

Lester... holding up a ruby lampshade, antique, good, but with cracked metal hangings; red glow against black. Lester yelping "home furnishings" and small dance, no shuffle. Gloria stepping right up. Wade selling it quick, dropping it cheap. "Gloria, three bucks. Gimmie something."

This crowd held mostly dealers, plus a few civilians. No society people were present. Country boys scattered through the crowd, but they were business-types who likely hadn't heard of the murder. If they had, they thought it none of their affair.

Wade made it through the first hour, and then faded. First it was a rough cough, then his hoarseness increased. Uneasiness ran through the crowd. The flow of the sale threatened to break. Fudd stood beside Lucky. "He's gonna quit. He's gonna have to shoot the rest off in one or two lots." Fudd stood ready to move in on the sale.

A big man, helpless, is a sad and sorry sight. Wade searched the crowd, looked for Jim; and Jim was wisely nowhere in sight. "Kid's too young anyway," Wade whispered. "The crowd wouldn't take him serious."

"Me," Lester whispered quick, like he didn't trust himself if he went slow. Lester sounded so nervous he didn't even sound pushy. "I can cut this, boss." Lester, like Wade, was a-sweat. His face glowed shiny beneath lights, his short hair almost dripping. He rubbed a black hand across a wet, black forehead. Paused. Lester standing on one foot then on the other. Lester sounding queasy.

Wade standing like a man breathless, like a man mule-kicked. Wade wiping sweat with a white hand across a white forehead. Wade looking at a sweaty black man, and in that moment Wade decided he'd better grow all-the-way-up. What he saw was a man working, and not a sweaty Negro. Wade had a thoughtless mouth, but give him credit.

"Give it a whirl," Wade said. "I can do grip." To the crowd, he croaked, "Got another auctioneer. Get with him." Wade stepped from his stool, and Lester ascended... Lester standing a good twelve inches above the crowd... Lester ascending like the blackest angel in God's good heaven.

Lester looking at the biggest damn crowd of white men that any colored man had ever seen... not true, of course, but so it seemed to Lester. After all, about the only time a colored man stood above white was when he was dangling from a rope. He felt a tug at his pant leg. "Give it hell, baby," Gloria said, and giggled friendly; and may the good Lord look down on Gloria.

He started nervous, and the rap sounded disjointed. He sold a couple of numbers, watched the crowd, and the crowd watched him. The crowd tried to make up its mind, individually, and collectively. A skinny black man running a sale?

A couple of the country boys whispered to each other. Waited. Lester fumbled. Daniels tossed in a bid. Gloria tugged again at Lester's pant leg. "Sounding good," Gloria whispered, "now spread a little crap."

"Sounds just how you'd expect," Fudd told Lucky. "Swartzer sounds illiterate. I don't put up with this." Fudd headed for the door.

"Fudd, one buck," yelped Lester.

Fudd stopped, turned, wondering what'n'hell? A box of mixed stuff, not much of it junk, was being set aside. With his name on it. O-boy. The box was probably worth seven bucks, or eight. Fudd turned back, discovering he was glad to put up with it.

"Nice pickup," Wade whispered to Lester. "You've got 'em. Start kickin'."

The rap began to smooth out, and it was different from Charlie Wheeler's remembered rap, and different from Wade's; though you could hear the influence of both. As Lester sold, the rap became metrical. He sold like he danced, lots of body, lots of emphasis on the roll of nouns, the same way he rolled his shoulders. Lots of Charlie Wheeler in there, lots of Wade; but lots of Dancer.

"Forty-one Hudson, look her over gents. Heater and radio, fire and a fiddle. Get enough traction and it'll drive straight up. Listen to her purr." Desire entered Lester's voice. His voice wanted that car so much, that everybody else wanted it as well. What a salesman. What an actor.

The filling station had tried to sell that car at two-and-a-quarter, and had failed. When the bid stalled at two-seventy, and Lester sold, Wade grinned like that proverbial fox in the henhouse. "Goddamn," Wade croaked, an impressed and happy man.

Being a grip is tiring. Being a buyer is tiring. But, selling is exhausting. By the time the sale ended, out at the rear of the store, out by the nighttime alley, Lester had absolutely nothin' left. When he stepped down after selling the last number, and when the adrenalin dropped off, he drooped. There wasn't a dance left in the man. There wasn't even a shuffle. But Lester carried a happy brain and a full heart.

"This is gonna work," Wade told him. "I think this is gonna work."

"Damndest thing I ever seen." One of the country boys talked to another. Jim stood by, waiting to check the guy out.

"Niggers taking over everything." This country boy looked like a heavyweight two years past his prime. His words sounded indignant, but his voice did not.

"It's the big city," the other country boy said. "I don't fret it a-tall." He was a small, dark-haired man named Sammy. A Hebrew from a real small town. "I'm ready to call auctioneer, not nigger." Sammy turned away.

"I'm ready to call him Lester," Jim said to the country boy. Jim, who weighed only a smidgen more than Howard, was nervous and ready to fight.

"Okay." The country boy sounded affable. "Do I give a fat rat's fanny? I'll get the big stuff tomorrow. Let's get the little stuff now."

And Jim, with a load of juvenile-jump, adrenalin-and-fight, found he had no place to put it. He worked quick, got the guy checked, then went looking for Howard.

Howard dawdled because Lucky dawdled. Lucky stood talking to other dealers, probably flipping a little b.s. just to stay in tune. Howard hung back, goofing off, but Howard watched Lester.

Howard's life had just changed, and Howard did not

understand, but he understood something.

"I'm going to have a store," he whispered to Jim. "I always thought I was, and now I know it." Howard watched Lester like Lester was President of the United States, or General of the Army. "Mother claims Lester is a credit to the race. I wish she was here. I wish she'd been here to see."

Thursday, September 18th

Check-Out
The Sixth Death

Lester left for work happy, early and eager; but not a little queasy. Life done changed, and Lester had lived long enough to know that good stuff and bad stuff generally mix.

He knew, for sure, that Howard told his momma about last night, and she would spread the word to every woman in church. The women would spread the word to their men, and the men would either praise Lester, or damn his innards to the lowest depths of the hot place. Lots of colored men had terrible times when other colored men succeeded. In that they were a hell of a lot like whites.

Then, there was the boss. Wade thought himself such a catfish among minnows, that he might start resenting Lester. On the other hand, Wade was practical as a brick. Have to step soft, wait and see.

When Lester got to Charlie Weaver's place he pulled over. The storefront had stripey-red awning. One of those new plastic signs, three times bigger than needed, swung from a tripod pole vertical to the street. *Candy Land* the sign said. Nothin' classy about that.

Over there to Cave Hill, Charlie lay to his rest. Charlie wasn't hardly even cold yet. Because here it was, not even the end of September, and Charlie dead only since the last week of August. It had been not quite two months, and everything changed. Charlie seemed like an echo of the past, like a sign of what 'used to be'. Still, it seemed like Charlie whispered friendly sounds in Lester's ear.

Charlie's old store, where Lester had put in his years, now had nothing going. Louisville-town was changing, but it sure wasn't finding itself. First, there had been a tea and coffee palace, and a joy-boy run out of town. Now, an ice cream store that would be gone by January. "Goddamit, Charlie," Lester whispered. "Just, you know, goddamit."

Drive on down the road. Nothin' else to do. When he got to Wade's auction, men stood out front waiting to load. Nary a colored in sight, but Daniels was there.

"Lester," Daniels said to the other men, "... last night Lester cut a fat piggie in the butt. Looks like Wade's got competition." Daniels clapped Lester on the shoulder, and the other men either grinned or shut up.

When Wade arrived he acted like he was shoving the world ahead of him, like always. His voice sounded raspy but improved, and he still sucked horehound. "We'll get these guys checked," he told Lester, "and talk later."

Odd, it is, how people who are busy can walk right past the most amazing stuff with never-a-notion. In early morning light goods moved out of the auction. Trucks pulled away, and other trucks pulled up to front and back doors. Men pushed, stacked, cussed, spread tarps, roped loads. Trucks squatted on their helper springs. Merchandise just poured onto the sidewalk, and not a soul looked toward Mrs. Samuels' sun porch. Not a soul.

Perhaps no one saw anything because sun, all goldy on Mrs. Samuels' sun porch, glazed the rusty screens making it hard to see beyond them.

Lucky parked a-ways from the auction, and walked. On this morning he found himself hopeful. Leaves of trees were in beginning change and morning air felt almost cool. If he knew anything about cops, and he did, the police were nearly burned out when it came to Jackson St. Maybe as early as today, things would return to normal.

And, the newspapers, for a change, seemed not so bad. True, they had been reporting on a man named Alger Hiss for a couple of months, and the new congressman Nixon pushed the investigation; spy stuff... some kind of rinky-dink about microfilm hidden in a pumpkin. A pumpkin?

So yes, the haters were busy. And true, a man on a white horse tried to clamber center stage.

But, it now looked like the new State of Israel had a chance of surviving. Money going to Israel would actually make a difference. And, in proof of that, Israel remained firm in opening its doors to all Jews, everywhere. It wasn't totally altruistic. Israel needed men and women for its army.

Perhaps because he thought of open doors and how Mrs. Samuels might have been illegal, Lucky stopped before her house. He looked through rusty, sun-sheened screens.

Small movement stirred behind dusty sunlight; little more than a tremble, a palsied hand, or a head falling sideways. Maybe it wasn't even human. Maybe a cat?

At Lucky's side, hotel furniture was being pushed or carried toward trucks: chests and beds and desks as utilitarian as crockery, but, still, symbols of civilization.

He stepped away from the auction and toward Mrs. Samuels' house. He stepped slow, telling himself that of all the things he didn't want, moving toward that house had to be number one. Charlie dead, Mrs. Samuels dead, her son dead, Jolly dead, plus the country fool. Lucky moved cautious and fearful.

When the light was just right, the man in the stuffed chair sat in plain view. The man looked like a thin child, too little for the littlest man. His face, what face he had, was only a fragile covering for his skull. His eyes, if his eyes saw anything, were seeing the floor because he could not lift his head. A blue tattoo, a number, stood vivid on a pale and sticklike forearm. Sighs, shallow as whispers dwelt around him like echoes of long forgotten thoughts. He breathed only well enough to sigh.

Lucky pushed the screen door. It was latched. He yelled. Smacked the screen with his fist, rusting wire parting so he could reach in for the latch. Blood welled from the back of his hand where the screen wire cut and scraped. He moved onto the porch, stood nearly helpless at first because he knew himself crazed. Then, having no time for helplessness, turned. Men standing on the sidewalk, gazed, responding to Lucky's yell... Lester appearing from the auction.

Lucky calmed himself. Firmed his voice. "Telephone," he said to Lester. "Get a doctor. There's gotta be a doctor someplace close." As Lester ran for the phone, Lucky spoke to the man. "Can you talk. Say a word."

Silence. Sighs. Behind Lucky, men crowded on the steps. Men peered in. All kinds of reactions.

"Need help?"

"I think I'm gonna puke."

"God-a-mighty, get help."

"Whose blood is that?"

"Where ta hell is Lester? I gotta finish this load."

When Wade arrived he pushed onto the porch. "You guys break it up." To Lucky he said, "What?" He stood watching. "We called a doc. Right down the street. Be here in a minute. What's wrong?"

"I think he's sick from starving... nobody ever saw a man so thin." Not a lie. Well, partly a lie. Pictures of German death camps had been printed in magazines, and shown in newsreels. There wasn't a Jew in the country who hadn't seen them.

The man died. He sounded a slightly deeper sigh. He tilted a little forward, and the sigh was so small it did not sound deadly. Lucky caught the man, kept him from falling, and Lucky did not understand the man was dead. A patch of blood appeared on the man's shirt, and Lucky did not understand the blood was his own. Lucky steadied the corpse, then felt it settling, all muscles deflated. Lucky still steadied, like he could not let the man go. He accepted death.

All around dwelt only silence, except from the sidewalk where a mirrored chest rumbled on its castors as it was pushed toward a truck.

"Go along," Lucky told Wade. "I'll stay." The weight of the man was no more than a bundle of kindling. The body tilted against Lucky, like the dead man had found friendly arms and could not break away. The body felt cool to the touch. Blood dripped on the man's shirt. It seemed a lot of blood for not much of a cut. The dead man's head leaned against Lucky's waist, and Lucky stood silent, waiting, waiting; knowing it was time to mourn, and beyond that, was past time to weep. The dead man's hair, what little there was, hung stringy; and rancid was the smell of death.

When the doctor arrived he worked quickly, as he and Lucky eased the man to the floor. No pulse, no breath, no life. Then, with time to really see the corpse, the doctor knelt stunned. He looked ready to weep, and he was no kid. As a doc in his fifties, he had seen his share of dying. He was a broad, tough-looking man, balding and with a gentle, gentle voice. "I'll take care of this," he told Lucky. "Keep people away."

"Police?"

"I don't doubt that police were part of his problem," the doc said. "But I'll see to it."

"You understand this?" Lucky, subdued, sounded so deep

in misery he had nothing left but tears. Of those he suddenly had a-plenty.

"This is not supposed to happen," the doc said. "Not in this country." Anger in his voice. More than anger. Fury. "... not supposed to happen, anywhere, ever. Again.

"Close that screen. Keep the fools and gawkers out. Let the man finally have some goddamn dignity. I need a phone." The doc took Lucky's hand, blood running from the cut and scrape, staining Lucky's sleeve. "Superficial," the doc said before he left, "but soap it good. You'll need a tetanus."

Lucky stood above the man and looked into the street. Trucks lined the curb. On a truck in front of the Samuels' house a stack of mattresses pooched beyond the tailgate. A driver hooked a red bandanna to the end of a mattress, flagging the load. Men worked. Life proceeded. Business as usual.

And, he told himself, why not? There was nothing those men could do except turn this death into a story over beer, or maybe a story to think of during quiet hours. These men had their work, and some of them, during the war, had probably been brave. He could not blame them for loading furniture. Somehow, though, he knew he could blame himself.

He turned and walked into Mrs. Samuels' house. Somewhere in the house there must be answers.

A 2 x 4 lay on the floor, and when Lucky checked, he saw brackets where the 2 x 4 had been used to bar the door. A radio aerial hung from one wall attached to a little tabletop Philco. Living room furniture was well-used, dusty, but unstained.

It was a shotgun house. A sun porch, a front bedroom, followed by a middle bedroom. There was nothing remarkable in the bedrooms except dust. The beds were bare, and a mattress was missing from one of them. Lucky shuddered, looked carefully around the room. Nothing.

The rest of the house split between small kitchen and bathroom. A back porch. It was a house built in a straight line; a workman's house, once company-owned from olden days.

These people had nothing unusual: a kitchen table, holding electric and water bills and papers. Kitchen chairs, a monitor top refrigerator. Old high-oven stove. Lucky pulled the switch on a dangling electric light. No electricity. He turned a faucet. No water. From somewhere above the ceiling, where an attic would be, came a scurry, a tumble, a squeak.

He picked up the stack of unpaid bills. Among them were sheets of lined paper, like kids used in school, and a packet of letters. Words on the lined paper were in trembly, but once elegant script. The language wasn't Russian. He was sure it wasn't Russian.

Lucky stepped onto the back porch. Brown grass in the backyard, a scraggy stand of chrysanthemums, a worn-out broom standing beside the door. Nothing. Just nothing.

Step into the yard, and look around. Next door, the side of Wade's place shone painted and shiny. From out back came the sound of men huffing and puffing, wrestling something big into a truck. Lucky looked around, looked more closely at the porch, and saw where the man had lived.

There was crawlspace beneath the porch, and a piece of plywood had been nailed to make a shield, or wall. A man could climb into the crawlspace, hide under the house, and the plywood would shield his entry.

Lucky knelt, peered, saw remains of an old mattress. Paper sacks and a few tin cans lay here and there, clean; maybe licked clean. If the man had food, why starvation? The cans carried little freckles of rust. Only humidity could have done that, because the ground was dry.

Lucky, who knew a good bit about the ways of the poor,

began to tremble. These were cans scavenged from garbage cans, doubtless scavenged late at night; and scavenged awhile back when the man still had strength.

The doc had said, "Never again. Not in this country."

"We didn't know," Lucky whispered to the old mattress and the rusting cans. "We didn't know."

He fumbled his way to the garage, stepped inside, and saw what Jim and Howard had seen. Dead flowers, wilting flowers, some sort of uniform, and a picture. He studied the picture and choked back tears. No one he knew. No one anyone knew.

And then he wept, and did not a first understand that the death of one man explained the death of millions. He leaned against the wall of the garage, objectivity gone, dispassion gone, even fear gone before the horror of knowing, and feeling, the cost of war and hatred.

He turned back to the house, still weeping. Blood from his cut had coagulated, and he still needed water to wash his hand. Before he left the kitchen he picked up the sheets of paper and packet of letters. Someone, somewhere, would know the language. Someone would be able to translate.

When Lucky got to the front porch the doc sat in one of the old chairs, and he watched the corpse. The doc wasn't talking. He waited for an ambulance or meat wagon. He looked at Lucky's face, at Lucky's tears. Then, remembering, he reached in his bag. "Tetanus," he said. "Goddamn."

Early Sunday Morning, September 20th

Jackson St.

The best city in the south, and one of the best in the country, lies sleeping in the nest of its great river. Along Jackson St. a patrol car drifts like slow footsteps along old brick. It slows even more beside the dark front of Sapphire Top Spot, then the cop gooses it a little and the car moves out. A cat crosses in front of headlights and the cop slows; the cat stepping prissy and sure of herself.

Along the alleys of the city, rats run, dogs rummage, cats hunt. Somewhere in the darkness the ghost of Jolly hovers, and in the alley beside Lucky's store three men and two women hunker down, drinking beer, thinking thoughts; folks with never a home to go to, or worse, afraid to go home for fear of a beating, or woman-scold.

"I want you have it baby, but I'm cuttin' my ass off. Can't do nothin' tonight...." ... a woman pleading her period, getting out of something.

"Albert gotta open. Man drink in a damn alley don't suit."

In his rooms, Lester dreaming dreams. Wade and Lester, a team, it might could be. Wade, ambitious, seeing ways to expand. Lester, satisfied for now with a raise in pay. Dreams, goddamn, sometimes do come true.

Howard at home, asleep, dreaming hopeful dreams.

Howard feeling safe because of his mother, because of Lester, because of Lucky.

And up on Bardstown road a traffic light winking at itself, red and yellow and green flashes regulating traffic that isn't happening. Red flash on the windows of drugstore and car dealership, red flash across the asphalt lot of Shell station, red flash reaching into the dark depths of White Castle.

Auction sitting dark and silent. Jim at home, dreaming ugly dreams; nightmare washing windows, washing and washing.

A single car, a '41 Cad cruises Bardstown Road, coming from deep in the Highlands. It stops before the red light. Nary a car in sight. Stores dark. The car sits through red, green, yellow, red. Then it hangs a right into Cherokee park, cruises; Lucky sleepless, Lucky telling himself it is unfair to Rachel if he allows himself to go crazy.

Because now he understands how a man can starve in the midst of plenty, and how a man can drive himself beyond all seeming depths of sorrow. And now he understands a million deaths, and death is real. And now he understands what his mind has tried to conceal through years of war and years of peace.

Must some men destroy so that other men learn? Learn what? Must Able kill Cain, or must Able kill Able?

Or is the root of all sorrow, simply hatred, the kind that stretches its long and vicious tongue across history? "Kill them, they are not like us."

Those words should be sung as a dark anthem, words hissing their song through all of human history. Because no matter how hard a man tried, or no matter how hard lots of men tried, the song kept hissing.

Roll along the dark and tree-lined roads of the park, Hogan's Fountain, Big Rock, drive round and round and round.

But the park is too beautiful. Go someplace sad.

Down Bardstown Road, past Charlie's old place now decked out like a carnival. Times changing. Maybe, not for the better. Charlie dead, and not two months... Charlie a symbol of what used to be... and some of it good, and some bad... and maybe it is just as well that Charlie lies in the cool, cool ground of Cave Hill.

Hang a left down Broadway, right at Jackson St. He pulled up to his store, smart enough to know why. At his store he felt like a man with purpose, a man who was not a cipher. He left his car and walked to his store. He unlocked, the lock clicking.

A shadowed face peered around the corner of the alley. "Lucky robbin' his own store," a voice whispered, but loud. "Gonna sue the insurance."

Once inside he did not turn on lights. Instead, he pulled up a stool behind the counter where he could watch and hear the silence of Jackson St. where southern ghosts might drift, and might be seen.

But no European ghosts would appear, except in his own mind; and that mind clouded because the tale, he knew, must always be incomplete. The tall man, the tall son of Mrs. Samuels, had been a Polish soldier. That much was certain. During the war the Jewish soldiers of Poland established a failed but heroic record, right along with the rest of the Polish army.

The peoples and wars of Europe have always ebbed and flowed. Refugees now fled from the northernmost points of Finland to the southernmost points of Greece. From the Balkans people flooded into western Europe.

And the tall man had somehow rescued, having traced, his brother. A miracle, because both men survived. In the middle of dispersion.

And they came to America, to a place where their father

had once had moderate success. All of that was speculative, but it was what 'had to have been'.

A police car cruised Jackson St. Lucky ducked behind his counter as a searchlight walked across the front of his store. The searchlight probed the alley. The cop car slowed, then, as the cop decided 'ta hell with it' speeded up. From the alley came the sound of muted cussing.

The rest of it was definite, because once translated, the lined pages of trembling script became a record. It was not a journal, exactly, or a diary. It explained, but mostly it grieved.

When Mrs. Samuels died, it was from diabetes. Her sons knew it was coming. She knew it was coming. She feared the cost of death, the expenditure of remaining money. The scrawled pages told about that. Then the pages recorded her sons' small satisfaction in the midst of great grief. She had died thinking her sons would live under a cloak of freedom.

And she died not knowing that her eldest son, savior of her youngest, was also dying from a wound; metal working its way in slow sureness toward death. The burden of that knowledge rested with the younger son.

The tall man, the oldest son, ended quickly. When his pain became too great, and while he thrashed about in semi-consciousness, his younger brother shot him... no depth of sin greater, no height of love greater.

The living brother moved the corpse, hid a bloody pillow, and planned to dig a grave in the garage. And then the horror began.

Discovery. Someone entering the garage. Only moments to hide beneath the house. Police breaking down the front door. To the mind of a man who spoke no English, police were police. Brown shirt or blue shirt. Storm trooper or cop. To the mind of a man who had been in a death camp, police meant only one thing.

And so he hid. And so he attended to the memory of his brother. And, late at night, he sorted through garbage. And then, becoming weak, and weaker, and weaker, plucked two flowers for his brother. And then in desperation he struggled toward the world of men, and made it only to his front porch. And then he died under no cloak of freedom.

Over east, over the tops of old brick houses along Jackson St., and beyond the river, first faint reaches of dawn stretched orange across the sky. From the alley came the distant sound of snoring, raspy, desperate in-drawing of drunken breath. From the hospital, over on Preston St., sounded an ambulance siren. Soon the city would wake, do business, make gossip, play politics. People would brag or complain, and some, like Howard, would get on with their dreams.

Lucky sat, watching, and telling himself that maybe a man couldn't win. Maybe the point was not winning. Maybe the point was to keep on trying; and what in the outrageous name of a fretful god did that mean? Above him, high on shelf, Lola the guinea hen seemed cluck-y, and Thomas, the Plymouth Rock rooster watched Jackson St.; Thomas, after these many hard weeks, looking even more crazy than he had ever looked, ever before.

WHAT CAME AFTER

And so they ended, those seven deadly weeks. They ended with the burial of that younger son (paid for by Lucky), and then the living turned back to the business of living. Some did well, and some badly.

Ozzie lasted until 1951 when he was shotgunned down at a crossroads in rural Arkansas. What brought him to such a deadly place no one knows, and not many cared. Blue took up with Zeke for a while, but couldn't stand him. In her early years she bore two kids, raised them at least better that she'd been raised, and today is an old lady in a housing project. She sits before TV and gossips with the next-door neighbor. Both ladies agree that youngsters, these days, do not own a speck of politeness.

Albert died of heart in '50, and Alfonzo the same in '55. Albert and Alfonzo left us before Jackson St. began to change. The Sapphire Top Spot passed to other hands and stayed open through 1967.

Fudd complained and bitched. He spent his last years absolutely sure someone was trying to steal from him, maybe as much as a dime. No one noticed when he passed. One day he wasn't there, and no one wondered.

Gloria is almost 90, and riding ramrod over the day room in a terribly expensive and snazzy nursing home.

241

Daniels, in the late '70s, traded to get himself a new Cadillac and eighty acres in Indiana. He covered the hillsides with goods. He had to build barns to hold "...one of every damn thing that has ever been made."

Wade and Lester did good for three years. They worked hand-in-glove until friction built. They groused at each other. They pissed and moaned. They became great friends.

And, then, in August of '51 a dry goods store that opened in Charlie Weaver's place went bust. With Wade chagrined, but cheering him on, Lester opened his own place; a black man standing where Charlie Weaver once sat; a black man jazzing where Charlie had once done dry humor.

Lester's business rocked along, almost making it, sometimes on the edge of going broke. And then it took a turn, because Lester and Miz Esther caught hold of each other, and held tight. Lester had found his woman.

Miz Esther went no-nonsense at the business. Lester's auction turned to consignment house, with auction on the side, and Lester joined the church. Miz Esther gave him a daughter, Marjorie, who now does social work in Chattanooga; and a son, Jackson, who runs a hospital laboratory; plus Howard.

Lester is a happy man. If, sometimes in the long reaches of night, he thinks of his communist girl Mona, it means not much. Who among us have not (one time or another) thought of our first loves?

These days Lester is retired, and, if not rich, awful comfortable. Rockin' chair kept stalking him, and finally caught him; but he rocks fast.

Wade bulled his way through the '50s, through the '60s, and just barely through the '70s. He worked hard. When he lost his wife to illness, his family fell into such sorrow and disarray it never really recovered.

Wade started drinking more than he ought, but kept working; because work is what he knew. Like Alfonzo and Albert, heart is what got him. When he died he left instructions that his body lie beside his wife, back in Blackford County. He claimed he didn't mind being caught dead there, he just didn't want to live in the damn place.

And his kids, who had spent their young lives fearing or detesting him, found that they missed him badly. As years passed that feeling did not change.

Wade's daughter, our beloved Miss Pushy, had stayed beside her dad. She married. Took over the auction. Finally moved it to better rooms on Oak St.

Mrs. Samuels' house stood for another year in disrepair. Then a carpet dealer bought it. He put on a roof and painted the place in green with red trim. He installed fluorescent lights. He swore like a maniac because there was no way in the world to get enough light into that house. Too much darkness, too many shadows. It made his inventory looked ratty. After another year the house was bulldozed and became a parking lot for White Castle.

Jim wandered. As a young man he went to sea for a while, then returned home. He married (but not auburn-haired Miss Stacy Hall who married... nobody seems to know). Jim's marriage didn't take. Nor did the second one, or third. He drifted here and there, learning things (half of which he wished he hadn't), made a living in various ways; and in his old age, having found the right woman, started writing small histories.

Howard, naturally enough, got his store. What with having two fathers, Lucky and Lester, it was predestined. Today, Howard has three stores, a wife (though not science teacher Miss Sarah Jones who married a fireman), two kids, and five grandkids. Howard is aging but active and still skinny; except with a little potbelly. He hires his relatives, plus other kids; young boys mostly, teaching them a trade.

Lucky, who had finally come fully alive to the haunts of history, mourned in the manner of good men. He mourned for the dead. He mourned for his country. He watched the political hounds who he feared, as they began to run in packs. He watched the awful witch hunts of the '50s, the high-striding mindlessness of Joe McCarthy, before Mr. Joe drank himself to death. And, though Lucky was not a drinking man, he was apt to mention in the presence of preachers that good red whiskey certainly had its charms, if it killed Senator Joe McCarthy.

Because, for quite a while, Lucky became bitter. Instead of seeking a fortune, he had stayed on Jackson St. where he was needed. In his quiet way he had set out to change the world for the better; and the world just got worse.

He remained bitter until 1954 when the Supreme Court ruled against school segregation and spanked the butt of Topeka. He perked up during the '60s when youngsters, ignorant and obnoxious, took rebellion to the streets. Lucky was not fooled about the youngsters—God knows, Lucky knew kids—but among all the howling ignorance of mostly-spoiled brats, there was a spirit that rebelled.

And he watched a series of Presidents, so enamored of their love affairs with themselves, that they forgot to love their country.

And he watched the rise of Israel, and he mourned as Israel struggled against a religious right that became what it hated; a right wing with the rhetoric of Nazis.

And yet, Lucky like so many Jews kept hoping, as Jews still hope; while fearing the next witch hunt, the next dispersion.

Lucky ran his store, until in the '70s Housing and Urban Development bulldozed most of Jackson St. and built a project. The heart just went out of Lucky, and he retreated into silence. He and Rachel retired to Miami.

He had set out, in that modest way, to change the world; and figured he had failed. None of us know, to this day, if he ever understood that he sure as hell changed part of it.

And Louisville-town, what of it?

Nothing good comes easy. In 1954 a white liberal named Carl Braden bought a house in a white subdivision, then sold it to a colored man named Andrew Wade. Crosses were burned. The house was bombed.

The Louisville establishment, including the liberal *Courier-Journal*, reacted like a man goosed with a cattle prod, whimpering and wondering "why, oh, why?" Most liberal white folks and liberal colored folks ran for cover. The police blamed Braden, and the police investigation was a sham.

Then, A. Scott Hamilton, public prosecutor, witch-hunter and red-baiter extrordinaire, tried Braden for sedition. A hick newspaperman named John Hitt incited action by screaming 'Communist'. And a lump of Ku Klux excrement named Millard Dee Grubbs, proclaimed that the Roosevelts (Franklin by then dead, but Eleanor still alive) were the power behind a communist move to place niggers in every white neighborhood of America.

Yes, Louisville went through a lot. But, also, by 1954 parks were integrated. There were other improvements. A colored man or woman could walk into any library in town and check out a book. The fire stations started mixing white and colored firemen.

Then came school integration. The man in charge was a dry stick who knew administration, but knew no more about teaching than a hog knows about a Bible. Omar Carmichael administered integration of the schools, and there was no violence. There was also not much integration. The schools stayed steady until the '70s when busing began. Then, for a while, all hell broke loose.

And today, it still isn't easy. White hatemongers circle the action, though not so loud, and black hatemongers circle as well. Suspicions between black and white are no longer universal, but too many of them remain in the streets. Perhaps it's as it should be. It gives the city something to work toward.

It's been a long haul, but today a black man or woman can buy a cup of coffee any place in town, and use the restroom as well. A white man and a black man can be friends, without too many murmurs about them. A black man or woman can go to the bus station and not wait in a separate room. Black ladies and white ladies can shop together, downtown. Black youngsters, and white youngsters, who haven't the foggiest notion of what earlier folks went through, act like most of this has always been.

And, today freeways crisscross the city, running above asphalt streets where once lay bricks and cobblestones. The best city of the south, like many cities in the south, has become more northerly.

Yet, magnolia trees still drop heavy perfume into summer nights. Lightning bugs flash tiny beacons. The river still runs, and in springtime rises to threaten the city. Old people still nod in the sun. There remains a southern aristocracy, but these days it is mostly mute.

On the flip side, the city remains a center of business; and in terms of the south, innovation. And, the city is still alive in at least one of its best traditions. It remains, in spite of true hell, and true high water, a center of culture and art.

JACK CADY was born in Ohio and raised in Indiana and Kentucky. He worked in a wide variety of jobs throughout the country, including stints as a tree high-climber, an auctioneer, a long-haul truck driver, and in the U. S. Coast Guard. He held teaching positions at the University of Washington, Clarion College, Knox College, the University of Alaska at Sitka, and Pacific Lutheran University.

Over a more than thirty-year career, the quality and diversity of his fiction was matched only by the quality and diversity of the honors and awards he received, including the *Atlantic Monthly* "First" Award, the Iowa Prize for short fiction, the National Literary Anthology Award, the Washington State Governor's Award, the Nebula Award, the Bram Stoker Award, the World Fantasy Award, and the Philip K. Dick Award (Special Citation).

Jack Cady died in January 2004.